The Joss
A Reversion

by

Richard Marsh

Double9
BOOKS

The Joss

A Reversion

by Richard Marsh

ISBN: 978-93-62762-70-2

Published by

DOUBLE 9 BOOKS

2/13-B, Ansari Road
Daryaganj, New Delhi – 110002
info@double9books.com
www.double9books.com
Tel. 011-40042856

This book is under public domain

ABOUT THE AUTHOR

English writer Richard Marsh (1857–1915) is most remembered for producing a large body of popular literature in the late 19th and early 20th century. He was born in England as Richard Bernard Heldmann and used the pen name "Richard Marsh" for his writing. When Marsh started writing in the 1880s, he was well known for his ability to write engrossing mysteries, suspense, and otherworldly stories. Although Marsh wrote in a variety of genres, such as science fiction, horror, mystery, and romance, his contributions to the Victorian and Edwardian ghost story tradition are arguably what made him most famous. His works frequently combined the macabre and the bizarre, drawing comparisons to other highly regarded writers of the day like Bram Stoker and H.G. Wells.

CONTENTS

BOOK I
UNCLE BENJAMIN

CHAPTER I
FIRANDOLO'S...9

CHAPTER II
LOCKED OUT..16

CHAPTER III
THE DOLL..24

CHAPTER IV
AN INTERVIEW WITH MR. SLAUGHTER 30

CHAPTER V
THE MISSIONARY'S LETTER...................................37

CHAPTER VI
SOLE RESIDUARY LEGATEE 44

CHAPTER VII
ENTERING INTO POSSESSION 52

CHAPTER VIII
THE BACK-DOOR KEY...58

BOOK II
84, CAMFORD STREET

CHAPTER IX
MAX LANDER...64

CHAPTER X
BETWEEN 13 AND 14, ROSEMARY STREET...........71

CHAPTER XI
ONE WAY IN 79

CHAPTER XII
THE SHUTTING OF A DOOR..86

CHAPTER XIII
A VISION OF THE NIGHT 93

CHAPTER XIV
SUSIE..100

CHAPTER XV
AN ULTIMATUM 108

CHAPTER XVI
THE NOISE WHICH CAME FROM THE PASSAGE 115

BOOK III
THE GOD OF FORTUNE

CHAPTER XVII
THE AFFAIR OF THE FREAK..119

CHAPTER XVIII
COUNSEL'S OPINION...127

CHAPTER XIX
THE RETICENCE OF CAPTAIN LANDER..133

CHAPTER XX
MY CLIENT—AND HER FRIEND 140

CHAPTER XXI
THE AGITATION OF MISS PURVIS...148

CHAPTER XXII
LUKE 156

CHAPTER XXIII
THE TRIO RETURN 164

CHAPTER XXIV
THE GOD OUT OF THE MACHINE..175

BOOK IV
THE JOSS

CHAPTER XXV
LUKE'S SUGGESTION 178

CHAPTER XXVI
THE THRONE IN THE CENTRE 185

CHAPTER XXVII
THE OFFERINGS OF THE FAITHFUL 192

CHAPTER XXVIII
THE JOSS REVERTS...199

CHAPTER XXIX
THE FATHER—AND HIS CHILD 206

CHAPTER XXX
THE MORNING'S NEWS..214

CHAPTER XXXI
THE TERMINATION OF THE VOYAGE OF
"THE FLYING SCUD." 221

CHAPTER XXXII
THE LITTLE DISCUSSION BETWEEN THE SEVERAL PARTIES......227

CHAPTER XXXIII
IN THE PRESENCE...231

BOOK V
AUTHOR'S POSTSCRIPT

CHAPTER XXXIV
HOW MATTERS STAND TO-DAY 235

BOOK I
UNCLE BENJAMIN

(MARY BLYTH TELLS THE STORY.)

CHAPTER I
FIRANDOLO'S

I had had an aggravating day. In everything luck had been against me. I had got down late, and been fined for that. Then when I went into the shop I found I had forgotten my cuffs, and Mr. Broadley, who walks the fancy department, marked me sixpence for that. Just as I was expecting my call for dinner an old lady came in who kept me fussing about till my set came up—and only spent three and two-three after all; so when I did go down alone there was nothing left; and what was left was worse than cold. Though I was as hungry as I very well could be I could scarcely swallow as much as a mouthful; lukewarm boiled mutton cased in solidified fat is not what I care for. Directly after I came up, feeling hungrier than ever, Miss Patten did me out of the sale of a lot of sequin trimming on which there was a ninepenny spiff. I was showing it to a customer, and before I had had half a chance she came and took it clean out of my hands, and sold it right away. It made me crosser than ever. To crown it all, I missed three sales. One lady wanted a veil, and because we had not just the sort she wanted, when she walked out of the shop Mr. Broadley seemed to think it was my fault. He said he would mark me. When some people want a triangular spot you cannot put them off with a round one. It is no use your saying you can. And so I as good as told him.

Not twenty minutes afterwards a girl came in—a mere chit—who wanted some passementerie, beaded. She had brought a pattern. Somehow directly I saw it I thought there would be trouble. I hunted through the stock and found the thing exactly, only there were blue beads where there ought to have been green. As there were a dozen different coloured beads it did not really matter, especially as ours were a green blue, and hers were a blue green. But that chit would not see it. She would not admit that it was a match. When I called Mr. Broadley, and he pointed out to her that the two were so much alike that, at a little distance, you could not tell one from the other, she was quite short. She caught up her old pattern and took herself away. Then Mr. Broadley gave it to me hot. He reminded me that that was two sales I had missed, and that three, on one day, meant dismissal. I did not suppose they would go so far as that, but I did expect that, if I missed again, it would cost me half-a-crown, at least. So, of course, there was I, as it were, on tenterhooks, resolved that rather than I would let anyone else go without a purchase I would force some elevenpence three-farthing thing on her; if I had to pay for it myself. And there was Mr. Broadley hanging about just by my stand, watching me so that I felt I should like to stick my scissors into him.

But I was doomed to be done. Luck was clean against me. Just as we were getting ready to close in came an old woman—one of your red-faced sort, with her bonnet a little on one side of her head. She wanted some torchon lace. Now, strictly speaking, lace is not in my department, but as we are all supposed to serve through, and most of the others were engaged—it is extraordinary how, some nights, people will crowd into the shop just as we are getting ready to close—Mr. Broadley planted her on me. She was a nice old party. She did not know herself what she wanted, but seemed to think I ought to. So far as I could make out, what she really did want was a four shilling lace at fourpence—which we could not exactly supply. At last I called Mr. Broadley to see if he could make her out. On which she actually turned huffy, and declaring that I would not take the trouble to show her anything at all, in spite of all that we could do or say, she marched straight out. Then I had a wigging. Broadley let himself go, before them all. I could have cried—and almost did.

I was three-quarters of an hour late before I got into the street. Emily Purvis was tired of waiting, and Tom Cooper was in a red-hot rage.

"My dear," began Emily, directly she saw me, "I hope you haven't hurried. We're only frozen to the bone."

"That's all right," said Tom. "It's just the sort of night to hang about this confounded corner."

It was disagreeable weather. There was a nasty east wind, which seemed to cut right into one, and the pavements were wet and slimy. It all seemed of a piece. I knew Tom's overcoat was not too thick, nor Emily's jacket too warm either. When I saw Tom dancing about to keep himself warm, all at once something seemed to go over me, and I had to cry. Then there was a pretty fuss.

"Polly!" exclaimed Emily. "Whatever is the matter with you now?"

And there, in the open street, Tom put his arm about my waist. I told them all about it. You should have heard how they went on at Broadley. It did me good to listen, though I knew it would make no difference to him. They had not had the best of luck either. It seemed that it had been one of those days on which everything goes wrong with everyone. Emily had not got one single spiff, and Tom had had a quarrel with young Clarkson, who had called him Ginger to his face—and the colour of his hair is a frightfully delicate point with Tom. Tom had threatened to punch his head when they went upstairs. I begged and prayed him not to, but there was a gloomy air about him which showed that he would have to do something to relieve his feelings. I felt that punching young Clarkson's head might do him good—and Clarkson no particular harm.

I do not think that either of us was particularly happy. The streets were nearly deserted. It was bitterly cold. Every now and then a splash of rain was driven into our faces.

"This is, for us, the age of romance," declared Emily. "You mightn't think so, but it is. At our age, the world should be alive with romance. We should be steeped in its atmosphere; drink it in with every breath. It should colour both our sleeping and our waking hours. And, instead of that, here we are shivering in this filthy horrid street."

That was the way she was fond of talking. She was a very clever girl, was Emily, and could use big words more easily than I could little ones. She would have it that romance was the only thing worth living for, and that, as there is no romance in the world to-day, it is not worth while one's living. I could not quite make out her argument, but that was what it came to so far as I could understand. I wished myself that there was a little more fun about. I was tired of the drapery.

"Shivering!" said Tom. "I'm not only shivering; I'm hungry too. Boiled mutton days I always am."

"Hungry!" I cried. "I'm starving. I've had no dinner or tea, and I'm ready to drop."

"No! You don't mean that?"

I did mean it, and so I told him. What with having had nothing to eat, and being tired, and worried, and cold, it was all I could do to drag one foot after another. I just felt as if I was going to be ill. I could have kept on crying all the time.

"Have either of you got any money?" asked Tom. Neither Emily nor I had a penny. "Then I'll tell you what I'll do; we'll all three of us go into Firandolo's, and I'll stand Sam."

I knew he had only enough money to take him home on Sunday, because he had told me so himself the day before. Cardew & Slaughter's is not the sort of place where they encourage you to spend Sunday in. He had been in last Sunday; and to stop in two Sundays running was to get yourself disliked; I have spent many a Sunday, loitering about the parks and the streets, living on a couple of buns, rather than go in to what they called dinner. And I knew that if we once set foot in Firandolo's we should spend all he had. Yet I was so faint and hungry that I did not want much pressing. I could not find it in my heart to refuse.

Firandolo's is something like a restaurant. Including vegetables, and sweets, and cheese, I have counted sixty-seven dishes on the bill of fare at one time, so that you have plenty of choice. For a shilling you can get a perfectly splendid dinner. And for sixpence you can get soup, and bread and cheese and butter; and they bring you the soup in a silver basin which is full to the brim.

At night it is generally crowded, but it was perhaps because the weather was so bad that there were only a few persons in the place when we went in. Directly after we entered someone else came in. He was a big man, and wore a reefer coat and a bowler hat. Seating himself at a table immediately opposite ours, taking off his hat, he wiped his forehead with an old bandanna handkerchief; though what there was to make him warm on a night like that was more than I could say. He had a fringe of iron-grey hair all round his head on a level with his ears. It stood out stiffly, like a sort of crown. Above and below it he was bald. He wore a bristly moustache, and his eyes were almost hidden by the bushiest eyebrows I had ever seen. I could not help noticing him, because I had a kind of fancy that he had been following us for some time. Unless I was mistaken he had passed me just as I had come out of Cardew & Slaughter's; and ever since, whenever I looked round, I saw him somewhere behind us, as if he were keeping us in sight. I said nothing about it to the others, but I wondered, all the same. I did not like his looks at all. He seemed to me to be both sly and impudent; and though he pretended not to be watching us, I do not believe he took his eyes off us for a single moment.

I do not know what he had; he took a long time in choosing it, whatever it was. We had soup. It was lovely. Hot and tasty; just the very thing I wanted. It made me feel simply pounds better. But, after we had finished, something dreadful happened. The bill came altogether to one and three;

we each of us had an extra bread. Tom felt in his pocket for the money. First in one, then in another. Emily and I soon saw that something was wrong, because he felt in every pocket he had. And he looked so queer.

"This is a bit of all right!" he gasped, just as we were beginning to wonder if he was all pockets. "Blessed if I have a single copper on me. I remember now that I left it in my box, so that I shouldn't spend it."

He looked at us, and we looked at him, and the waiter stood close by, looking at us all. And behind him was the proprietor, also with an observant eye. Emily and I were dumbfounded. Tom seemed as if he had not another word to say. Just as the proprietor was beginning to come closer, the stranger who had been following us got up and came to us across the room, all the time keeping his eyes on me.

"Pardon me if I take a liberty, but might I ask if I'm speaking to Miss Blyth?"

An odd voice he had; as if he were endeavouring to overcome its natural huskiness by speaking in a whisper. Of course my name is Blyth, and so I told him. But who he was I did not know from Adam. I certainly had never set eyes on him before. He explained, in a fashion; though his explanation came to nothing, after all.

"I knew a—a relative of yours. A pal, he was, of mine; great pals was him and me. So I naturally take an interest in a relative of his." He turned to Tom. "If so be, sir, as you've left your purse at home, which is a kind of accident which might happen to any gentleman at any time, perhaps I might be allowed to pay your little bill."

Tom had to allow him, though he liked it no more than I did. But we none of us wanted to be sent to prison for obtaining soup on false pretences, which I have been given to understand might have happened. Though, for my part, I would almost as soon have done that as be beholden to that big, bald-headed creature, who spoke as if he had lost his voice, and was doing all he knew to find it. When he had paid the one and three, and what were Tom's feelings at seeing him do it was more than I could think, because I know his pride, the stranger came out with something else.

"And now, ladies, might I offer you a little something on my own. What do you say to a dozen oysters each, and a bottle of champagne? I believe they're things ladies are fond of."

He smiled—such a smile. It sounded tempting. I had never tasted oysters and champagne; though, of course, I had read of them in books, heaps of times. And it is my opinion that Emily would have said yes, if I had given her a chance. But not me. I stood up directly.

"Thank you; but I never touch oysters and champagne—at this time of night."

"Might I—might I be allowed to offer a little something else. A Welsh rarebit, shall we say?"

Now, as it happens, a Welsh rarebit is a thing that I am fond of, especially when eaten with a glass of stout. I was still hungry, and my mouth watered at the prospect of some real nice, hot toasted cheese. It needed some resolution to decline. But I did. Hungry as I was, I felt as if I had had more than enough of him already.

"I am obliged to you, but I want nothing else. I have had all that I require."

It was not true; but it seemed to me that it was a case in which truth would not exactly meet the situation. The stranger came close to me, actually whispering in my ear.

"May I hope, Miss Blyth, that you'll remember me when—when you want a friend?"

I was as stand-offish as I could be.

"I don't see how I can remember you when I don't even know your name."

He spoke to me across the back of his hand.

"My name is Rudd—Isaac Rudd; known to my friends, of whom, the Lord be praised, I've many, as Covey. It's a—a term of endearment, so to speak, Miss Blyth."

That anyone could apply a term of endearment to such a man as he seemed to be, was more than I believed to be possible.

"If you will let me take your address, Mr. Rudd, I will see that you have your one and three."

"My address? Ah! Now there you have me. I don't happen to have an—an address just now. In fact, I'm—I'm moving."

We were going towards the door. I was beginning to fear that he intended to accompany us home. Nor did I see how we could prevent him, since he was at liberty to take such measures as he chose which would ensure the return of the money he had paid for us. But, as we drew near the entrance, he started back; and his demeanour changed in the most extraordinary way.

"Good-night," he stammered, retreating farther and farther from us. "Don't—don't let me keep you, not—not for another moment."

We went out. Directly we were in the open air Tom drew a long breath.

"Geewhillikins! A nice scrape I nearly got you in, and myself as well. A pretty hole we should have been in if that fellow hadn't turned up in the very nick of time. He's the sort I call a friend in need with a vengeance."

Emily struck in.

"Polly, why wouldn't you let us sample his oysters and champagne? Considering he's a friend of yours, you seemed pretty short with him."

"My dear, he's not a friend of mine, nor ever could be; and as for his oysters and champagne, they'd have choked me if I'd touched them."

"They wouldn't have choked me, I can tell you that. There is some romance in oysters and champagne, and, as you know very well, romance is what I live for. There's precious little comes my way; it seems hard it should be snatched from my lips just as I have a chance of tasting it."

"Hollo! Who on earth— —"

It was from Tom the exclamation came. He stopped short, with his sentence uncompleted. I turned to see what had caused him to speak—to find myself face to face with the most singular-looking individual I had ever seen.

CHAPTER II
LOCKED OUT

At first I could not make out if it was a man or woman or what it was. But at last I decided that it was a man. I never saw such clothes. Whether it was the darkness, or his costume, or what it was, I cannot say, but he seemed to me to be surprisingly tall. And thin! And old! Nothing less than a walking skeleton he seemed to me, the cheekbones were starting through his skin which was shrivelled and yellow with age. He wore what looked to me, in that light, like a whole length piece of double width yellow canvas cloth. It was wrapped round and round him, as, I am told, it is round mummies. A fold was drawn up over his head, so as to make a kind of hood, and from under this his face looked out.

Fancy coming on such a figure, on a dark night, all of a sudden, and you can guess what my feelings were. I thought I should have dropped. I had to catch tight hold of Tom's arm.

"Tom," I gasped, "what—whatever is it?"

"Come on," he muttered. "Let's get out of this. Looney, he looks to me."

Lunatic or not, he did not mean that we should get away from him quite so easily. He took Emily by the shoulder—you should have heard the scream she gave; if it had been louder it would have frightened the neighbourhood. But the lunatic, or whatever the creature was, did not seem to be in the least put out. He held her with both his hands, one on either shoulder, and turned her round to him, and stared at her in the most disgraceful way. He put his face so close to hers that I thought he was going to bite her, or something awful. But no; all at once he thrust her aside as if she was nothing at all.

"It is not she," he murmured, half to himself, as it seemed, and half to us.

And before I could guess what he was going to do, he laid his hands on me. It was a wonder I did not faint right then and there. He gripped my shoulders so tight that I felt as if he had me screwed in a vice, and for days after my skin was black and blue. He thrust his face so close to mine that I felt his breath upon my cheeks. There was an odd smell about it which made me dizzy. He had little eyes, which were set far back in his head. I had a notion they were short-sighted, he seemed to have to peer so long and closely. At last his lips moved.

"It is she," he said, in the same half-stifled voice in which he had spoken before. He had a queer accent. There was no mistaking what he said, but it was certain that his tongue was not an Englishman's. "You will see me again—yes! Soon! You will remember me?"

Remember him? I should never forget him, never! Not if I lived to be as old as Methuselah. That hideous, hollow-cheeked, saffron-hued face would haunt me in my dreams. I do have dreams, pretty bad ones sometimes. I should see him in them many a time. My head whirled round. The next thing I knew I was in Tom's arms. He was holding me up against Firandolo's window. He spoke to me.

"It's all right now; he's gone."

I sighed, and looked round. The wretch had vanished. What had become of him I did not ask, or care to know. It was sufficient for me that he had vanished. As I drew myself up I glanced round towards the restaurant door. Mr. Isaac Rudd's face was pressed against the glass. Unless I was mistaken, when he perceived I saw him he drew back quickly. I slipped my arm through Tom's.

"Let's get away from here; let's hurry home as fast as we can."

Off we went, we three. Emily began to talk. Tom and I were silent. It was still as much as I could do to walk; I fancy Tom was thinking.

"It is a wonder I didn't faint as well as you; if you hadn't I should. But when you went I felt that it would never do for two of us to go, so I held myself tight in. Did you ever see anything like that awful man? I don't believe he was alive; at least, I shouldn't if it wasn't for the way in which he pinched my shoulders. I shall be ashamed to look at them when I've got my dress off, I know I shall. My skin's so delicate that the least mark shows. What was he dressed in? And who could the creature be? I believe he was something supernatural; there was nothing natural about him that I could see. Then his eye! He looked a thousand years old if he looked a day."

She ceased. She glanced behind her once or twice. She drew closer to Tom. When she spoke again it was in a lower tone of voice.

"Mr. Cooper, do you mind my taking your arm? There's—there's someone following us now."

Tom looked round. As he did so, two men came past us, one by me, the other one by Emily. The one who passed me was so close that his sleeve brushed mine; as he went he turned and stared at me with might and main. He was short, but very fat. He was shabbily dressed, and wore a cloth cap slouched over his eyes. When he had gone a yard or two the other man fell in at his side. They talked together as they slouched along; we could not but see that, while both of them were short, one was as thin as the other was stout.

"Are you sure they've been following us?" whispered Tom to Emily.

"Certain. They've been sticking close at our heels ever since we came away from Firandolo's."

The fact was put beyond dispute before we had gone another fifty yards. The two men drew up close in front of us, in such a way that it would have been difficult for us to pass without pushing them aside.

"Which of you two ladies is Miss Blyth?" asked the stout man, in the most impudent manner.

On a sudden I was becoming the object of undesired attention which I did not at all understand, and liked, if possible, still less. The fellow looked us up and down, as if we had been objects offered for sale.

"What has it to do with you?" returned Tom. "Who are you, anyhow?"

The thin man answered; the stout man had spoken in a shrill squeaky treble, he had the deepest possible bass.

"We're the young lady's friends; her two friends. Ain't that gospel, Sam?"

"It's that, William; it's gospel truth. Truer friends than us she'll never have, nor none what's more ready to do her a good turn."

"Not if she was to spend the rest of her days sailing round the world looking for 'em, she'd never find 'em, that she wouldn't. All we ask is for her to treat us as her friends." The thin man spat upon the pavement. "Now then, out with it; which of you two ladies is Miss Blyth?"

"I'm not," cried Emily.

Which I thought was distinctly mean of her, because, of course, it was as good as saying that I was. Once more the stout man looked me up and down.

"You're her, are you? So I thought. The other's too pretty, by chalks. You're a chip of the old block, and there wasn't no beauty thrown away on him; plain he was, as ever I saw a man; and plainer."

The fellow was ruder than ever. I am aware that Emily Purvis is a beauty, and that I am not, but at the same time one does not expect to be stopped and told so by two perfect strangers, at that hour of the night.

"For goodness' sake," I said to Tom, "let's get away from these dreadful persons as fast as we possibly can."

I made him come. The fat man called after us—in his squeaky treble.

"Dreadful, are we? Maybe you'll change your mind before you've done. Don't you be so fast in judging of your true friends, it don't become a young woman. There's more dreadful persons than us about, as perhaps you'll find."

"It is to be hoped," I observed to Tom, and paying no attention whatever to Emily Purvis, who I knew was smiling on the other side of him, "that we shall meet no more objectionable characters before we get safely in."

"They're friends of yours, my dear."

This was Emily.

"I don't see how you make that out, seeing that I never saw them before, and never want to again."

"Some of us have more friends than we know, my love." Her love! "We've seen four of yours already; I shouldn't be surprised if we saw another still before we're in."

As it happened, in a manner of speaking, it turned out that she was right; though, of course, to speak of the creature we encountered, even sarcastically, as a friend of mine, would be absurd. We were going along the Fenton Road. As we were passing a street, which branched off upon our right, there popped out of it, for all the world as if he had been waiting for us to come along, a man in a long black coat, reaching nearly to his heels, and a felt hat, which was crammed down so tight, that it almost covered his face as well as his head. I thought at first he was a beggar, or some object of the tramp kind, because he fell in at our side, and moved along with us, as some persistent beggars will do. But one glance at what could be seen of his features was sufficient to show that he was something more out of the common than that. He had a round face; almond-shaped eyes which looked out of narrow slits; a flat nose; a mouth which seemed to reach from ear to ear. There was no mistaking that this was a case of another ugly foreigner. The consciousness that he was near made me shudder; as he trudged along beside us I went uncomfortable all over.

"Go away! Make him go away!" I said to Tom.

Tom stood still.

"Now then, off you go! We've nothing for you. The sooner you try it off on somebody else, the less of your valuable time you'll waste."

Tom took him for a beggar. But he was wrong, and I was right; the man was not a beggar.

"Which is little lady?"

I don't pretend that was exactly what he said. Thank goodness, I am English, and I know no language but my own, and that is quite enough for me, so it would be impossible for me to reproduce precisely a foreign person's observations; but that is what he meant. Tom was angry.

"Little lady? What little lady? There's no lady here, big or little, who has anything to do with you; so, now then, you just clear off."

But the man did nothing of the kind. He hopped to Emily, and back again to me, peering at us both out of his narrow eyes.

"Which of you is Missee Blyth?"

"Miss Blyth! Is the whole world, all at once, on the look-out for Miss Blyth? What is the meaning of this little game? You, there, hook it!"

But instead of hooking it, to use Tom's own language, and gentlemen will use slang, the man grew more and more insistent. He must have gone backwards and forwards between Emily and me half-a-dozen times.

"Quick! Tellee me! Which is Missee Blyth? Quick, quick! tellee me! I have something to give to Missee Blyth."

"I am Miss Blyth."

I did not suppose, for an instant, that he really had anything to give me. But the man seemed to be in such a state of agitation, that I felt that perhaps the best way to put an end to what was becoming a painful situation would be for me to declare myself without delay. However, to my surprise, hardly were the words out of my lips, than the man came rushing to me, thrusting something into my hand. From what I could feel of it, it appeared to be something small and hard, wrapped in a scrap of paper. But I had no chance of discovering anything further, because, before I had a chance of even peeping, the two short men, the fat and thin one, came rushing up, goodness only knows from where, and I heard the thin one call out, in his deep bass voice, to the other:

"He's given it her—I saw him! At her, Sam, before she has a chance of pouching it."

The stout man caught me by the wrist, gave it a twist, which hurt me dreadfully, and, before I could say Jack Robinson, he had the little packet out of my hand. It was like a conjuror's trick, it all took place so rapidly, and before I had the least notion of what was going to happen. The foreign person, however, seemed to understand what had occurred better than I did. Clearly he did not want courage. With a sort of snarl he sprang at the stout man, and with both hands took him by the throat, as, I have heard, bulldogs have a way of doing. The stout man did not relish the attack at all.

"Pull him off me, William," he squeaked.

The thin man endeavoured to do as he was told. And, in a moment, out in the open street there, the most dreadful fight was going on. What it was all about I had not the faintest idea, but they attacked each other like wild beasts. The foreign person did not seem to be at all dismayed by the odds of two to one. He assailed them with frightful violence.

Plainly it would be as much as they could do to deal with him between them. I certainly expected every second to see someone killed. Emily went off her head with terror. She rushed, screaming up the street. Tom dashed after her, whether to stop her or not I could not tell. And, of course, I rushed after Tom. And the three men were left alone to fight it out together.

Emily never drew breath till we were quite close to Cardew & Slaughter's. Then a church clock rang out. It struck the half-hour. It might have struck her, she stopped so suddenly.

"Half-past eleven!" she cried. "My gracious! whatever shall we do?"

It was a rule of the firm that the assistants were to be in by half-past ten. Between the half-hour and the quarter there was a fine of sixpence, and between the quarter and the hour one of half-a-crown. After eleven no one was admitted at all. The doors had been closed for more than half-an-hour! We stood, panting for breath, staring at one another. Emily began to cry.

"I daren't stop out in the streets all night—I daren't!"

"I know a trick worth two of that," declared Tom. "There's a way in which is known to one or two of us; I've had to use it before, and I daresay I can use it again."

"It's all very well for you," cried Emily. "But we can't climb windows; and, if we could, there are no windows for us to climb."

Tom hesitated. I could see he did not like to leave us in the lurch. The gentlemen slept right up at the other end of the building; there was no connection between his end and ours. I had heard of what Tom hinted at before; but then things are always different with gentlemen. As Emily said, for the ladies there was no way in but the door. Somehow I felt that, after all we had gone through, I did not mean to be trampled on.

"You go, Tom, and get in as best you can. Emily and I will get in too, or I'll know the reason why."

Away went Tom; and off started Emily and I to try our luck. She was not sanguine.

"They'll never let us in, never!"

"We'll see about that."

I gritted my teeth, as I have a trick of doing when I am in earnest. I was in earnest then. It is owing to the firm's artfulness that there are no bells or knockers on the doors leading to the assistants' quarters. When they are open you can get in; when they are closed there are no means provided to call attention to the fact that you require admission. They had been unloading some packing-cases. I picked up two heavy pieces of wood which had been left lying about; with them I started to hammer at the door. How I did hammer! I kept it up ever so long; but no one paid the slightest heed. I began to despair. Emily was crying all the while. I felt like crying with her. Instead, I gritted my teeth still more, and I hammered, and I hammered. At last a window was opened overhead, and the housekeeper, Mrs. Galloway, put her head out.

"Who's that making this disgraceful noise at this hour of the night?"

"It's Miss Purvis and Miss Blyth. Come down and let us in; we've been nearly robbed and murdered."

"I daresay! You don't enter this house to-night; you know the rules. And if you don't take yourselves off this instant I'll send for the police."

"Send for the police, that's what we want you to do. The police will soon see if you won't let us in."

Mrs. Galloway's head disappeared; the window was banged. Emily cried louder than ever.

"I told you she'd never let us in."

"We'll see if she won't."

Off I started again to hammer. Presently steps were heard coming along the passage. Mrs. Galloway's voice came from the other side of the door.

"Stop that disgraceful noise! Go away! Do you hear me, go away!"

"If we do it will be to fetch the police. They'll soon show you if you can keep us out all night when we've been nearly robbed and murdered."

The door was opened perhaps three inches; as I believed, upon the chain. I knew Mrs. Galloway's little tricks. But if it was upon the chain what occurred was odd. Someone came hurrying up the steps behind us. To my amazement it was the dreadful old man in the yellow canvas cloth. I was too bewildered to even try to guess where he had come from; I had never supposed that he, or anybody else, was near. He pointed to the door.

"Open!" he said, in that queer, half-stifled voice in which he had spoken to me before.

The door was opened wide, though how the housekeeper had had time to remove the chain, if it was chained, was more than I could understand. Emily and I marched into the passage—sneaked, I daresay, would have been the better word. As I went the stranger slipped something into my hand; a hard something, wrapped in a scrap of paper.

CHAPTER III
THE DOLL

I do not know what it was, but something prevented Mrs. Galloway from giving us the sort of talking to I had expected. She is a woman with as nasty a tongue as you would care to meet. I had never before known her lose a chance of using it. And there was a chance! But, instead, there she stood mumchance, and before she had even so much as said a word, Emily and I were off upstairs. I was on the second floor, and Emily was on the third. When I stopped to go into my room I called out to her, "Good night!" but she ran on, and never answered. She was in such a state of mind, what with the fright, and her crying, and the cold biting us through and through while we waited on the doorstep, that all she cared for was to get between the sheets.

In my room most of the girls were wide awake. It was not a large room, so there were only nine of us, and that was including Miss Ashton. She was the senior assistant, a regular frump, thirty if a day. She came to bed a quarter of an hour after we did, and after she had come to bed no one was supposed to talk. If any girl did talk Miss Ashton reported her, and the girl was fined, and half the fine, whatever it was, went into Miss Ashton's pockets. So, of course—since, sometimes, her pockets were bulging out with our money—no love was lost between us.

When I went in, although I knew that most of the girls were awake, because of Miss Ashton no one spoke a syllable, until Lucy Carr, who had the next bed to mine, whispered as I stood by her:

"Whatever have you been up to?"

"I've been nearly robbed and murdered, that's what I've been up to."

"Miss Blyth, I shall report you for talking after midnight."

This was Miss Ashton, cold, and hard, and short as usual. Trust her to go to sleep while there was a chance to snatch at somebody else's penny!

"Very well, Miss Ashton, you can report me, and you can say, at the same time, that it's a wonder that I was alive to talk at all, for what I've gone through this day, and this night, I alone can tell."

I plumped down on my box, and I leaned my back against the wall, and I had to cry. Then all the girls set off together. Lucy Carr sat up in bed, and she put her arms about my neck; she was a nice girl, was Lucy Carr, we hardly ever quarrelled.

"Never mind her, my love; you know what she's like; she can't help it, it's her nature. Don't you cry, my dear."

And then there were such remarks as "It's a shame!" "Poor dear!" and "How can people be so cruel?" from the others. But Miss Ashton was not touched, not she; she simply said, in her cold, hard tones:

"Miss Carr, Miss Sheepshanks, Miss Flick, Miss James, I shall report you for talking after midnight."

"That's right," said Lucy, "and much good may our money do you. I wish it would burn a hole in your pocket!"

Then the girls were still. Of course they did not want to lose all their money, and there was no knowing what the fine might be for talking at that time of night, and especially for keeping on. So I sat on my box, and I wiped my eyes; I never do believe much in crying, and somehow I felt too mad for a regular weep. I should like to have given Miss Ashton a real good shaking—everything would go wrong!

Just as I was beginning to undress—I actually had unhooked my bodice—I thought of what the object in the grey canvas cloth had slipped into my hand. What had become of it? In my agitation I had forgotten all about it. I was holding it when I came into the room—I remembered that. What had become of it since? I felt on my knee; it was not there. I had not put it in my pocket. It must have dropped on the floor. Intending to start a search I put out my foot and touched something with my toe. I reached out my hand; it was the scrap of paper.

As I picked it up I knew quite well that there could be nothing in it of the slightest consequence. People don't give things worth having to perfect strangers, especially such people as that creature in the canvas cloth. Yet there had been a good deal of fuss. First the man in the long black coat had given me a scrap of paper; then the thin man had egged on the stout man to snatch it from me like a hungry lion; then, to regain it in his possession the black-coated man had attacked the two others like some mad wild beast; finally, to crown all, the canvas cloth creature had put into my hand what seemed to be the identical scrap of paper as I stood on the threshold of the door. There must be something of interest connected with the thing; or why had these persons, in spite of what Emily had said, all utter strangers to me, behaved in such an extraordinary manner?

I was both tired and sleepy, but I was more worried than either. Part of my worry had to do with that scrap of paper. What was in it? I was sure I should never sleep until I knew. It was about half an inch broad, and an inch and a half long. As I pressed it with my fingers, I could feel that something was inside, something queer-shaped and hard. The room was pretty dark. All the light there was came through the sides of the badly fitting blind from the lamp on the opposite side of the street. I could not get the paper open. It was fastened in some way I did not understand. As I held it up against the shaft of light which came through the side of the blind, to make out, if possible, what the trick of the fastening was, a queer thing took place.

Something moved inside, and tore the paper open. It was only a little thing, but it took me so completely by surprise that it affected me almost as much as if the ceiling had fallen in. What could there have been inside to move? I sat staring, in the darkness, with my mouth wide open. Suddenly there came Miss Ashton's voice from the other end of the room.

"Miss Blyth, are you not going to get into bed at all to-night?"

At that moment I myself could not have told. I was holding in my hand something which gleamed at me. What it was I could not even guess. I only knew that two specks of light, which looked like eyes, were shining at me through the darkness; and that the thing had moved. There was Miss Ashton's voice again.

"Do you hear me, Miss Blyth? Are you going to bed? or am I to summon Mrs. Galloway?"

Without answering her a word I dropped what I was holding on to the bed. I was convinced that it moved as I did so, as if to cling to my fingers. It was silly, but I was never so frightened in my life. I saw the two bright spots of light shining up at me from the counterpane as if they were watching me. I hardly dared to breathe. I slipped off my bodice, and the rest of my things, moving as little as I possibly could, and stood in my night-gown shivering by the bed. Had I not been afraid, I would have asked Lucy to let me get into bed with her. But I knew Miss Ashton would hear, and would rout me out again, and then there would be worse to follow. I should get Lucy into trouble as well as myself. And there was trouble enough in store for all of us already. Better face what there was to face alone, than drag anybody else into the ditch into which I seemed to be continually tumbling.

It was too ridiculous to be afraid to get into bed because that thing with the shining spots was lying on the counterpane. I was sensible enough to be aware of that. Yet I was afraid. Was it alive? If I could only have made sure that it was not, I should not have minded. But it was too dark to see; and I could not touch it.

"Miss Blyth, are you going to get into bed?"

"Well, Miss Ashton, there's something on my bed, and I don't know what it is."

"Something on your bed? What do you mean? What nonsense are you talking?"

"Have you any matches? If you'll lend me some, I shall be able to see what it is. I can't get in until I know."

"Is it a fresh trick you are playing me? I never heard anything so ridiculous. Here are some matches. Be quick; and don't be sillier than you can help."

I went and took the box of matches she held out to me. Returning, I lit one and held it over the counterpane. Some of the girls lifted their heads to watch me. Lucy Carr leaned right out of her bed towards mine.

"Whatever is it?" she whispered.

My hand shook so, with the cold, and the state I was in, that it was all I could do to keep it steady enough to prevent the match from going out. I held it lower.

"I believe it's a frog."

"A frog!" cried Lucy. She drew herself back with a little shriek.

"It's—it's something horrid."

Two or three of the girls sat up, drawing the bedclothes to their chins.

"Miss Blyth, what is the cause of this confusion? Are we never to have any sleep to-night?"

Miss Ashton, getting out of bed, came across the room to see what was the matter. The match went out. The red-hot end dropped on to the counterpane. I brushed it off with my fingers. As I did so I touched the thing. My nerves were so strung up that I gave a scream. There came an echo from the girls. Miss Ashton was at my side before I could strike another match. She was in a fine rage.

"Give me the box!" She snatched it from me. "Have you been misbehaving yourself? or are you mad? I'll soon see what is the cause of all this nonsense, and then I'll be sorry for whoever is at the bottom of it."

The first match she tried would not light. The second burst into vivid flame. She stooped down.

"What is this thing upon your bed? It's some painted toy. You impudent girl!"

Picking it up, she threw it on to the floor into the corner of the room. Her match went out. There was a sound like a little cry of pain.

"Whatever's that?" asked Lucy.

"It's nothing," replied Miss Ashton. "It was only the thing striking against the floor."

"I believe it's alive," I said. "It shrieked."

"I believe you have been drinking."

"Miss Ashton!"

"I have heard of people who have been drinking seeing things—that appears to be your condition now. Are you going to get into bed? You will have something to shriek for when the morning comes."

I got into bed, feeling so cowed, that I could not even resent, with a proper show of dignity, her monstrous accusation. That anyone could have been wicked enough to accuse me of such a thing! I was trembling all over. I believed that the thing had shrieked, and was haunted by a horrible doubt that it was alive. Never before was I in such a state of mind and body. My brain was all in a whirl. I could do nothing but lie there shivering; my joints and muscles seemed to be possessed by an attack of twitching spasms, as if I had been suddenly smitten with some hideous disease.

I heard Miss Ashton return to her own bed. Then a voice whispered in my ear, so gently that it could have been audible to no one but me—

"Never mind, dear. She's a beast!"

It was Lucy. I put out my hand. She was leaning over me.

"Kiss me," I muttered.

She kissed me. It did me good. I held her, for a moment, to me. It comforted me to feel her face against mine.

"Now go to sleep! and don't you dream!"

It was easy enough to talk; it was harder to do. I did not often dream. Not nearly so much as some of the other girls, who were always telling us of the things they dreamed about. Rubbish it mostly was. I always said they made up three parts of it, not believing that such stuff could get into the heads of sensible people, even when they were asleep. That night I dreamt while I was wide awake. I was overcome by a sort of nightmare horror, which held me, with staring eyes and racking head, motionless between the sheets, as if I had been glued to them. It was as if the thing which Miss Ashton had thrown on the floor was in an agony of pain, and as if it had communicated its sufferings to me.

At last I suppose I must have gone to sleep. And then it was worse than ever. What I endured in my sleep that night no one could conceive. It was as if I were continually passing through endless chambers of nameless horrors. With it all were mixed up the events of the evening. I saw Isaac Rudd, and the creature in the canvas cloth, and the two short men, and the person in the long black coat. They kept popping in and out, always in full enjoyment of my tortures. There were Emily and I, standing at the top of an enormous flight of steps, in pitch-black darkness, in frightful weather, outside the door of some dreadful place, and there were those dreadful creatures jeering at us because no one would let us in. And Tom—I knew that somewhere near Tom was crying. And the thing which was in the scrap of paper was with me all the night. It was always on me somewhere; now on my throat, biting through the skin; now on my breast, drawing the life right out of me; now on my toes, hampering my feet, so that I could scarcely lift them up and down; now inside my mouth, filling me with a horrible choking sense of nausea.

But perhaps the strangest part of it all was that, when I awoke, there actually was something on my forehead. I felt it against my chin. Giving my head a sudden shake it slipped off on to the pillow at my side. I sat up. It was broad day. I saw it as plain as could be. A little painted thing, tricked out in ridiculously contrasting shades of green, and pink, and yellow. As Miss Ashton had said, it might have been a toy. I had seen things not unlike it in the shop, among the Japanese and Chinese curiosities. Or it might have been a tiny representation of some preposterous heathen god, with beads for eyes.

CHAPTER IV
AN INTERVIEW WITH MR. SLAUGHTER

That was a curious day. More things happened on it than on any day of my life before. It was the beginning of everything and the end of some things. From morning to night there was continual movement like in the transformation scene in a pantomime. When, since one was born, nothing has taken place, and nothing changed, it makes such a difference.

I got up feeling dreadfully stale; an up-all-night sort of feeling. Not that I ever have been up all night; but I know what the sensation is like because of the descriptions I have read. Miss Ashton was disagreeable, and the girls were snappish—even Lucy Carr was short; and, I daresay, I was not too nice. But then there often is a little show of temper in the morning; it is human nature. They had all begun when I got down to breakfast, and, of course, I got black looks for that. I caught sight of Emily Purvis as I sat down. She nodded; but it struck me that she was not looking brilliant, any more than I was.

Breakfast stuck in my throat. The butter was bad as usual—cheap margarine just rank enough to make pastry taste. The bread seemed as if it had been cut for hours, it was so hard and dry. I did manage to swallow a mouthful of tea; but the water was smoked, and I do not like condensed milk which is just going off, so I could not do much even with that. On the whole I did not feel any better for the meal when I got into the shop. I am not sure that I did not feel worse; and I knew I should be sinking before dinner came. Mr. Broadley began at me at once. He set me re-packing a whole lot of stock, which he declared I had not put tidily away; which was perfectly untrue, because, as a matter of fact, it was Miss Nichols who had had it last, and it was she who had put it back again. And, anyhow, some of those trimmings, when they have been once shown, will not set neatly; they are like hats, they cannot be made to go just so.

It was past eleven, and I had not had a single customer; it was miserable weather, and perhaps that had something to do with it, because scarcely a soul came into the shop. Mr. Broadley kept me at putting the shelves in order, almost as if I had been stock-taking. Not that I cared, for I hate doing nothing; especially as, if you so much as speak to one of the other young ladies, he is fit to murder you; that is the worst of your married shopwalkers, directly a girl opens her mouth he jumps down it. Still, I did not like it all the same; because I was getting tired, and hungry too; and, when you are hungry, the only way to stave the feeling off is to be kept busy serving; then you cannot stop to think what you would like to eat.

At last, just as a customer entered the shop, and was coming toward me, up sailed Mr. Broadley.

"Miss Blyth, you're wanted in the office."

My heart dropped down with a thump. I had half expected it all along, but now that it had come I went queer all over. I had to catch hold of the counter to keep up straight. Miss Nichols, seeing how it was with me, whispered as she went past:

"It's all right, Pollie, don't you worry, it's nothing. Buck up, old girl."

It was nice of her to try to cheer me up; but there was a choking something in my throat which prevented me from thanking her. Broadley was at me again.

"Hurry up, Miss Blyth, don't stand mooning there. Didn't you hear me tell you that you are wanted in the office?"

He was a bully, he was, to the finger-tips. I knew that he was smiling at me all the time; enjoying my white face, and the tremble I was in. When I got away from the counter I felt as if my knees were giving way beneath me. Everyone stared as I went past—I could have cried. They knew perfectly well that being summoned to the office during working hours meant trouble.

Outside the office was Emily Purvis. I had been wondering if she would be there, yet it was a shock to see her all the same. She was quite as much upset as I was. I knew that her nearest friends were down in Devonshire, and that she was not on the best of terms with them; so that if there was going to be serious trouble, she would be just as badly off as I was, without any friends at all. Her pretty face looked all drawn and thin, as if she were ten years older than she really was. It would only want a very little to start her tears. Her voice shook so that I could hardly make out what she said.

"Pollie, what do you think they'll do to us?"

"I don't know. Where's Tom? Did he get in all right? Has he—been sent for?"

"How can I tell? I don't know anything about Mr. Cooper. You know, Pollie, it was not my fault that I was in late."

"So far as I know it was neither of our faults. I wonder if Tom got in all right."

"Bother Tom! It's very hard on me. I wonder if they'll fine us?"

Before I could answer Mr. Slaughter put his head out of the office.

"Come in there! Stop that chattering! Are you the two young women I sent for?"

We went in, standing like two guilty things. Mr. Slaughter sat at his desk.

"Which of you is Mary Blyth?"

"I am, sir."

"Oh, you are, are you?"

He leant back in his chair, put his hands in his pockets, and looked me up and down, as if he was valuing me. He was a little man, with untidy hair and a scrubby black beard. I could not have been more afraid of him if he had been a dozen times as big. He had a way of speaking as if he would like to bite you; and as if he wished you to clearly understand that, should he have to speak again, he would take a piece clean out of you. Everybody about the place was more frightened of him than of Mr. Cardew. It was he who had made it what it was. In the beginning it had been nothing; now there were all those shops. He was a thorough man of business, without a grain of feeling in him. We all felt that he looked on us assistants as if we were so many inferior cattle, not to be compared, for instance, to the horses which drew his vans.

I could have sunk through the ground as he continued to stare at me. It was more than I could do to meet his eyes; yet something seemed to say that he did not think much of what he saw. His first words showed that I was right.

"Well, Mary Blyth, it seems that you're an altogether good-for-nothing young woman. From what I find upon this paper it seems that there's everything to be said against you, nothing in your favour; no good for business, no good for anything. And you look it. I can't make out why you've been kept about the place so long; it points to neglect somewhere. It appears that you're habitually irregular; three times yesterday you missed making a sale, and you know what that means. We don't keep saleswomen who send customers away empty-handed; we send them after the customers. You were impertinent to Mr. Broadley. And, to crown all, you were out last night till something like the small hours. On your return you made a riot till they let you in, and more riot when you were in. Miss Ashton, who is far too gentle, does not like to say that you had been drinking, but she says that you behaved as though you had been. In short, you're just the type of young woman we don't want in this establishment. You'll go and draw whatever is due to you, if anything is due; and you'll take yourself and your belongings off these premises inside of half an hour. That, Mary Blyth, is all I have to say to you."

For the moment, when he had finished, I was speechless. It was all so cruel and unjust; and there was so much to be said in reply to every word he uttered, that the very volume of my defence seemed to hold me paralysed. I could only stammer out:

"It is the first time I have been reported to you, sir."

"As I have already observed, there has evidently been neglect in that respect. The delay amounts to a failure of duty. I will make inquiries into its cause."

"It was not my fault that I was late, sir."

"No? Was the gentleman to blame?"

My face flamed up. I could have slapped him on the cheek. What did he mean by his insinuations?

"You have no right to speak to me like that!"

"When young women in my employment misbehave themselves as you have done I make plain speaking a rule. A man was with you, because one was seen. You can apportion the blame between you." I could not tell him it was Tom; it might have been bad for him. "None of your airs with me; off you go. Stay! This other young woman heard me talk to you; now you shall hear me talk to her. Is your name Emily Purvis?"

"Yes, sir. It's the first time—I never meant it—it wasn't my fault."

Emily broke into stammering speech; he cut her short.

"Don't you trouble yourself to talk; I'll do all the talking that's required. You were out after hours with Miss Blyth. I'm not going to ask any questions, and I'll listen to no explanations; young women who scour the streets at midnight are not the sort I like. We are judged by the company we keep. You were Mary Blyth's companion last night; you'll be her companion again. With her, you'll draw what is due to you; with her, you'll clear yourself off these premises inside half an hour. Now, stop it!"

Emily began crying.

"Oh, Mr. Slaughter, I've done nothing! it isn't fair! I've nowhere to go to!"

"Oh, yes, you have, you've outside this office to go to. Now, no nonsense!" He struck a hand-bell; a porter entered. "Take these young women out of this; let them have what's due to them; see they're off the premises inside half an hour."

"Oh, Mr. Slaughter!" wailed Emily.

It made me so angry to see her demean herself before that unfeeling thing of wood, that I caught her by the wrist.

"Come, Emily! don't degrade yourself by appealing to that cruel, unjust, hard-hearted man. Don't you see that he thinks it fine sport to trample upon helpless girls?"

"Come, none of that."

The porter put his hand upon my shoulder. Before I knew it we were out of the office and half a dozen yards away. I turned upon him in a flame of passion.

"Take your hand from off my shoulder! If you dare to touch me again you'll be sorry!"

He was not a bad sort. He seemed scared at the sight of me.

"I don't want to do anything to you. Only what's the good of making a fuss? You know he's master here."

"And, because he's master here, I suppose, if he tells you to behave like a miserable coward, you would?"

"What's the use of talking? If he says you've got to go, you've got to, and there's an end of it. You take my advice, and don't be silly."

"Silly! Your advice! When I ask you for your advice, you give it, not before."

I stood and glared. I do not think he altogether liked the look of me; I am sure that had he touched me I should have flown at him, and I rather suspect he knew it. While he hesitated I heard someone speaking in loud tones in the office from which we had just now been ejected. It was a man's voice.

"I want to see Miss Blyth."

It was Mr. Slaughter who replied.

"I say you can't see Miss Blyth, so you have my answer, sir."

"But that is an answer which I am unable to accept. I must see Miss Blyth, and at once, on a matter of grave importance."

"Don't talk to me, sir; my time is valuable. This is neither the hour nor the place at which we are accustomed to allow a stranger to see the young women in our employ. And as, in any case, this particular young woman is no longer in our employ, I repeat that you cannot see Miss Blyth."

"Oh, yes, you can—for here is Miss Blyth."

Darting past the porter, who seemed pretty slow-witted, I was back again in the office. A stranger was confronting the indignant Mr. Slaughter. I had just time to see that he was not old, and that he was holding a top hat, when he turned to me.

"Are you Miss Mary Blyth?"

"I am, Mr. Slaughter knows I am."

"My name is Paine, Frank Paine. I am a solicitor. If you are the Mary Blyth I am in search of I have a communication to make to you of considerable importance."

"Then make it outside, sir." This was Mr. Slaughter.

The porter appeared at the door.

"What's the meaning of this, Sanders? Didn't I tell you to see this young woman off the premises?"

"I was just seeing her, sir, when she slipped off before I knew it."

I flashed round at Sanders.

"You've assaulted me once, don't you dare to assault me again; this gentleman's a solicitor. If you're a solicitor, Mr. Paine, I want you to help me. Because I was accidentally prevented from returning till a few minutes after time last night, Mr. Slaughter wishes to send me away at a moment's notice, without a character."

"Is that the case, Mr. Slaughter?"

"What business is it of yours? Upon my word! I tell you again to leave my office."

"You appear to wish to carry things off with a high hand."

"A high hand! Mr. Slaughter thinks that he has only to lift his little finger to have us all turned into the street."

"If that is so, he is in error. Miss Blyth is my client. As her solicitor I would advise you to be sure that you are treating her with justice."

"Her solicitor!" Mr. Slaughter laughed. "I wish you joy of the job, you won't make a fortune out of her!" He waved his hands. "Any communication you have to make, you make through the post. For the last time I ask you to leave my office."

"Come, Mr. Paine, we will go. He need not ask us again. As he says, we can communicate with him through the post; and that will not necessitate our being brought into his too close neighbourhood."

I shook the dust of the office off my feet. Mr. Paine seemed puzzled. Outside was Emily, still crying. I introduced her.

"This is Emily Purvis, another victim of Mr. Slaughter's injustice. Emily, this is my solicitor, Mr. Paine."

She stared, as well she might. For all I knew, it might have been a jest of his, he might not have been a solicitor at all. The truth is I was quite as anxious to carry things off with a high hand as Mr. Slaughter could be; so I held my head as high as ever I could.

"Mr. Paine, we are going to draw our salaries. They are sure to get as much out of us in fines as they can. Will you come and see that they don't cheat us more than can be helped?"

"Fines!" Mr. Paine looked grave. "I doubt if they have any right to deduct fines without your express permission."

So he told them. That book-keeper had a pleasant time—the wretch! He made out that the princely sum of fifteen shillings was due to each of us; and off this, he wanted to dock me nine and six, and Emily five. Mr. Paine would not have it. He put things in such a way that the book-keeper referred to Mr. Slaughter. Mr. Slaughter actually sent back word to say that he was to give us our fifteen shillings and let us go. Then Mr. Paine handed in his card, and said that if we did not receive, within four and twenty hours, a quarter's salary in lieu of notice, proceedings would be immediately commenced for the recovery of the same.

So, in a manner of speaking, Emily and I marched off with flying colours.

CHAPTER V
THE MISSIONARY'S LETTER

The question was, what was to become of us? With no friends one cannot live long on fifteen shillings. Even if we got fresh situations in a fortnight it would only be with management that the money could be made to last that time; and, if we did, then we should be more fortunate than I expected to be.

Mr. Paine, however, postponed the solution of the difficulty by suggesting that I should arrange nothing until I had had a talk with him. I was willing; though what he had to do with it was more than I could guess; unless, like they used to do in the fairy tales, he was all of a sudden going to turn out to be my fairy godpapa. One thing I insisted on, that Emily should come with me. So, after I had scribbled a note to Tom—"Dear Tom, Emily and I have got the sack. Meet me after closing time at the usual place. Yours, as ever, Pollie. P.S.—Hope you're all right"—which Sanders, who was a good sort, promised to see he got—we all three got into a four-wheeled cab, with our boxes on top, and away we rattled.

"Good bye, Slaughter!" I said. "And may we never want to see your face again. And now, Mr. Paine, where are you taking us to?"

"To my offices in Mitre Court. What I have to say to you may take some time, and require a little explanation, and there we shall have the necessary privacy."

It sounded mysterious, and I began to wonder more and more what he had to say. I daresay I should have put my wonder into words, only just at that moment, who should I see, peeping at us round the corner of the street which we were passing, but the man who paid our bill at Firandolo's, and who said his name was Isaac Rudd. The sight of him gave me quite a shock.

"There's Isaac Rudd!" I cried.

"Isaac—who?" asked Emily. She can be dull.

"Why, the man who paid the bill last night."

Then she understood. Out went her head through the window.

"Where? I don't see him."

"No, and he'll take care you won't. Unless I'm mistaken, directly he knew I saw him he took himself away; but he's got his eye upon us all the same."

I looked at Emily, and she at me. Mr. Paine saw that something was up.

"Who was that you're speaking of? Someone who has been annoying you?"

"No—nothing. Only there was something a little queer took place last night."

I sat silent, thinking of Isaac Rudd; as, I daresay, was Emily too. Putting two and two together, it was odd that he should be just there at that particular moment. Especially as, a little farther on, I saw, standing in the shadow of a doorway, a man in a long black overcoat, with his hat crushed over his eyes, who bore the most amazing resemblance to the foreigner who had given me the something in a scrap of paper.

Suddenly I jumped up from my seat. I was so startled that I could not help but give a little scream. They both stared at me.

"What is wrong?" asked Mr. Paine.

"Why, look at that!"

There, sitting, as it were, bolt upright on my knee was the something which had been in the scrap of paper. Mr. Paine eyed it.

"What is it?"

"That's what I should like to know; also where it's come from; it wasn't there a moment back, and that I'll swear."

"May I look at it?"

"Certainly; and throw it out of the window too, for all I care."

Mr. Paine took it up. He turned it over and over.

"It looks like one of the images, representatives of well known deities, which are used as household gods on some of the Pacific coasts. People hang them over their beds, or over the thresholds of their doors, or anywhere. Imitations are sold in some of the London shops. Perhaps Messrs. Cardew & Slaughter keep them in stock."

"That I am sure they don't. And, if they do, that's not out of their stock. That was given to me last night by a foreigner in yellow canvas cloth. It jumped out of the scrap of paper in which it was wrapped——"

"Jumped?"

"If it didn't jump I don't know what it did do; I can tell you it took me aback. Miss Ashton threw it on to the floor; yet, when I woke up this morning, it was on my forehead, though how it got there I know no more than the dead."

"Are you in earnest, Pollie?"

"Dead earnest. It's my belief I left it in the bedroom, though I might have put it in my pocket, but how it came on to my knee is just what I can't say."

Mr. Paine was dividing his attention between me and the thing.

"This is very interesting, Miss Blyth. Especially as I also have had a curious experience or two lately. Can you describe the person who gave it you?"

I described him, to the best of my ability.

"That is—odd."

His tone seemed to suggest that something in my description had struck him; though what it was he did not explain.

"You'd better throw that thing out of the window," I said. "I've had enough of it."

"Thank you; but, if you have no use for it, if you do not mind, I should like to retain it in my own possession. It's a curiosity, and—I'm interested in curiosities."

He slipped it into his waistcoat pocket. I noticed that once or twice he felt with his fingers, as if to make sure that it still was there.

Mr. Paine was very civil to us when we reached his office—a funny, dark little place it was. He got out some cake, and biscuits, and a decanter of wine, and Emily and I helped ourselves, for I was starving. Sitting at a table in front of us, he took some papers out of a drawer, and began to look at them. Now that I could notice him more I could see that he was tall and well set up; quite the gentleman; with one of those clear-cut faces, and keen grey eyes, with not a hair upon it—I mean upon his face, of course, because I particularly observed that his teeth and eyelashes were perfect.

"Before I go into the subject on which I have ventured to bring you here, I am afraid I shall have to ask you one or two questions, Miss Blyth."

His manner was just what it ought to have been, respectful, and yet not too distant.

"Any answers I can give you, Mr. Paine, you are welcome to."

"What was your mother's maiden name?"

"Mary Ann Batters. She died six years ago next month, when I was fourteen. My father's name was Augustus. He was a most superior person, although unfortunate in business; and though he died five years before my mother, I've heard her say, almost to her last hour, that she had married above her—which I believe she did."

"Had your mother any relations?"

"None."

"Think again."

"Well, in a manner of speaking, there was one; but about him least said soonest mended; although he was her brother—that is, until she cast him off."

"What was his name?"

"Benjamin. Although I do not remember ever hearing her mention it, and, indeed, she was opposed to speaking of him at all; I learned it was so through finding some letters of his in one of her boxes after she was dead, and those letters I have unto this day."

"That is fortunate; because it is as the representative of Mr. Benjamin Batters that I am here."

"Indeed? You don't mean to say so. This is a surprise."

And not a pleasant one either. I had heard of Mr. Benjamin Batters, though not for years and years, but never had I heard anything to his credit. A regular all-round bad lot he must have been, up to all sorts of tricks, and worse than tricks. I had reason to believe he had been in prison more than once, perhaps more than twice. When you have a relation like that, and have forgotten all about him, and are thankful to have been able to do it, you do not like to have him come flying, all of a sudden, in your face. I was not obliged to Mr. Paine for mentioning his name. If that was all he had to talk about I was sorry I had come.

"I may take it, then, that Mr. Benjamin Batters is an uncle of yours."

"In a manner of speaking. Although, considering my mother, his sister, cast him off, and that I myself never set eyes upon the man, it is only by a figure of speech that you can call him so."

"Mr. Benjamin Batters, Miss Blyth, is dead."

"Then that alters the case. And I can only hope that he died better than, I have been told, he lived."

"I should mention that I myself never met Mr. Batters, nor do I, really, know anything at all about him. My connection with him is rather an odd one. A little more than a week ago I received this package." He held out a bundle of papers. "Its contents rather surprised me. Among other things was this letter, which, with your permission, I will read to you. 'Great Ka Island, lat. 5° South; long. 134° East'—that is the heading of the letter; the address at which it purports to have been written. A curious one, you will perceive it is. There actually is such an island. It lies some three hundred miles off the western coast of New Guinea, in the Arafura Sea; and that, practically, is all I have hitherto been able to learn about it. I have made inquiries, in the likeliest places, for someone who has ever been there, but I have not, as yet, been able to light on such a person. Ships, it appears, trade among the islands thereabouts. To the captain of one of those the letter may have been handed. He may have transferred it to the captain of an English vessel engaged in the Australian trade, who bore it with him to England, and then posted it to me; for that it was posted in London there is the postmark on the original package to witness. I am informed, however, that letters from those out-of-the-way corners of the world do reach England by circuitous routes, so that, in itself, there is nothing remarkable in that.

"There is a discrepancy, I am bound to add, which, considering what the letter purports to be, is a distinct misfortune—it is undated. But I will read it, and then you yourself will see my point.

"'Dear Sir', it runs, 'I write to inform you that this morning, at 10.45, there died here, of enteric fever in my presence, Benjamin Batters. From what I have heard him say, I believe he was in his sixty-first year, though, latterly, he looked more, and was, at one time, of Little Endell Street, Westminster.'"

"That was where mother lived when she was a girl," I interposed.

Mr. Paine read on:

"'At his particular request I send you this intimation, together with the documents which you will find enclosed. Set apart from the world as here I am I cannot say when an opportunity will arise which will enable me to despatch you this, nor by what route it will reach you; but, by the mercy of an All-seeing Providence, I trust that it will reach you in the end.

"'Mr. Batters suffered greatly towards the close; but he bore his sufferings with exemplary patience. He died, as he had lived, at peace with all men.

"'I am, Dear Sir, your obedient servant,

"'Arthur Lennard, Missionary.

"'P.S.—I may add that I have just buried poor Batters, with Christian rites, as the shadows lengthened, in our little graveyard which is within hearing of the sea.'"

Mr. Paine ceased; he looked at us, and we at him.

"That's a funny letter," I remarked.

"Funny!" cried Emily. "Pollie, how can you say so? Why, it's a romance."

"Precisely," said Mr. Paine. His voice was a little dry. "It is, perhaps, because it is so like a romance that it seems—odd."

I had a fancy that he had meant to use another word instead of "odd;" I wondered what it was.

"According to that letter my Uncle Benjamin must have changed a good deal before he died; I never heard of his being at peace with anyone. Mother used to say that he would fight his left hand against his right rather than not fight at all."

"From what you have been telling us a marked alteration must have taken place in his character. But then, when people are dying, they are apt to change; to become quite different beings—especially in the eyes of those who are looking on." Again there was that dryness in the speaker's tone. I felt sure there was a twinkle in his eye. "You will see, Miss Blyth, that this letter is, to all intents and purposes, a certificate of your uncle's death; you will understand, therefore, how unfortunate it is that it should be undated. We are, thus, in this position; that, although his death, and even his burial, are certified, we do not know when either event took place; except that, as it would appear from the context, he was buried on the same day on which he died—which, in such a climate, is not unlikely. Our only means of even remotely guessing at the period of his decease is by drawing deductions from the date of his will."

"His will! You don't mean to say that my uncle Benjamin left a will?"

"He did; and here it is."

"I expect that that's all he did leave."

"You are mistaken; he left a good deal more."

"To whom did he leave it?"

"It is to give you that very information, Miss Blyth, that I ventured to bring you here."

I gasped. This was getting interesting. A cold shiver went down my back. I had never heard of a will in our family before, there having been no occasion for such a thing. And to think of Uncle Benjamin having been the first to start one! As the proverb says, you never can tell from a man's beginning what his end will be—and you cannot.

Emily came a little closer, and she took my hand in hers, and she gave it a squeeze, and she said:

"Never mind, Pollie! bear up!"

I did not know what she meant, but it was very nice of her, though I had not the slightest intention of doing anything else. But, as my mother used to say, human sympathy is at all times precious. So I gave her squeeze for squeeze. And I wished that Tom was there.

CHAPTER VI
SOLE RESIDUARY LEGATEE

Mr. Paine unfolded a large sheet of blue paper.

"This is, it appears, the last will and testament of your late uncle, Benjamin Batters. It is, as, when you have heard it, I think you will yourself agree, a somewhat singular document. It came with the letter from Mr. Lennard which I have just now read you. It is, so far as I know, authentic; but it is my duty to inform you that the whole affair is more than a little irregular. This document seems to be a holograph—that is, I take it that it is in your uncle's own writing. Do you recognise his handwriting?"

He gave me the paper. I glanced at it. Emily peeped over my shoulder.

"Well, I shouldn't exactly like to go so far as that, but I have some letters of his, and, so far as I remember, the writing seems about the same. But you can see them if you like; then you will be able to compare it."

"I should be very much obliged, Miss Blyth, if you would allow me to do so. A very important point would be gained if we could prove the writing. As matters stand at present I am in a position in which I am able to prove absolutely nothing. Mr. Batters was a stranger to me; he seems, also, to have been a stranger to you; I can find nobody who knew him. All we have to go upon is this letter from the other end of the world, from a person of whom no one knows anything, and which may or may not be genuine. Should another claimant arise we should be placed in a very awkward situation."

"Is there going to be another claimant? And what is there to claim?"

"So far as I know there is going to be none; but in legal matters it is necessary to be prepared for every emergency. As to what there is to claim, I will tell you."

I gave him back the blue paper. He began to read. Emily came closer. I could feel that she was all of a flutter.

"'This is the last will and testament of me, Benjamin Batters.

"'On condition that she does as I hereby direct I give and bequeath to my niece, Mary Blyth, the daughter of my sister,

Mary Ann Batters, who married Augustus Blyth, and who when I last heard tell of her was assistant at Cardew & Slaughter's, a life income of Four Hundred and Eighty Eight Pounds Nineteen Shillings and Sixpence a year, interest of my money invested in Consols.'"

Mr. Paine stopped.

"I may say that bonds producing that amount were enclosed in the package. Here they are."

"Four Hundred and Eighty Eight Pounds Nineteen Shillings and Sixpence a year!" said Emily. "I congratulate you, Pollie!"

She kissed me, right in front of Mr. Paine. For my part, I felt a queer something steal all over me. My heart began to beat. To think of Uncle Benjamin, of all people in the world, leaving me such a fortune as that! And at the very moment when all my expectations in this world amounted to exactly fifteen shillings! There need be no more waiting for Tom and me. We would be married before the year was out, or I would know the reason why.

Mr. Paine went on.

"The will is by no means finished, ladies. The greater, and more remarkable part of it is to follow. When you have heard what it is I am not sure that Miss Blyth will consider herself entitled to congratulations only."

What could he mean? Had the old rascal changed his mind in the middle of his own will?

"'This money,' Mr. Batters goes on to say, 'was earned by hard labour, the sweat of my brow, and sufferings untold, so don't let her go and frivol it away as if it was a case of lightly come and lightly go.'"

"If that's true, Uncle Benjamin must have altered, because I've heard my mother say, over and over again, that he never could be induced to do an honest day's work in all his life."

"People sometimes do alter—as I have observed. 'On condition, also, that she does as I tell her,' continues Mr. Batters, 'I bequeath to her the life tenancy of my house, 84, Camford Street, Westminster, together with the use of the furniture it contains.'"

"What!" interrupted Emily, "a house and furniture too. Why, Pollie, what else can you want?"

I wondered myself. But I was soon to know. Mr. Paine read on:

"'I give and bequeath the above to my niece, Mary Blyth, on these conditions. She is to live in the house at 84, Camford

Street. She is never to sleep out of it. She is never to be away from it after nine o'clock at night or before nine o'clock in the morning. She is only to have one companion, and she must be a woman. They are to have no visitors, neither she nor her companion. She is to choose a companion, and stick to her. If the companion dies, or leaves her, she is not to have another. She is afterwards to live in the house alone. She is not to let any woman, except her companion, enter the house. She is not to allow any man, under any circumstances whatever, to come inside the house, or to cross the doorstep. These are my wishes and orders. If she disobeys any one of them, then may my curse light on her, and I will see that it does, and the house, and the income, and everything, is to be taken from her, and given to the Society for Befriending Sailors.

"'Signed, Benjamin Batters.'"

"That, Miss Blyth, is what purports to be your uncle's will."

"But," I gasped, "what is that at the end about stopping in the house, and letting no one come in, and all the rest of it?"

"Those are the conditions on which you are to inherit. Before, however, touching on them I should like to point out in what respect the will seems to me to be most irregular. First of all, it is undated. There could hardly be a more serious flaw. There is nothing to show if it was made last week or fifty years ago. In the interim all sorts of things may have happened to render it null and void. Then a signature to a will requires two witnesses; this has none. Then the wording is extremely loose. For instance, should you fail to fulfil certain conditions, the property is to pass to the Society for Befriending Sailors. So far as I can learn there is no such society. Societies for befriending sailors there are in abundance, but there is not one of that exact name, and it would become a moot point which one of them the testator had in his mind's eye."

"All of which amounts to—what?"

"Well, it amounts to this. You can receive the money referred to, and live in the house in question, at your own risk, until someone comes forward with a better title. It will not need a very good title, I am sorry to say, Miss Blyth, to be better than that which is conferred on you by this document. I am not saying this by way of advice, but simply as a statement of the case as it appears to me."

"What I want to know is, what's the meaning of those conditions? I suppose, by the way, there is such a house."

"There certainly is. Camford Street is an old, and not particularly reputable street, one end of which leads into the Westminster Bridge Road. No. 84 is in a terrace. From the exterior—which is as much as I have seen of it—it looks as if it had not been occupied for a considerable period of time. Indeed, according to the neighbours, no one has lived in it for, some say ten, others fifteen, and others twenty years."

"That sounds nice," cut in Emily. "If no one has lived in it for all that time I shouldn't be surprised if it wanted a little cleaning."

"Not at all improbable, from what it looks like outside. The shutters are up at the window—on that point, I may mention, a man who has a small chandler's shop on the opposite side of the road, tells rather a singular story. He informed me that, to the best of his knowledge and belief, the last occupant of the house was a man named Robertson. He was an old man. Mr. Kennard, my informant, says that what became of him he does not know. He did not move; there was no attempt to let the place; he simply ceased to be seen about. Nor has a living soul been seen in the house for years. But, he says, some months ago, he is not sure how many, when he got up one morning to open his shop, on looking across the road he saw that all the windows inside were screened by shutters. He declares that not only were there no shutters there the night before, but dirty old blinds which were dropping to pieces, but that he never had seen shutters there before, and, indeed, he doubted if there were such things at any other house in the terrace. If his tale is true, it seems an odd one."

"It sounds," said Emily, "as if the house were haunted."

"Without going so far as that, it does seem as if the shutters could hardly have got there of their own accord, and that someone must have been inside on that particular night, at any rate. No one, however, was seen, either then or since. There the shutters are, as one can perceive in spite of the accumulated grime which almost hides the windows. No one seems to know who the house belongs to, or ever did belong to; and I would observe that, since no title deeds were in the package, or any hint that such things were in existence, we have only Mr. Batters' bare word that the property was his. I should hasten to add that there is a small parcel addressed to Miss Blyth, whose contents may throw light, not only on that matter, but on others also."

He handed me a parcel done up in brown paper. It was addressed, in very bad writing, "To be given to my niece, Mary Blyth, and to be opened by her only." I cut the string, and removed the wrapper. In it was a common white wood box. Emily leaned over my shoulder.

"Whatever is inside?" she asked.

The first thing I saw when I lifted the lid, gave me a start, and I own it—there, staring me in the face, was the own brother of the little painted thing which was in the packet which the foreigner had slipped between my fingers.

"Why," I cried, "if there isn't another!"

"Another!" Mr. Paine gave a jump. "That's very odd." He was fishing about in his waistcoat pocket. "I thought you gave me the one you had."

"So I did. You put it in the pocket in which you're feeling."

"I thought I did. But—have you noticed me taking it out?"

"You've not taken it out, of that I'm sure."

"But—I must have done. It's gone."

His face was a study. I hardly knew whether to laugh or not.

"It strikes me," he remarked, "that someone is playing a trick on us; and, as I'm not over fond of tricks which I don't understand, I'll put an end to this little joke once and for all."

There was a fire burning in the grate. Laying the box down on a chair, taking the little painted thing between his finger and thumb, off he marched towards the fireplace. As he was going, all of a sudden he gave a little jump, as I suppose, loosened his hold, and down the thing dropped on to the floor. He stood staring at his hand, and at the place where it had fallen, as if startled.

"Where's it gone?" he asked.

"It must have rolled under the table." This was Emily.

But it had not. We searched in every nook and cranny. It had vanished, as completely as if it had never been.

"This is a pretty state of affairs. If it goes on much longer we shall begin to take to seeing things. If the rest of the contents of the box are of the same pattern, you might have kept it, Mr. Paine, for all I care."

But they were not. The next thing I took out was a key. It was a little one, and the queerest shape I ever saw. It was fastened to a steel chain; at one end of the chain was a padlock. Attached to the handle of the key was a kind of flying label; on it this was written:

> "To Mary Blyth. This is the key of 84, Camford Street. The lock is high up on the left-hand side of the door. There is no keyhole. You will see a green spot. Press the key against the spot and it will enter the lock. Push home as far as it will

go, then jerk upwards, and the door will open. Don't try to enter when anyone is looking. Directly you get it, tear off this label and burn it. Then pass the chain about your waist, underneath your dress, and snap the padlock. If you lose the key, or let it go for a moment from your possession, may the gods burn up the marrow in your bones. And they will."

"That's cheerful reading," I observed, when I had read the label to an end. I passed it to Mr. Paine.

"It is curious," he admitted. "In which respect it's of a piece with all the rest."

When Emily read it her eyes and mouth opened as wide as they very well could do.

"I never!" she cried. "Isn't it mysterious?"

"What shall I do?" I asked, when the chain and key had been returned to me.

Mr. Paine considered.

"You had better do as instructed — burn the label; that is, after we have taken a copy. There is nothing said against your doing that; and, if you have a copy, it will prevent your memory playing you false. As for the key itself — will it do you any harm to fasten it to your waist in the manner directed?"

"Except that it's a bit too mysterious for my taste. Some folks like mysteries; I don't."

"My dear," cut in Emily, "they're the salt of life!"

"Then I don't like salt. Perhaps it's because I'm a plain person that I like plain things. Here's more mystery."

The only thing left in the box was an envelope. When I took it out I found that on it this was written:

"This envelope is for Mary Blyth, and is not to be opened by her till she is inside 84, Camford Street."

I showed it to Mr. Paine, who was copying the label.

"What shall I do with that?"

"As you are told. Open it when you are in the house, and afterwards, if it is not expressly forbidden, you can, if you choose, communicate the contents to me."

While he copied the label I went with Emily into an inner room, which turned out to be his bedroom; put the chain about my waist inside my bodice, and closed the padlock; and it was only when I had done so that I discovered that it had no key, so that how I was to open it, and get the chain off again, goodness only knew. Emily kept talking all the while.

"Pollie, isn't it all just lovely? In spite of what you say, your Uncle Benjamin must have been a really remarkable man. It's like a romance."

"I wish my Uncle Benjamin hadn't been such a remarkable man, then he might have left me the money and the house without the romance. Bother your romance, is what I say."

"You're a dear," she affirmed, and she held up her hands—and very pretty hands they were. "But you have no soul."

"If that's what you call soul," I answered, "I'm glad I haven't."

When we got back to Mr. Paine, I began at him again.

"Now let me clearly understand about those conditions. Do you mean to say that I'm to stop in the house all alone?"

"You may have a companion—who must be a woman."

"I'll be your companion! Do let me be your companion, Pollie!"

I looked at Emily, who stood in front of me with flushed cheeks and eager eyes; as pretty a picture as you could wish to see.

"Done!" We shook hands upon it. "I only hope you won't have too much romance before you've been my companion long."

"No fear of that! The more there is the more I'll like it."

I was not so certain. She spoke as if she were sure of herself. But, for my part, I felt that it remained to be seen. I went on:

"What was that about being in before nine?"

"You are never to sleep out of the house. You are always to be in it before nine at night, and never to leave it before nine in the morning."

"That's a nice condition, upon my word!" I turned to Emily. "What do you think of that? It's worse than Cardew & Slaughter's."

"It does seem rather provoking. But"—there was a twinkle in her eye—"there may be ways of getting out of that?"

"What was that about no man being allowed in the house?"

"No man, under any circumstances, is to be allowed to cross the doorstep; nor, indeed, is anyone, except the lady you have chosen to be your companion."

"But what about my Tom?"

"Your—Tom? Who is he?"

"Mr. Tom Cooper is the gentleman to whom I am engaged to be married."

"I am afraid that, by the terms of the will, no exception is made even in his favour."

I did not answer. But I told myself that we would see about that. If, as Emily hinted, there were ways of getting the better of one condition, it should not be my fault if means were not found to get the better of the other too.

Almost immediately afterwards we started for the house; all three of us again in the four-wheeler which had been waiting for us the whole of the time. I wondered who was going to pay the fare. It would make a hole in my fifteen shillings.

CHAPTER VII
ENTERING INTO POSSESSION

It was Mr. Paine who settled with the cabman. It had not struck me that we had been passing through an over-savoury neighbourhood; we drew up in front of a perfectly disreputable-looking house. Not that it was particularly small; there were three storeys; but it looked so dirty. And if there is one thing I cannot stand it is dirt. I could easily believe that no one had lived in it for twenty years; it was pretty plain that the windows had not been cleaned for quite as long as that.

"Well," I declared as I got out of the cab, "of all the dirty-looking places I ever saw! If no one is to be allowed to set foot inside except Emily and me, who do you suppose is going to clean those windows?"

"That, I am afraid, is a matter which you must arrange with Miss Purvis; the will makes no exception in favour of window cleaners."

"Then all I can say is that that's a nice thing." I turned to Emily. "This is going to turn out a pretty sort of romance—charwomen is what we shall have to commence by being."

"I'm not afraid of a little work," she laughed.

I looked at the door.

"That writing on the label said that we were not to go into the house when anyone was looking. How are we going to manage that? Are you and the cabman to turn your backs?"

"I don't think that that is necessary; this shall be an exception. After you've opened the door we'll hand the luggage to you when you're inside."

Mr. Paine and the cabman were not by any means the only two persons who were looking. Our stoppage in front of No. 84 had created quite a wave of interest. People were watching us at doors and through windows, and a small crowd of children had gathered round us in a circle on the pavement. As it was out of the question for us to wait till all eyes were off us, I straightaway disobeyed at least one of the directions which were on the label.

What looked like an ordinary opening for a latchkey was in its usual place on the right hand side of the door, but when I slipped my key into that it turned round and round without producing any visible effect whatever. So I examined the other side. There, sure enough, so high up as to be almost beyond my reach, was what looked like a small dab of green paint. When I pushed the key against it it gave way. The key went into the apparently solid wood-work right up to the handle. I gave it an upward jerk; the door was open. However neglected the windows were, that lock seemed to be in good condition.

The door had opened about an inch. We all stared at it as if something wonderful had happened. I confess that I was a little startled, because I had used so little force that it was a wonder to me how it had come open. The children, giving a sort of cheer, came crowding close round. Mr. Paine had to order them back. I pressed my hand against the door. As it swung upon its hinges a bell sounded somewhere in the house. It seemed to come from upstairs, with a shrill, metallic clanging.

"There might be someone in already, who wanted to have warning of anyone's approach."

This was Emily. She was staring into the passage as if she expected to see something strange.

"Come," said Mr. Paine. "Let me help you in with the luggage; then I must leave you. People are taking a greater interest in the proceedings than is altogether desirable. You may find them a nuisance if you don't look out."

The crowd was being reinforced by children of an older growth. Loiterers were stopping to stare. People were coming out of their houses. As Mr. Paine said, their interest was becoming too demonstrative. He helped the cabman to get our boxes into the passage. Then he went. We shut the door after him in the faces of the crowd. Emily and I were left alone.

It was an odd sensation which I felt during those first few moments in which I realised that she and I were alone in my Uncle Benjamin's old house. I was conscious of a foolish desire to call the crowd to keep us company. Emily Purvis was hardly the kind of girl I should myself have chosen to be my sole companion in a tight place; and I had a kind of feeling that before very long it might turn out that I was in a tight place now.

It had all come on me so suddenly. More things had happened in a few hours than in all my life before. Yesterday I had thought myself a fixture at Cardew & Slaughter's; with marriage with Tom in the far-off distance; when the skies had fallen; or he had become a shopwalker and I a buyer; or we had saved up enough to start a small shop of our own. Now, Cardew

& Slaughter's had gone from me for ever. So far as money went I was free to marry Tom next week. But there was this horrid house—already I was calling it horrid—and my uncle's absurd conditions. If I was to observe them during the rest of my life I might as well write myself a nun at once, and worse. Better Cardew & Slaughter's—or anything.

We could hear the sound of traffic and voices in the street. Within the house all was still. There was no window over the door. In the passage it was so dark that it was as much as we could do to make out where we were. Emily put her hand upon my arm, as if she wished to make sure that I was close.

"It's no good our stopping here," I said. "We'd better light a candle and look about us. If the whole house is as light as this it must be a cheerful place to live in."

Acting on Mr. Paine's suggestion, as we had come along in the cab we had bought some candles and matches, and enough provisions to carry us on to to-morrow. Routing out a box, I struck a match. I gave Emily a candle and took one myself.

"Now to explore!"

We were brought to a standstill at the very start. In front of us was a door which led into a room opening out of the passage, or ought to have done. When I tried the handle I found that it was locked. I shook it, I even thumped at the panels, I searched for a key; it was no good. Against us the door was sealed.

"This is a comfortable beginning! If all the doors are locked it will be really nice. Perhaps Uncle Benjamin intended that I should merely have the run of the passage and the stairs."

Such, however, fortunately or otherwise, was not the case. The room behind the one which was closed was the kitchen; that was open, and a delightful state it was in. Not only was it inches thick in dust, but it was in a state of astonishing confusion. Pots and pans were everywhere. The last person who had used that kitchen to cook a meal in had apparently simply let the utensils drop from her hand when she had done with them, and left them lying where they fell. There was a saucepan here, a frying-pan there, a baking tin in the corner. Another thing we soon became conscious of—that the place was alive with cockroaches.

"What is it we are stepping on?" asked Emily.

"Why, it's beetles."

She picked up her skirts, she gave a scream, and back she scurried into the passage. I am not fond of the creatures; I never met anyone who was; but I am not afraid of them, and I was not going to let them drive me out of my own kitchen.

"There's one thing wanted, and that's light and fresh air. Only let me get those shutters down, and the window open, and then we'll see. I should say from the smell of the place that there has never been any proper ventilation since the house was built."

But it was easier said than done. Those shutters would not come down. How to begin to get them down was more than I could understand. To my astonishment, when I rapped them with my knuckles, they rang.

"I do believe," I said, "they're made of iron—they're a metal of some kind. They seem to have been built into the solid wall, as if they had never intended them to be moved. No wonder the place smells like a vault, and beetles, and other nice things, flourish, if they're fixtures."

A scullery led out of the kitchen. It was in the same state. One crunched blackbeetles at every step. There was a shutter before the window, which had evidently never been meant to be taken down. Where, apparently, there had been a door leading into a backyard or something, was a sheet of solid metal. No one was going to get out that way in a hurry; or in either.

"But what can be the meaning of it all?" I cried. "There must be an object in all this display of plate armour, or whatever it is. The place is fortified as if it were meant to stand a siege. I shall begin to wonder if there isn't a treasure hidden somewhere in the house; a great store of gold and precious stones, and that Uncle Benjamin made up his mind that at any rate thieves should not break through and steal."

"Oh, Pollie, do you think there is? Perhaps it's in the next room—perhaps that's why the door is locked."

"Perhaps so; and perhaps the key's upstairs, waiting for us to come and find it. Anyhow we'll go and see."

When I rejoined Emily it struck me that she was not looking quite so happy as she might have done; as if the romance was not taking altogether the shape she either expected or desired. I led the way upstairs. There was a carpet on them; but by the illumination afforded by a guttering candle, it only needed a glance to see that, if you once took it up, you would probably never be able to put it down again—it would fall to pieces. We had hardly gone up half-a-dozen steps when there came a clitter-clatter from above. Emily, who was behind, caught me by the skirt.

"Pollie! Stop! Whatever's that? There's someone there!"

"Rats, most likely. In a house like this there are sure to be all sorts of agreeable things. Where there aren't blackbeetles there are rats; and where there's either there's probably both."

Rats it was. Before we had mounted another tread two or three came flying down, brushing against our skirts as they passed. You should have heard Emily scream.

"Don't be silly," I said. "You talk about liking romance, and you make all that fuss because of a rat or two."

"It isn't exactly that I'm afraid of them, but—they startled me so. I daresay I shan't mind them when I've got used to them, only—I've got to get used to them first."

She was likely to have every opportunity. Presently two or three more came down. They seemed to be in a hurry. One, which was not looking where it was going, struck itself against my foot, and squeaked. Emily squealed too. When we reached the landing we could hear them scampering in all directions.

On that floor there were three rooms and a cupboard. The cupboard was empty. So was one of the rooms; that is, so far as furniture was concerned. But it was plain where, at any rate, some of the rats were. When I went into the room I stepped on a loose board. As it gave way beneath my tread I never heard such an extraordinary noise as came from under it. Apparently a legion of rats had their habitations underneath that flooring. I half expected them to rush out and make for us. I was out of the room quicker than I went in, and took care to close the door behind me. Emily had turned as white as a sheet.

"I can't stop in this place—I can't."

I was scornful.

"I thought you couldn't. You'll remember I told you that you wouldn't be my companion long. I knew that was the sort you were."

"It isn't fair of you to talk like that—it isn't. I don't mind ordinary things—and I'll not leave you, you know I won't. But all those rats! Did you hear them?"

"I heard them, and they'll hear me before long. There's going to be a wholesale slaughter of rats, and blackbeetles. There'll soon be a clearance when they've sampled some of the stuff I know of. I'm not going to be driven out of my own house by trifles."

One of the other rooms was a bedroom, a sort of skeleton of one. There was some carpet on the floor, or what had been carpet. There was an iron bedstead, on which were the remains of what might have been a mattress. But there were no signs of sheets or blankets; I wondered if the rats had eaten them.

After what we had seen of the rest of the house, the third room, which was in front, was a surprise. It was a parlour; not the remnants of one, but an actual parlour. There was what seemed to be a pretty good carpet on the floor. There was a round table, with a tapestry cover. There were two easy chairs, four small ones, a couch. On the sideboard were plates and dishes, cups and saucers. On the stove, which was a small kitchener, was a kettle, two saucepans, and a frying pan, all of them in decent order. Although the usual shutters screened the window, the place was clean, comparatively speaking. And when I went to a cupboard which was in one corner, I found that in it there were coals and wood.

"It is not twenty years since this room was occupied, there's that much certain; nor, from the look of it, should I say it was twenty hours. I should say there had been a fire in that stove this very day, and there's water in the kettle now."

"What's this?"

Emily was holding out something which she had picked up from the floor. It was a woman's bracelet, a gold bangle; though I had never seen one like it before. It was made of plain, flat gold, very narrow, twisted round and round; there was so much of it that, when it was in its place, it must have wound round the wearer's arm, like a sort of serpent, from the wrist to the elbow. At one end of it was something, the very sight of which gave me quite a qualm.

CHAPTER VIII
THE BACK-DOOR KEY

"Look!" I said. "Look!"

"Look at what? What's the matter with you, Pollie? Why are you glaring at me like that?"

"Don't you see what's at the end of it?"

She turned the bangle over.

"It isn't pretty, but—it's some sort of ornament, I suppose."

"It's that thing which was in the scrap of paper, or its double."

"Pollie! Are you sure?"

"Certain. I'll back myself to know that wherever it turns up."

Taking the bracelet from her I eyed it closely. There was no mistaking the likeness; to one end was attached the very double of that painted little horror. Emily criticised it as she leant over my shoulder.

"It looks as if it were meant for a man who mostly runs to head. And what a head it is! Look at his beard, it reaches to what may be meant for feet. And his hair, it stands out from his scalp like bristles."

"Don't forget his eyes, how they shine. They must be painted with luminous paint, or whatever they call the stuff, which lights up in the dark. The other night they gleamed so I thought the creature was alive. And his teeth—talk about dentist's advertisements! I believe it's meant for one of those heathen gods who are supposed to live on babies, and that kind of thing. He looks the character to the life. But fancy your picking it up from the floor! That's not lain there twenty years. There's not a speck of rust upon it. It's as bright as if it had just come off somebody's arm."

"Pollie, do you think there's anybody in the house besides we two?"

"My dear, I haven't the faintest notion; you can use your senses as well as I can, and are quite as capable of putting two and two together. One fact's obvious, it's not long since somebody was in this room. But we've the rest of the house to see; I can tell you more when we've seen it. Come, let's go upstairs."

Putting the bracelet on the table, I left the room. Emily seemed reluctant to follow. I fancy that if she had had her way she would have postponed the remainder of our voyage to later on—a good deal later on. And, on the whole, I hardly wondered, because, directly we began to go upstairs, such a noise came from above, and, indeed, from everywhere, that you would have thought the whole place was alive; and so it was—with rats. I had heard of the extraordinary noises the creatures could make, but I had never realised their capacity till then. Emily stood trembling on the bottom step.

"I daren't go up, I daren't."

"Very well, then; stop where you are. I dare, and will."

Off I started; and, as I expected, directly I moved, she rushed after me.

"Oh, Pollie, don't leave me, don't. I'd sooner do anything than have you leave me."

On that top floor there were again three rooms. And again, one of them was empty. It was a sort of attic, at the back. So far as I could make out it had no window at all; it was papered over if it had one. But talk of rats! It was a larger room than the one below, and seemed to be still more crowded. We could not only hear them, we could see them. There they were, blinking at the candlelight out of the floor and walls, and even ceiling. It was a cheerful prospect. I had heard of rats, when they had got rid of everything else, eating human beings. We two could do nothing against these multitudes; I felt sure that the mere fright of being attacked would be enough to kill Emily. I said nothing to her, but I thought of it all the same.

The door next to the attic was fastened. Whether it was locked or not I could not make out. It felt as solid as if it never had been opened, and had been never meant to open. When I struck it with my knuckles, it returned no sound. That it was something else besides a mere wooden door was obvious.

"Another treasure room!" I laughed.

But Emily did not seem pleased.

"I don't like these locked-up rooms. What is there on the other side?"

"I thought you were so fond of mystery."

"Not mystery like this." She lowered her voice. "For all we know there may be people inside, who, while we can't get at them, can get at us whenever they choose."

I laughed again; though conscious there was sense in what she said.

"Let's go and look at the other room and see if that's locked up too."

But the door of that yielded at a touch. It, also, had had occupants less than twenty years ago—a good deal less. It was furnished as a bedroom. There was a chest of drawers, a washstand, toilet-table, chairs, and a bed. On the latter the bedding was in disorder; sheets, blankets, pillows tumbled anyhow, as if somebody, getting out of it in a hurry, had had no time to put it straight. There was a lamp upon the toilet table, the blackened chimney of which showed it had been smoking; even yet the smell of a smoky lamp was in the air. The drawers were all wide open. One, which had been pulled right out, was turned upside down upon the floor, as if the quickest way had been chosen to clear it of its contents.

"It looks," said Emily, standing in the doorway, looking round her with doubtful eyes, and speaking as if she were saying something which ought to have been left unspoken, "as if someone had just got out of bed."

Throwing the bedclothes back, I laid my hand against the sheets. It might have been my imagination, but they seemed warm, as if, since someone had been between them, they had not had time to cool. Not wishing to make her more nervous than she was already, I hardly knew how to answer her; more especially as I myself did not feel particularly comfortable. If, as appearances suggested, somebody had been inside that bed, say, within the last half-hour, who could it have been? and what had become of him or her, or them? Crossing to the dressing-table, I touched the lamp-glass. It was hot, positively hot. I could have sworn that it had been burning within the last ten minutes or quarter of an hour. That was proof positive that someone had been there—lamps do not burn unless somebody lights them, and they do not go out unless somebody puts them out. Who could it have been? The discovery—and the mystery!—so took me aback that it was all I could do to keep myself from screaming. But, as Emily was nearly off her head already, and I did not want to send her off it quite, I just managed to keep my feelings under. All the same, I did not like the aspect of things at all.

To stop her from noticing too much, I tried my best to keep on talking.

"This is our bedroom, I suppose. How do you like the look of it? Not over cheerful, is it?"

"Cheerful?" I could see she shuddered. "Does any light ever get into the room?"

Where the window ought to have been were the usual massive and immovable shutters.

"The person who put up those shutters wasn't fond of either light or air. But you wait, I'll have them down, I like plenty of both. You heard Mr. Paine's story about the shutters having made their appearance in a night? If they did, then there was witchcraft used, or I'm a Dutchman. It took weeks, if not months, to get them there. If the walls have to be pulled to pieces I'll have them moved. Give me a week or two and you won't know the place. I'll turn it inside out and upside down. Because Uncle Benjamin had his ideas of what a house ought to be like, dark as pitch, and alive with rats, not to name blackbeetles, it doesn't follow that his ideas are mine, so I'll show him."

"We can't do all that, you and I alone together."

"Catch me trying! Before we're many hours older I'll have an army of workmen turned into the house."

"What about the conditions? No one is to be allowed to enter except us two, especially no man."

"Bother the conditions! Do you think I mind them? Uncle Benjamin must have been stark staring mad to think that I would. If I'm only to live in such a place as this on such terms as those, then I'll live out of it—that's all. By the way, where's the envelope which was in that box? I took it out of my dress pocket. 'This envelope is for Mary Blyth, and is not to be opened by her till she is inside 84, Camford Street.' Well, now Mary Blyth is inside 84, Camford Street—a nice, sweet, clean, airy place she's found it! So I suppose that now she may open the envelope. Let's hope that the contents are calculated to liven you up, because I feel as if I wanted something a little chirrupy."

Inside was a sheet of blue writing paper. It was not over clean, being creased, and thumb-marked, and blotted too. On it was a letter, written by somebody who was not much used to a pen. I recognised Uncle Benjamin's hand in a moment, especially because I remembered how, in his letters to mother, which I had in my box, the lines kept getting more and more slanting, until the last was screwed away in a corner, because there was no room for it anywhere else. And here was just the same thing. He began straight enough, right across the page, but, long before he had reached the bottom, he was in the same old mess.

"I need no ghost to tell me that this is from my venerated uncle. I remember his beautiful neatness. Look at that, my dear, did you ever see anything like those lines for straightness?"

I held up the page for Emily to see. She actually smiled, for the first time since she had been inside that house.

"Now let's see what the dear old creature says. Do hope it's something comforting. What's this?" I began to read out aloud.

"'Dear Niece,—Now that you are once inside the house, you will never sleep out of it again.' Shan't I? We shall see. Nice prospect, upon my word. 'You may think you will, but you won't. The spell is on you. It will grow in power. Each night it will draw you back. At your peril do not struggle against it. Or may God have mercy on your soul.' This is—this is better and better. My dear, Uncle Benjamin must have been very mad. 'You are surrounded by enemies.' Am I? I wasn't till I had your fortune. I'm beginning to wonder if I shouldn't have been better off without it. 'Out of the house you are at their mercy. They watch you night and day. When you are out, they are ever at your heels. Sooner or later they will have you. Then again may God have mercy on your soul. But in the house you are safe. I have seen to that. Do not be afraid of anything you may see or hear. *There is That within these walls which holds you in the hollow of Its hand.*' That last line, my dear, is in italics. It strikes me that not only was Uncle Bennie mad, but that writing novels ought to have been his trade. As you are so fond of saying, this is something like a romance; and I wish it wasn't. Emily, what's the matter with you now?"

She had come to me with a sudden rush, gripping my arm with both her hands—I doubt if she knew how hard. I could see that she was all of a tremble.

"I—I thought I heard someone downstairs."

"Not a doubt of it—rats."

"It—it wasn't rats. It sounded like footsteps in the room beneath."

"When I've finished uncle's letter we'll investigate; but I think you'll find it was rats—they've got footsteps. Let me see, where was I? Oh, yes— '*Its hand.* Go out as little as you can.' To be sure. I'm not fond of going out— especially with such a house as this to stop in. 'Be always back before nine. It is then the hour of your greatest peril begins. Should you ever be out after nine—which the gods forbid—let no one see you enter. They will be watching for you in the front. Go to Rosemary Street at the back. Between thirteen and fourteen there is a passage. At the end there is a wall. Climb it. There are two stanchions one above the other on the right. They will help you. Drop into the yard. Go to the backdoor. You will see a spot of light shining at you. Put the key in there. Turn three times to the left. The door will open. Enter and close quickly lest your enemies be upon you. If they enter with you may God have mercy on your soul. From your affectionate uncle, Benjamin Batters. P.S.—You will find the back door key on the parlour table.' Shall I? That's story number one at any rate. I haven't found any back door key on the parlour table, and I never saw one there. Did you?"

"There—wasn't one—I noticed—there was nothing on the table—when you put that bangle down."

I wished Emily would not speak in that stammering way, as if there was a full stop between each word or two. But I knew it was not the slightest use my saying so just then; that was how she felt.

"Of course. I did leave that bangle on the table, didn't I? That's one thing which we've found in uncle's dear old house which seems worth having; and one thing's something. Let's go and have another look at it."

Down the stairs again we went; Emily sticking close to my side as if she would rather have suffered anything than have let me get a yard away from her. One of the pleasantest features of my new possession seemed to be that every time we moved from one room to another about a hundred thousand rats got flurried; it sounded like a hundred thousand by the din they made. And Emily did not like them scurrying up and down the stairs when she was on them; nor, so far as that went, did I either.

When we reached the parlour, I made a dart at the table.

"Why, where's that bangle? I put it down just there, I remember most distinctly. Emily, it's gone! Whatever's this? I do believe—it's that back-door key!"

It was, at any rate, a key; and bore a family likeness to the one which was attached to the chain which was about my waist. I stared, scarcely able to credit the evidence of my own senses. Between our going from that room and our returning to it a miracle had happened; a transformation had taken place; a bangle—and such a bangle! had become a key. Apparently the back-door key of Uncle Benjamin's "P.S.!"

BOOK II
84, CAMFORD STREET

(THE FACTS OF THE CASE ACCORDING TO EMILY PURVIS.)

CHAPTER IX. MAX LANDER

Talk about romance! I never could have believed that after wishing for a thing your whole life long you could have had enough of it in so short a space of time. In the morning Pollie Blyth heard, for the very first time, that a fortune and a house had been left to her, and, before the night of that same day was over, she wished that it had not. And here had I been looking, ever since I was a teeny-weeny little thing, for a touch of romance to give existence a real live flavour, and then, when I got it, the best I could do was to wonder how I had been so silly as ever to have wanted it.

Poor Pollie! That first night in Camford Street she would go out. She said she must go and see her Tom. That he would be waiting, wondering what had become of her, and that nothing should keep her from him. Nothing did. I could not. And when I suggested that it might be as well for her to be a little careful what she did that very first night, she actually proposed that I should stop in that awful house by myself, and wait in it alone till she returned.

I would not have done such a thing for worlds, and she knew it. As a matter of fact I could not have said if I was more unwilling to leave the place, or to stay in it, even with her. The extraordinary conditions of her dreadful old uncle's horrible will weighed on me much more than they seemed to do on her. I felt sure that something frightful would happen if they were not strictly observed. Nothing could be clearer than his repeated injunction not to be out after nine, and her appointment with Mr. Cooper was for half-past eight.

Cardew and Slaughter are supposed to close at eight, but she knew as well as I did what that really meant. It was a wonder if one of the assistants got out before nine. Mr. Cooper was in the heavy, and the gentlemen in that department were always last. If he appeared till after nine I should be surprised, and, if we were at the other end of London at that hour, with the uncle's will staring us in the face, what would become of us? Being locked out of Cardew and Slaughter's was nothing to what that would mean.

But Pollie would not listen to a word. She is as obstinate as obstinate when she likes, though she may not think it.

"My dear," she said, "I must see Tom. Mustn't I see Tom? If you were in my place, and he was your Tom, wouldn't you feel that you must see him?"

There was something in that I acknowledged. It was frightful that you should be cut off from intercourse with the man you loved simply because your hours would not fit his. But then there was so much to be said upon the other side.

"I'm sure he'll be punctual to-night, he'll be so anxious. And you know sometimes he can get off a little earlier if he makes an effort. You see if he isn't there at half-past eight. I'll just speak to him, then start off back at once. He'll come with us, we shall be back here before nine, and then he'll leave us at the door."

That was how it was to turn out, according to her. I had my doubts. When you are with the man to whom you are engaged to be married half an hour is nothing. It's gone before you know it's begun.

It was eight o'clock when we left the house. I thought we should never have left it at all. We could not open the door. It had no regular handle; no regular anything. While we were trying to get it open the house was filled with the most extraordinary noises. If it was all rats, as Pollie declared, then rats have got more ways of expressing their feelings than I had imagined. It seemed to me as if the place was haunted by mysterious voices which were warning us to be careful of what we did.

"Of course if we're prisoners it's just as well that we should know it now as later on. How do you open this door?"

Just as she spoke the door opened.

"How did you do that?" I asked.

"I don't know." She seemed surprised. "I was just pushing at the thing when—it came open. There's a trick about it I expect; we'll find out what it is to-morrow, there's no time now. At present it's enough that it's open; out you go!"

When we were out in the street, and she pulled it to, it shut behind us with an ominous clang, like the iron gates used to do in the barons' castle which we read about in the days of old. We took the tram in the Westminster

Bridge Road, then walked the rest of the way. It was half-past eight when we arrived. As I expected, of course Mr. Cooper wasn't there.

"Pollie, we ought not to stop. We ought to be in before nine this first night, at any rate. We don't know what will happen if we're not."

"You can go back if you like, but I must and will see Tom."

Nine o'clock came and still no Mr. Cooper. I was in such a state I was ready to drop. It was nearly a quarter-past before he turned up. Then they both began talking together at such a rate that it was impossible to get a word in edgeways. When I did succeed in bringing Pollie to some consciousness of the position we were in, and she asked Mr. Cooper to start back with us at once, he would not go. He said that he had had such a narrow escape the night before, and had had such difficulty in getting in—so far as I could make out he had had to climb up a pipe, or something, and had scraped a hole in both knees of his trousers against the wall—that he had determined that it should be some time before he ran such a risk again, and had therefore made up his mind that he would be in extra early as a sort of set-off. It was no good Pollie talking. For some cause or other he did not seem to be in the best of tempers. And then, when she found that, after all our waiting, he would not see us home, she got excited. They began saying things to each other which they never meant. So they quarrelled.

Finally Mr. Cooper marched off in a rage, declaring that now she had come into a fortune she looked upon him as a servant, and that though she had inherited £488 9s. 6d. a year, and a house, he would not be treated like a lackey. She was in such a fury that she was almost crying. She assured me that she would never speak to him again until she was compelled, and that they would both be grey before that time came. All I wanted to do was to keep outside the quarrel, because they had behaved like a couple of stupids, and to find myself in safe quarters for the night.

"I don't know, my dear Pollie, if you're aware that it's past half-past ten. Do you propose to return to Camford Street?"

"Past half-past ten!" She started. Her thoughts flew off to Mr. Cooper. "Then he'll be late again! Whatever will he do?"

"It's not of what he'll do I'm thinking, but of what we're going to do. After what your uncle said, do you propose to return to Camford Street at this hour of the night?"

"We shall have to. There's nowhere else to go. I wish I'd never come to see him now; it hasn't been a very pleasant interview, I'm sure." I cordially agreed with her—I wished she had not. But it was too late to shut the stable-door after the steed was stolen. "Let's hurry. There's one thing, I've got the back-door key in my pocket, if the worst does come to the worst."

What she meant I do not think she quite knew herself. She was in a state of mind in which she was inclined to talk at random.

We had not gone fifty yards when a man, coming to us from across the street, took off his hat to Pollie. I had noticed him when she was having her argument with Mr. Cooper, and had felt sure that he was watching us. There was something about the way in which he kept walking up and down which I had not liked, and now that Mr. Cooper had gone I was not at all surprised that he accosted us. He looked about thirty; had a short light brown beard and whiskers, which were very nicely trimmed; a pair of those very pale blue eyes which are almost the colour of steel; and there was something about him which made one think that he had spent most of his life in open air. He wore what looked, in that light—he had stopped us almost immediately under a gas-lamp—like a navy blue serge suit and a black bowler hat.

"Miss Blyth, I believe, the niece of my old friend Batters. My name is Max Lander. Perhaps you have heard him speak of me."

His manner could not have been more civil. Yet, under the circumstances, it was not singular that Pollie shrank from being addressed by a stranger. Putting her arm through mine, she looked him in the face.

"I don't know you."

"Have you never heard your uncle speak of me—Max Lander?"

"I never knew my uncle."

"You never knew your uncle?" He spoke, in echoing her words, almost as if he doubted her. "Then where is your uncle now?"

"He is dead."

"Dead?"

"If you knew my uncle, as you say you did, you must know that he is dead. Come, Emily, let us go. I think this gentleman has made a mistake."

"Stop, Miss Blyth, I beg of you. Where did your uncle die?"

"I don't know where exactly, it was somewhere in Australia."

"In Australia!" I never saw surprise written more plainly on a person's face. "But when?"

"If, as you say, you knew him, then you ought to know better than I, who never did."

"When I last saw Mr. Batters he didn't look as if he meant to die."

He gave a short laugh, as if he were enjoying some curious little joke of his own.

"Where did you see him last?"

"On the *Flying Scud*."

"The *Flying Scud*? What's that?"

"My ship. Or, rather, it was my ship. The devil knows whose it is now."

"Mr. Lander, if that really is your name, I don't know anything about my uncle, except that he is dead. Was he a sailor?"

"A sailor?" He seemed as if he could not make her out. I stood close to him, so that I saw him well; it struck me that he looked at her with suspicion in his eyes. "He was no sailor. At least, so far as I know. But he was the most remarkable man who ever drew breath. In saying that I'm saying little. You can't know much of him if you don't know so much. Then, if he's dead, where's Luke?"

He spoke with sudden heat, as if a thought had all at once occurred to him.

"Luke? What is Luke?—another ship?"

"Another ship? Great Cæsar!" Taking off his hat, he ran his fingers through his short brown hair. "Miss Blyth, either you're a chip of the old block, in which case I'm sorry for you, and for myself too, or, somewhere, there's something very queer. Hollo! Who are you?"

While we had been talking a man had been sidling towards us along the pavement. He had on a long black coat, and a hat crammed over his eyes. As he passed behind Mr. Lander he stopped. Mr. Lander spun round. On the instant he tore off as if for his life. Without a moment's hesitation Mr. Lander rushed full speed after him. Pollie and I stood staring in the direction they had gone.

"Whatever is the matter now?" I asked. "What did the man do to Mr. Lander?"

"Emily, that's the man who slipped the paper into my hand last night—you remember? There's a cab across the road; let's get into it and get away from here as fast as we can."

We crossed and hailed the cabman. As he drew up beside the kerb, and we were about to enter, who should come tearing over the road to us again but Mr. Lander. He was panting for breath.

"Miss Blyth, I do beg that you will let me speak to you. If not here, then let me come with you and speak to you elsewhere."

"I would rather you did not come with us, thank you, I would very much rather that you did not."

He stood with his hand on the apron of the hansom in such a way that he prevented us from entering.

"Miss Blyth, you don't look like your uncle—God forbid! You look honest and true. If you have a woman's heart in your bosom I entreat you to hear me. Your uncle did me the greatest injury a man could have done. I implore you to help me to undo that injury, so far as, by the grace of God, it can be undone."

He spoke in a strain of passion which I could see that Pollie did not altogether relish. I didn't either.

"I will give you my solicitor's name and address, then you can call on him, and tell him all you have to say."

"Your solicitor! I don't want to speak to your solicitor; he may be another rogue like your uncle. I want to speak to you."

Before Pollie could answer, another man came up. He touched his hat to Mr. Lander.

"I beg your pardon, sir, but this is the young lady I told you about. Miss Blyth will remember me, because I was so fortunate as to do her a small service last night. May I hope, Miss Blyth, that you have not forgotten me?"

The man spoke in a small, squeaky voice, which was in ridiculous contrast to his enormous size. It was actually the creature who had paid the bill for us the night before at Firandolo's—one shilling and threepence! My impulse was to take out my purse, give him this money, and be rid of him for good and all. But, before I had a chance of doing so, Mr. Lander turned upon him in quite a passion.

"What do you mean by thrusting in your oar? Get out of it, Ike Rudd!"

"I beg your pardon, sir, I'm sure, if I'm intruding, and the young lady's; but, seeing that I was able to do her a little service, I thought that perhaps she might be willing——"

Mr. Lander cut him short with a positive roar.

"Don't you hear me tell you to take yourself out of this, you blundering ass!"

In his anger with Mr. Rudd he moved away from the cab. Without a moment's delay Pollie jumped into it, and dragged me after her.

"Drive off, and don't stop for anyone!"

It was done so quickly that before Mr. Lander had an opportunity to realise what was happening the driver gave his horse a cut of the whip. The creature gave a bound which it was a wonder to me did not upset the hansom, and when his master struck him again he galloped off as if he were racing for the Derby.

After we had gone a little way—at full pelt!—the driver spoke to us through the trap-door overhead.

"Where to, miss?"

"Is he following us?"

"Not he. He tried a step or two, but when he saw at what a lick we were going he jerked it up. He went back and had a row with the other chap instead, the one who came up and spoke to him I mean. They're at it now. Has he been bothering you, miss?"

"I don't know anything at all about him. He's a perfect stranger to me. I think he must be mad. Drive us to the Westminster Bridge Road, if you are sure that he's not following."

"I'll see that that's all right, you trust me." He swung round a corner. "He's out of sight now, I should think for good; but if he does come in sight again I'll let you know. What part of the Westminster Bridge Road?"

Pollie hesitated.

"I'll tell you when we get there."

CHAPTER X
BETWEEN 13 AND 14, ROSEMARY STREET

A church clock struck as we rolled along.

"That sounds like nine—a quarter-past eleven. What shall you do if we can't get in at all?"

"Not get into my own house? My dear, this is not a case of Cardew and Slaughter's. What is going to keep me out of my own house—if I choose to enter it with the milk!—I should like to know."

I did not know. I could not even guess. But all the same I had a sort of feeling that someone could—and might. "My own house" came glibly from her tongue. That morning there had been ten shillings between her and the workhouse; already she had become quite the woman of established means. I might have been the same had the case been mine. You never know. It must be so nice to have something of your very own.

We were nearing the Westminster Bridge Road. Again the driver spoke to us from above; he had hardly slackened pace the whole of the way.

"Coast clear, miss; not had a sight of the party since we lost him. Where shall I put you down?"

"I'll stop you in a minute; keep on to the left." Pollie spoke to me. "What did it say in the letter was the name of the street in which is the entrance to the back door?"

"Rosemary Street."

"Of course! I couldn't remember its stupid name."

"But I shouldn't tell him to put us down just there. You don't know who may be waiting for us."

I was leaning over the front of the cab, keeping a sharp look-out. There were the crowded trams and omnibuses, and many people on the pavements; but I noticed nothing in any way suspicious.

"Who should be waiting for us? Haven't we shaken Mr. Lander off? Didn't the cabman say so?"

"Yes. But—you never know."

"What do you mean? What are you driving at?"

"Nothing. Only it's past nine. The letter said that it was the time your greatest peril began."

"What nonsense you do talk! Do you think I pay attention to such stuff? Lucky I'm not nervous, or you'd give me the fidgets. The sooner everybody understands that I intend to go in and out of my own house at any time I please the less trouble there is likely to be. I'm not a child, to be told at what time I'm to come home."

I was silent. She spoke boldly enough; a trifle too boldly I thought. There was an unnecessary amount of vigour in her tone, as if she wished to impress the whole world with the fact that she was not in the least concerned. But she acted on the hint all the same—she stopped the cab before we reached our destination.

"It's all right now, miss," said the driver. It was rather a novel sensation for us to be riding in cabs, and the fare we paid him did make a hole in one's purse. It was lucky there was that four hundred and eighty-eight pounds nineteen shillings and sixpence to fall back upon. "You've seen the last of that fine gentleman, for to-night at any rate. Good-night, miss, and thank you."

I was not so sure that it was all right. We might have seen the last of "that fine gentleman," as the cabman called Mr. Lander, though there was nothing particularly "fine" about him that I could see; but there might be other gentlemen, still less "fine," who had yet to be interviewed. When the hansom had driven off, as we walked along the pavement, I felt more and more uncomfortable, though I would not have hinted at anything of the kind to Pollie for worlds.

"Have we passed Camford Street?" she wondered. "I don't know which side of it is Rosemary Street."

"I'm sure I don't. You had better ask."

We were standing at the corner of a narrow street, a pretty dark and deserted one it seemed. Pollie turned to make enquiries of some passer-by. A man came towards us.

"Can you tell me which is Rosemary Street?" she said.

"This way! this way!"

He took her by the arm and led her into a gloomy-looking street, as if he were showing her the way. She must have been purblind, or completely off her guard, to have been tricked by him so easily, because directly he spoke I recognised him as the person in the long black coat who had fled from Mr. Lander. I myself was taken by surprise, or I would have called out and warned her. But I suppose that I was bewildered by his sudden and wholly unexpected appearance, because, instead of bidding her look out, I went after her into the narrow lane, for really it seemed to be no more.

The moment we were round the corner two other figures appeared out of the darkness as if by magic. But by now Pollie had taken the alarm.

"Let me go!" she cried to her conductor. "Take your hand away from my arm!"

He showed no inclination to do anything of the kind.

"This way! this way!" he kept repeating, as if he were a parrot. He spoke with a strong foreign accent—as if his stock of English was not a large one.

But Pollie was not to be so easily persuaded. She stood stock still, evincing every disposition to shake herself free from his grasp.

"Let me go! let me go!"

The taller of the two newcomers uttered some words in a language which I had never heard before. Giving Pollie no time to guess what he was about to do he produced a cloth and threw it over her head. The other man sprang at her like a wild animal. Between them they began to bear her to the ground. I was not going to stand quietly by and see that kind of thing go on. I may not be big, and I do not pretend to be brave, but I am not an absolute coward all the same.

The smaller of the newcomers had taken me by the arm. I did my best to make him wish that he had not. I flew at him.

"You villain! Let me go, or I'll scratch your eyes out!"

The little wretch—he was little; I do not believe he was any bigger than I was, or perhaps I should not be alive to tell this tale—actually tried to throw a cloth over my head. When I put up my arms, and stopped his doing that, he began to dab it against my mouth, as if to prevent my screaming. There was a nasty smell about that cloth. It was damp. All of a sudden it struck me that he was trying to take away my senses with chloroform, or some awful stuff of that kind. And then didn't I start shrieking; I should think they might have heard me on the other side of the bridge.

In less than no time—or so it seemed to me—a policeman came round the corner. Apparently he was the only one who had heard; but he was quite enough.

"What's the matter here?" How I could have kissed him for his dear official voice. "What's the meaning of all this?"

Those three cowards did not wait to explain. Really before the words were out of his lips they were off down the lane like streaks of lightning. All my man left behind him was the smell of his horrid cloth. Beyond disarranging my hat and my hair, and that kind of thing, I knew that he had not damaged me almost before, so to speak, I examined myself to see.

"Has he hurt you?" asked the constable. "What was he trying to do?"

"He has not hurt me, thanks to you; but in another half second I'm quite sure he would have done. He was trying to chloroform me, or something frightful, I smelt it on his cloth."

"Who's this on the ground?"

It was Pollie. In my excitement I had quite forgotten to notice what had become of her. She lay all of a heap. Down I plumped on my knees beside her.

"Pollie!" I cried. "Has he killed you?"

"No fear," said the policeman. "She's only a bit queer. I shouldn't be surprised if they've played the same sort of trick on her they tried to play on you."

It was so. That policeman was a most intelligent man, and quite good-looking, with a fair moustache which turned up a little at the ends. They had endeavoured to stupefy her with some drug; the policemen said he didn't think it was chloroform, it didn't smell like it. I didn't know—to my knowledge I have never smelt chloroform in my life, nor do I ever want to. They had so far succeeded that she had nearly lost her senses, but not entirely. When I lifted her head she gave several convulsive twitches, so that it was all I could do to retain my hold. Then she opened her eyes and she asked where she was.

"It's all right," I told her. "They've gone. I hope they haven't hurt you."

She sat up, and she looked about her. She saw me, and she saw the constable, which fact she at once made plain.

"Oh, you're a policeman, are you? It's as well that there are such things as policemen after all." Her meaning was not precisely clear, but I hardly think it was altogether flattering to the force, which was ungrateful on her part. "I don't think they've hurt me. I believe it was the keys they were after, though they've left them both behind. Perhaps that was because they hadn't time to properly search for them." She was feeling in her pocket. "But they have taken Uncle Benjamin's letter—the one in which he told us how to get in at the back door."

There was a pause. I realised all that the abstraction might mean. If it had told us how to enter, it would tell them too. It was lucky they had had to go without the key.

"Do you know the men?" inquired the officer. "You had better charge them."

"Charge them?" She put her hand up to her head, as if she were dazed. I rather fancied she was making as much of her feelings as she could. Unless I was mistaken she was endeavouring to gain time to consider the policeman's words. Under the circumstances it might not be altogether convenient to charge them, even though they had proved themselves to be such utter scoundrels. "But I don't know what men they were."

"That doesn't matter; I daresay we know. You mustn't allow an outrage like this to pass unnoticed; they might have murdered you. I'll take the charge."

"Thank you." She stood up. He had produced his notebook. "I don't think I'll trouble you. There are circumstances connected with the matter which render it necessary that I should think it over."

"What's there to think about? It was an attempt to rob with violence, that's what it was; as clear a case as ever I knew. Come, give me your name, miss, then I'll have the particulars. What name?"

"I'm afraid you must excuse me. When I've thought the matter over you shall hear from me again, but I cannot act without consideration. Thank you all the same."

She carried it off with an air which took the constable aback. He was not best pleased. He eyed her for a second or two, then he closed his notebook with a snap.

"Very good. Of course, if you won't make a charge I can't take it. All I can say is, that if you find yourself in the same hole again, it'll about serve you right if no one comes to help you. It's because people won't go into court that there's so much of this sort of thing about. What's the good of having laws if you won't let them protect you."

Off he strode in a huff. I stared after him a little blankly.

"I don't think, Pollie, that you need have been quite so short with him. What he says is true; we might have been murdered if it hadn't been for him."

"I wasn't short with him; I didn't mean to be. But I couldn't charge them—could I? Besides, I want to get in. I didn't want to have him hanging about, for I don't know how long, watching us."

"Someone else may be watching us."

"No fear of that; they've had enough of it for to-night."

"So you said before, and hardly had you said there was nothing to fear when they had us at their mercy. It's my belief that what your uncle said in that letter—which now they've got—is true, and that we are in peril, dreadful peril, and that though we mayn't know it someone is watching us all the time. For my part I should like that policeman to have kept his eye upon us until we were safe indoors."

"After what my uncle said about allowing no one to see us enter?"

"It's a pity you are not equally particular about everything your uncle said, my dear."

Off we started down the lane, or street, or whatever it was. If I had had my way, after all that had happened, I would not have attempted to enter the house until at any rate next morning; I would rather have wandered about the streets all night. But I could see that she was set on at least trying to get in. I did not wish to quarrel, or to be accused of a wish to desert her after promising to be her companion. So I stuck to her side. Presently she spoke.

"Do you know, Emily, I believe I haven't got the very clearest recollection of the directions in uncle's letter. Didn't he say something about a passage?"

"He said that there was one between 13 and 14 Rosemary Street. The question is, is this Rosemary Street? We don't know."

"We'll soon find out. Which are 13 and 14? It's so dark it's hard to tell."

It was dark; which fact lent an additional charm to the situation. On one side were the backs of what seemed like mews; all they presented to us was a high dead wall. On the other was a row of cottages. If they were occupied all the inhabitants were in bed. There was not a light to be seen at any of the windows. Pollie began to peer at the numbers on the doors.

"This is 26." She passed on. "And this is 25; so 13 and 14 must be this way." We went farther along the street. "Here is 14—and here's the passage."

There was a passage, between two of the mean little houses. But so narrow an one that, if we had not been on the look-out for it, we should have passed it by unnoticed. Such was the darkness that we could not see six feet down it, so that it was impossible to tell where it led to, or what was at the end. I did not like the idea of venturing into it at all. I would have given almost anything to have flown down the street and sought the protection of that nice policeman. My heart was going pitter patter; I could feel it knocking against my corsets. I did not know if Pollie really was nervous, though I do not believe that it was in feminine human nature to have been anything else; but she behaved as though she wasn't. I could not have made believe so well. She apparently did not hesitate about what was the best, and proper, and only thing to do. There was not even a tremor in her voice.

"What did uncle say—at the end there is a wall?"

"I—I think he did."

"Then now for the wall."

She dashed into the passage. I was afraid to do anything else—and she did not give me a chance to remonstrate—so I went after her. I am thankful to say that nothing happened to us as we went, though I seemed to see and hear all sorts of things. After we had gone what appeared to be a mile Pollie suddenly stopped.

"Here is the wall. Now to climb it. Didn't uncle say we should find two stanchions? Was it on the right or on the left? Here they are, on the right; at least, I suppose they're stanchions. They feel like two pieces of iron driven into the brickwork. Now for a climb. One good thing—the wall isn't high."

Since I could only perceive her dim outline, and didn't wish to have her vanish altogether in the darkness, I had kept my hand on her. I could feel, rather than see, her going through the motions of climbing. I was conscious she had reached the top.

"Now, Emily, you come. It's easy; give me your hand."

I gave her my hand. In a second or two I was beside her, on the crest of the wall.

"Now let's go together, it's nothing of a drop."

As she said, it was nothing of a drop, and we went together. I suppose the wall was not much, if at all, over five feet in height. We landed on what felt like a pavement of bricks.

"It's a pity it's so dark. Here it's worse than ever. I can't see my hand before my face, can you?"

I could not. I told her so.

"Well, we'll have to feel, that's all; and we'll hope that we're in the right backyard. It would be something more than a joke if we weren't; they might take us for burglars. Come on; give me your hand again; we'll feel our way—tread carefully whatever you do. Hollo! here is a door. And—Emily, there's the spot of light! Do you see it there upon the door? As uncle says, it shines at us. Whether it's luminous paint, or whether it's something much more wonderful, truly, it lightens our darkness. Doesn't it, my dear? Where is that key?"

I could see, straight in front of us, a round spot of something which gleamed. It was not bigger than a threepenny piece. It might have been a monster glow-worm. Or, as Polly said, a dab of luminous paint. But there was no time to ascertain what it was, because, almost as soon as I saw it, I heard something too.

"Pollie, there's someone coming along the passage."

In the silence, there was what was obviously the sound of feet, feet which were apparently moving as if they did not wish to be heard.

CHAPTER XI
ONE WAY IN

I heard her fumbling with her pocket.

"I can't find the thing; I had it just now; I can't have dropped it."

"Oh, Pollie! Quick! they're at the wall!"

There was a scraping noise from behind; a muffled whispering. It sounded as if someone was endeavouring to negotiate the obstacle we had just surmounted. Still Pollie was continuing her researches.

"Where can I have put the thing?"

"Can't you find it? Oh, Pollie!"

Someone was on the wall; had dropped softly to the ground. The sound of his alighting feet was distinctly audible. There was a pause, as if for someone to follow. It was the pause which saved us. As I waited, with my heart actually banging against my ribs, my legs giving way at the knees, expecting every second that someone would come darting at us through the darkness, just in time to save me from toppling in a heap on to the ground Pollie found the key.

"I've got it! What did uncle say I was to do with it? Push it against the spot of light—and then? I've got it into the keyhole; can't you remember what uncle said I was to do with it then? It turns round and round."

"Pollie!—they're coming!"

They were. There was the sound of advancing footsteps. Approaching forms loomed dimly through the darkness. That same instant Pollie caught the trick of it; the door opened.

"Inside!" she gasped.

I was inside, moving faster than I had ever done in my life before. And Pollie was after me. The door shut behind us, seemingly of its own accord, with a kind of groan.

"That was a near thing!"

It could hardly have been nearer. Whoever was upon our heels had almost effected a simultaneous entrance with ourselves.

"He made a grab at my skirt; I felt his hand!"

But the door had closed so quickly that whoever was there had had no time to make an attempt to keep it open. It was pitch dark within, darker almost than it had been without. Pollie pressed close to my side. The fingers of one of her hands interlaced themselves with mine; she gripped me tighter than she perhaps thought. Her lips were near my ear; she spoke as if she were short of breath.

"There's a good spring upon that door; it moved a bit too fast for them; it shuts like a rat-trap. Listen!"

There was no need to bid me to do that; already my sense of hearing was on the strain. Someone, apparently, was trying the door; to see if it was really shut; or if it could not be induced to open again.

There were voices in whispered consultation.

"There's more than one; I wondered if there was more than one."

"There are three," I said.

Presently someone struck the door lightly, with the palm of the hand, or with the fist. Then, more forcibly, a rain of blows. Unless I was mistaken, the assault came from more than one pair of hands; it was like an attack made in the impotence of childish passion. The voices were raised, as if they called to us. They were like none which either of us had ever heard before; there was a curious squeakiness about them, as if their natural tone was a falsetto. What they said was gibberish to us; it was uttered in an unknown tongue. The voices ceased. After an interval, during which, one suspected, their owners had withdrawn a step or two to consider the situation, one was raised alone. It had in it a threatening quality, as if it warned us of the pains and penalties we were incurring. The fact that we were being addressed in a language which was, to us, completely strange, seemed at that moment to have about it something dreadful. Audibly, we paid no heed. Only I felt Pollie's grip growing tighter and tighter. I wondered if she knew that she would crush my fingers if she did not take care.

The single speaker ceased to hurl at us his imprecations. I felt sure it was bad language he was using. All was still.

"What are they doing?"

So close were Pollie's lips her whispered words tickled my ear. We had not long to wait before the answer came—in the shape of a smashing blow directed against the door.

"They're trying to break it down; they'll soon wake up the neighbourhood if they make that noise. Let's get farther into the house. Why—whatever's that?"

She had turned. In doing so she had pulled me half round with her. Her words caused me to glance about in the darkness, searching for some new terror. Nor was I long in learning what had caused her exclamation. There, glaring at us through the inky blackness in flaming letters, a foot in length, were the words "*TOO LATE!*" Beneath them was some hideous creature's head.

For a second or two, in the first shock of surprise, I imagined it to be the head of some actual man, or, rather, monster. As it gleamed there, with its wide open jaws, huge teeth and flashing eyes, it was like the vivid realisation of some dreadful nightmare. It was as if something of horror, which had haunted us in sleep, had suddenly taken on itself some tangible shape and form. So irresistible was this impression, so unexpected was the shock of discovering it, that I believe, if Pollie had not caught hold of me with both her hands, and held me up, I should have fallen to the floor. As it was I reeled and staggered, so that I daresay it needed all her strength to keep me perpendicular. It was her voice, addressing me in earnest, half angry, expostulation which reassured me—at least in part.

"You goose! Don't you see that it's a picture drawn with phosphorus, or luminous paint, or something, on the wall. It won't bite you; you're not afraid of a picture, child."

It was a picture; and, when you came to look into it, not a particularly well-drawn one either. Though I could not understand how we had missed seeing it so soon as we had entered—unless the explanation was that it had only just been put there. And, if that was the case, by whom? and how? A brief inspection was enough to show that the thing was more like one of those masks which boys wear on Guy Fawkes' day than anything else. It was just as ridiculous, and just as much like anything in heaven or earth.

"Let's get out of this; let's go into the house; why do you stop in this horrid place? Where's the door?"

"That's the question—Where is it? Uncle Benjamin's ideas of the proper way of getting in and out of a house are a little too ingenious for me; we seem to be in a sort of entry with nothing but walls all round us. Haven't you a match? Didn't you take a box out with you? For goodness sake don't say you've lost it."

I had not lost it, fortunately for us. I gave it to her. She struck a light. As she did so, the face and the writing on the wall grew dimmer. They were only visible when, standing before the flame, she cast them into shadow.

"Well, this is a pretty state of things, upon my word! There doesn't seem to be a door!"

There did not. The flickering match served to show that we were in what looked uncommonly like an ingenious trap. We were in what seemed to be a sort of vault, or cell, which was just large enough to enable us to turn about with a tolerable amount of freedom, and that was all. Semblance of a door there was none, not even of that by which we had entered. So far as could be judged by that imperfect light on all four sides were dirty, discoloured, bare walls, in not one of which was there a crack or crevice which suggested a means of going out or in. As Pollie had said, it was indeed a pretty state of things. It seemed that we were prisoners, and in a prison from which there was no way out. Our situation reminded me of terrible stories which I had read about the Spanish Inquisition; of the sufferings of men and women, and even girls, who had spent weeks, and months, and years, in hidden dungeons out of which they had never come alive again.

Just as I had begun to really realise the fact that there did not seem to be a door, Pollie's match went out. That same moment there came a fresh crash from without. And, directly after, another sound, or, rather, sounds. Something was taking place outside which, to us, shut in there, sounded uncommonly like a scrimmage, or the beginning of one, at any rate. Someone else, apparently, had climbed over the wall, a weighty someone, for we heard him descend with a ponderous flop. Without a doubt, the first comers had heard him too, with misgivings. Something fell, with a clatter— perhaps the tool with which they had been assailing the door. There was a scurrying of feet, as of persons eager to seek safety in flight. An exclamation or two, it seemed to us in English; then a thud, as if some soft and heavy body had come in sudden contact with the ground. A momentary silence. Then what was unmistakably an official voice, a beautiful and a blessed voice it sounded to me just then.

"All right, my lads! A little tricky, aren't you? I daresay you think you did that very neat. You wait a bit. Next time it'll be my turn, then perhaps I'll show you a dodge or two."

"Pollie," I exclaimed, "it's that nice policeman!"

"Hush! What if it is?"

What if it is? Everything—to me. It meant the flight of mystery, and an opportunity to breathe again. If I could have had my way I would have rushed out into the back yard and hugged him. But Pollie was so cold, and—when she liked and her precious Tom wasn't concerned—so self-contained. She froze me. I could hear his dear big feet stamping across the yard. He thumped against the door—and I perhaps within an inch of him and not allowed to say a word.

"Inside there! Is there anyone in there?" There was; there was me. I longed to tell him so, only Pollie's grasp closed so tightly on my arm—I knew it would be black and blue in the morning—that I did not dare. "Isn't there a bell or a knocker? This seems to be a queer sort of a house. There's something fishy about the place, or I'm mistaken."

I could have assured him that he was not mistaken, and would if it had not been for Pollie. I could picture him in my mind's eyes flashing the rays of his bull's-eye lantern in search of something by means of which he could acquaint the inhabitants within of his presence there without—in his innocence! As if we did not know that he was there. For some minutes—it seemed hours to me—he prowled about, patiently looking for what he could not find. Then, giving up the quest in despair, he strode across the yard, climbed heavily over the wall, stamped along the passage; we could hear his footsteps even in the street beyond.

Then I ventured to use my tongue.

"Pollie, why wouldn't you let me speak to him? Why wouldn't you let me tell him we were here?"

"And a nice fuss there'd have been. No, thanks, my dear. Before I call in the assistance of the police I should like to turn the matter over in my mind. It begins to strike me that where my Uncle Benjamin had reasons for concealment, I may have reasons too, at any rate until I know just what there is to conceal."

"In the meanwhile, how are we to get out of here? We're trapped."

"It's the ingenuity with which Uncle Ben, or somebody, has guarded the approach to his, or, rather, my, premises which makes it clear to me that there may be something about the place on which it may be as well not to be in too great a hurry to turn the searchlight of a policeman's eye. As to getting out of this—we'll see."

She struck another match, and saw. Either we had been the victims of an ocular delusion, or something curious had taken place since she had struck the first, for where, just now, there was a blank wall, in which was no sign of any opening, a door stood wide open. I could not credit the evidence of my own eyes.

"I declare," I cried, "it wasn't there just now."

"It was not visible, at any rate. I tell you what, my dear, we mayn't be the only occupants of this establishment, that's about the truth of it. It's possible that there's someone behind the scenes who's pulling the strings."

I did not like the ideas which her words conjured up at all.

"But—who can it be?"

"That's for us to discover."

There was a grimness about her tone which suggested what was, to me, a new side of Pollie's character. My impulse was to get away from the place as fast as ever I could and never return to it again. She spoke as if she were not only resolved to remain, and defied anyone to turn her out who could, but as if she had a positive appetite for any—to put it mildly—disagreeable experiences which her remaining might involve. The first horror she encountered then and there. If she did not mind it—I only wish that I could say the same of myself!

"You left the candle in the hall; let's go and fetch it."

As soon as we set foot outside that entry there was a pandemonium of sounds, as of a legion rushing, scrambling, squeaking. It was rats—myriads. The whole house swarmed with them; they were everywhere. They were about our feet; I felt them rushing over my boots, whirling against my skirts. One rat is bad enough, in the light, but in the dark—that multitude! I had to scream; to stumble blindfold among those writhing creatures, and keep still, was altogether too much for my capacity.

"Pollie!—light a match!—quick!—they're all over me!—Pollie!"

She struck a match. I do not know that it was any better now that we could see them. The light only seemed to make them more excited. In fact, their squeaking increased so much that, thinking that it angered them, I had half a mind to tell Pollie to put it out again. But she never gave me a chance. Taking me by the arm she dragged me along the passage so that we were at the front door before I knew it. When we went out we had left a candle on the floor in the passage so that it might be ready for us when we came back. Pollie stooped to pick it up. But, instead of doing so at once, she remained in the same position for a second or two, as if she were staring at something. Then she broke into a laugh.

"Well, that beats anything. That was a new candle when we went out; look at it now."

I looked; the candle had vanished. In its place what seemed to be a greasy piece of twine trailed over the side of the candlestick. The candle itself had been consumed by the rats; they had presented us with an object lesson, by way of showing us what they could do if they had a chance. I shuddered. I had heard of their fondness for fat. I am not thin. I thought of them picking the plumpness off my bones as I lay sleeping.

"Let's get out of this awful house. Do, Pollie, do! The rats will eat us if we stay in it."

"Let 'em try. They'll find us tougher morsels than you think. If a rat once has a taste of me he won't want another, I promise you that, my dear."

It was a frightful thing to say. It made my blood run cold to hear her. I felt absolutely convinced that if rats once started nibbling at me they would never rest content till they had had all of me that they could eat. I was sure that there was not enough that was tough about me. In that hour of trial I almost wished that there had been.

CHAPTER XII
THE SHUTTING OF A DOOR

We went upstairs to get another candle. A pound had been left on the parlour mantelpiece wrapped up in a stout brown paper. The rats had climbed up on to the shelf, they alone knew how, torn the paper to shreds, and made a meal off the contents. Pieces of candle were left, but not one whole one. Other things had been on that mantelpiece—tea, butter, bread, sugar, bacon, eggs, all the food we had. Practically the whole of it was gone. More of the tea was left than anything; possibly they had not found it altogether to their palates. But the butter had been entirely consumed; of the bacon, only the rind remained, and of the eggs the shells. I had heard, and I had read, a good deal about the voracity of rats, but never had I seen an example of it before. Pollie seemed to look on it as quite a joke. She only hoped, she said, that the quality of the provisions was good, so that they would not give them indigestion. But I could not see the fun at all. If that was a sample of their appetite, who could doubt that they would at any rate try to make a meal of us. I had been told of their devouring people's toes as if they were toothsome dainties. I did not want them to stay their stomachs with mine if I could help it. With such calmness as I could command I did my best to explain my views upon the matter. But Pollie only laughed. She would not be sensible. So I then and there made up my mind that, sleep or no sleep, I would not take off my clothes that night. If I was to be devoured they should eat their way through my garments before they could get at me.

Pollie lit one of the stumps of the candles. The rest she slipped into her pocket. If we left them there again, she remarked, they would probably vanish completely directly our backs were turned, and candles were precious, which was true enough; but there were other things which were precious as well as candles. I asked her what she was going to do.

"Investigate, that's what I'm going to do. I'm going to find out what's behind those two closed doors. If it's something alive I'd like to know. Also, in that case, I'd like to know just what it is. I'm not partial to rats, but I'm still less partial to strangers, who may be up to all kinds of tricks for all that I can tell, roaming about my house while I'm wrapped in the arms of Morpheus, so if anyone's going to roam I should like to make their acquaintance before they're starting."

There was something callous in her demeanour, a sort of bravado, which made me momentarily more uncomfortable. This was quite a new Pollie to me. She spoke as if we were enjoying ourselves, with an apparently entire unconsciousness of the frightful situation we actually were in. I was positively beginning to be afraid of her.

"Do let us go upstairs to the bedroom, Pollie, and lock ourselves in till the morning comes."

She glanced at her watch.

"It's morning now; the midnight chimes have sounded long ago. Would you like to have your throat cut in the silence of the night?"

"Pollie!"

"It wouldn't be nice to wake up and find it slit from ear to ear, would it? So don't be a goose. There's a door locked downstairs and another up. Before I rest I'm going to do my best to find out why those two rooms are not open to me, their rightful owner. If it's because they harbour cut-throats, it's just as well that we should know as soon as we conveniently can. So I'm off on a voyage of discovery. You can go to bed if you like."

Of course I went with her. It was a choice of two evils—frightful evils— but, under the circumstances, nothing would have induced me to go to bed by myself. I would far rather have had my throat cut with her than be eaten by rats alone. She began to hunt about the room.

"I'm looking for some useful little trifle which might come in handy in breaking down a solidly-constructed door or two. Here's a poker, heavy make—there's some smashing capacity in that; a pair of tongs; a fender— there's a business end to a fender; furniture—I have heard of chairs being used as battering-rams before to-day. My mother used to tell of how once, when his landlady locked him out because he wouldn't pay the rent of his rooms, my Uncle Benjamin burst his way into the house with the aid of a chair, snatched off a passing cart which was laden with somebody else's goods, so I can't see how he could object to my trying the same kind of thing in the house which was once his own. But I won't—not yet. To begin with I'll give the poker a trial, and you might take the tongs."

I took the tongs, though the only thing against which I should be likely to use them would be rats, even if I ventured to touch them. Indeed, the mere idea of squelching a wriggling, writhing, squeaking rat between a pair of tongs made an icy shiver go all down my spine. Pollie whirled the poker round her head with a regular whoop. What had come to her I could not imagine. Her eyes flamed; her cheeks were flushed; she was transformed. I verily believe that if half-a-dozen men had rushed in at the door that very second, she would have flown at them with a shriek of triumph. I had always known that one of her worst faults was a fondness for what she called "a bit of a scrimmage," and that in an argument very few people got the better of her; but I had never dreamed that she would go so far as she was going then. She seemed as if she were perfectly burning for someone to attack her.

Down the staircase she went, brandishing the poker over her head. I could not keep so close to her as I should have liked for fear of it. She stamped so as she descended that near the bottom she put her foot clean through one of the steps. No doubt the wood was rotten, but still she need not have insisted on treading as heavily as she possibly could. And as soon as she reached the passage, without giving me an opportunity to say a word, she dashed at the door of the room, which was locked, and hit it with all her might with the end of the poker. I expected to see her go right through it, but, instead of that, she gave a sort of groan, and down fell the poker with a clatter to the floor.

"Pollie, what is the matter? What have you done?"

The expression of her countenance had changed all in an instant. A startled look, a look almost of pain, had come upon her features. She was rubbing her arms and feeling her shoulder-blades.

"More than I intended. If you had exerted all your strength to drive a poker through what seemed a panel of ordinary wood, and discovered that it was sheet iron instead, you'd find that you'd done more than you intended—it sort of jars."

She picked up the poker again, and tapped it, much more gingerly, against the door. It gave forth a metallic ring.

"Iron, real iron! Not a shadow of a doubt of it. Pity I was not aware of the fact before I dislocated both my arms. Inside there! Do you hear me calling? If anyone is inside there, perhaps you'll be so good as to let me know. I'm Pollie! Pollie Blyth!"

Not a sound came from within, for which, personally, I was grateful. She hammered and hammered, but not the slightest notice was taken of the noise she made, except by the rats, who sounded to me as if they had gone stark mad. What we should have done if anyone had replied to her summons from within is more than I can tell. We certainly should have been no better off than before. We never could have got at them. Pollie tried all she could to get that door to open, without, so far as we could judge, producing the least impression of any sort or kind. She thought of forcing the lock, but when she endeavoured to insert the end of the poker into the keyhole, it turned out that it was such a tiny one that nothing very much thicker than a hatpin could be induced to enter.

"There's a mystery behind that door. Mark my words, Emily Purvis! It may take the form of decaying corpses, with their brains dashed out, and their throats all cut, and their bones all broken, in which case they'll haunt us while we slumber, pointing at us spectral fingers as we lie on our unquiet beds——"

"Pollie!"

"What's the matter, my dear? They'll be quite as cheerful anyhow as rats, and they won't take bites at us. At least, it's to be hoped they won't. Ugh! Fancy murdered spectres making their teeth meet in your flesh!"

"Pollie, if you talk like that I shall be ill; I know I shall. It isn't fair of you. I wish you wouldn't. Don't!"

"Very well, my love, I won't. I've only this remark to make—if the mystery doesn't take that form, it takes another, and probably a worse one. And let me tell you this. My Uncle Benjamin was a curiosity while he lived— my mother used to say that there never was such a devil's limb as he was, and she was his only sister, and disposed to look upon his eccentricities— and they were eccentricities—with a lenient eye; and it's my belief that he was quite as big a curiosity when he died. There were spots in his eventful life—uncommonly queer ones—which he would not wish revealed to the public eye. Unless I'm wrong, some of them are inside there; we're almost standing in their presence now, and I wish that we were quite."

She rattled the poker against the panels as a kind of parting salute. I had rather she had not. Every time she made a noise—and she kept on making one—it set my nerves all tingling. What with the things she said, and the way that she went on, and everything altogether, I was getting into such a state that I was beginning to hardly know whether I was standing on my head or heels. As for Pollie, she seemed in the highest possible spirits. It was incomprehensible to me how she dared. And the way she kept on talking!

"Before I'm very much older I will get the other side of you, or I'll know the reason why; the idea of not being allowed the free run of my own premises is a trifle more than I can stand. If I have to blow you down, I'll get you open."

Bang, bang, she went at it again.

"It sounds hollow, doesn't it? Perhaps that's meant by way of a suggestion, and is intended to let us understand that it's only a hollow mystery after all. Well, we shall see—and you shall see too, if you have curiosity enough."

I doubted if I had. I certainly had not just then. I wished, with all my heart, that she would come away from the horrid door, which presently she did, though not at all in the spirit I should have preferred, nor with the intentions I desired.

"There's a second Bluebeard's chamber upstairs. I may have better luck with that; perhaps it's not guarded with sheet iron. Uncle Benjamin must have spent a fortune at the ironmonger's if it is, which fortune should have been mine. We'll go and see."

I endeavoured to expostulate.

"Pollie, let's leave it till to-morrow. What's the use of making any more fuss to-night. I'm dying for want of sleep."

"Are you?" She looked at me with what struck me as being suspicious eyes; though what there was to be suspicious about is more than I can pretend to say. "But don't you see, my dear, that if you were to have that sleep for which you're dying, before you wake from it you may be dead. That second Bluebeard's chamber is next our bedroom. Suppose someone were to come out of it, while we were sunk in innocent repose, and — —" She drew her thumb across her throat with a gesture which made me shudder. "That wouldn't be nice, you know."

"Pollie, if you keep on talking like that I'll walk straight out of the house, I don't care what time of the night it is, and whether you'll come with me or whether you won't."

"I shouldn't if I were you. It would seem so irregular for a young lady to be taking her solitary walks abroad during the small hours, don't you know. Now up you go—up those stairs. We'll continue this conversation at the top. You vowed to be my companion to the death, and my companion to the death you're going to be."

I had never done anything of the kind, as she was perfectly well aware. But she did not give me a chance to contradict her. She bundled me up the staircase as if I were a child, with such impetuosity that I was breathless when we reached the landing. She was laughing. We might have been enjoying a romp. As if that were the place or season for anything of the sort!

"I trod upon a rat. Did you hear it squeal? I think it was its tail. I believe the little beast turned and flew at me, it felt as if it did. I hope I scrunched its silly little tail. What is one rat's tail among so many? Now for Bluebeard's Chamber No. 2. This time we'll beware of iron."

She made a preliminary sounding, luckily for her. Even a slight tap with the poker produced the ring of metal.

"Iron again, so that's all right. Now what shall we do? Shall we confess ourselves baffled after all, and leave a formal attack until the morning, or shall we try the effect of a little more poker smashing? What ho, within! Is anyone inside there, living or dead? If so, would you be so very obliging as to just step forth, and let us see what kind of gentleman you are."

There was no response, thank goodness. I took her by the arm.

"Pollie, do let's leave it to the morning, and do let's go to bed!"

"We'll go to bed!"

We went; at least we went into the bedroom. I did not feel much happier when we were there. To begin with, after the way in which she had been talking, my first thought was to do as much as possible to keep anyone out who might try to enter. But there was no key in the lock, the handle was loose, the hasp a bad one, so that the door would not even keep closed without our propping something up against it. I wanted Pollie to help me pile up a sort of barricade, consisting of chairs, the washhand stand, chest of drawers, and everything, as I had read of people doing in books. She only laughed at me.

"What good will it do? Who do you suppose it will keep out? Spectres? My dear, spectres will walk through stone walls. They pay no heed to trivial obstacles. Creatures of flesh and blood? You may take my word for it that if there are any of that sort alive and kicking in this house to-night, and they mean to come in here, they'll come in just when and how they choose, and they'll treat your ingenious barricade as if it wasn't there."

"Do you really think that there's anyone in the house beside ourselves?"

She shrugged her shoulders.

"I tell you what I do think, that if I'd known as much before as I do now, I'd have treated myself to a revolver, and you should have had one too."

"A revolver! Whatever should I have done with a revolver?"

"I can't say what you'd have done. I know what I'd have tried to do. I only wish that I had something loaded handy at this moment, there's more persuasive power in bullets than in your barricade, my dear. If the worst does come to the worst, and we have to protect ourselves against goodness alone knows what, if I could only have had my grip upon a pistol I don't fancy that all the scoring would have been upon the other side."

Whether she talked like that simply to make my hair stand up on end, or whether she was really in earnest, was more than I was able to determine. But as I looked at her I felt a curious something creep all over me. There was an expression on her face, a smile on her lips, a light in her eyes, which made me think of her Uncle Benjamin, to whose peculiarities we owed our presence there, and wonder if not only his blood, but something of his spirit too, was in her veins. I was persuaded that she perceived something actually agreeable in a situation in which I saw nothing but horror. And it was I who had supposed myself to be romantic!

She began to bustle about the room.

"I thought you were dying for want of sleep. Aren't you going to get between the sheets? There is a bed, and there are sheets, though I should hardly like to swear that they have been washed since someone slept between them last. When are you going to begin to undress?"

"Undress? Do you imagine that I intend to remove so much as a stitch of clothing while I remain beneath this roof?"

"Do you propose to sleep in your boots then?"

"If I am to sleep at all, and I am more than half disposed to hope that sleep may not visit my eyelids till I am out of this dreadful place, I propose to do so in what I stand up in. Pollie, have you ever heard of people's hair turning white in the course of a single night? I shouldn't be at all surprised if mine did. It feels as if it were changing colour now."

She stared as if she could not make me out. I wondered if she was noting the transformation which was taking place in my hair; if it had already become so obvious. Then she broke into peal after peal of laughter. The tears started to my eyes. Just as I was about to really cry there came a crash which shook the house.

It sounded as if someone had opened a door in the passage and shut it with a bang.

CHAPTER XIII
A VISION OF THE NIGHT

In a second Pollie was across the room, through the door, and on the landing. Before I could stop her she was tearing down the stairs, crying,

"Now we'll see who that is?"

I was in a dreadful position, not wanting to descend and be murdered as a result of seeing "who that is," nor daring to remain behind alone. I did not even venture to call out and try to stay her, not knowing who might hear my voice below. She had gone off with our only piece of candle and left me in the dark. All I could do was to steal after her as quickly as possible, keeping as close to her as I was able. Pollie was at the bottom almost before I started; she had gone down with a hop, skip, and a jump; I had to struggle with the darkness and the rats. Leaning over what was left of the banisters I could see the gleam of her candle in the passage. I expected to hear her shriek, and sounds of a struggle. The candle flickered, as if she were moving here and there in an endeavour to discover the cause of the commotion. Presently her voice came up to me.

"Emily!"

"Yes?"

I spoke in a much lower tone than she had done.

"No one's murdered, unless it's you up there. In case you're not, you might come down."

I went. She appeared disgusted, rather than otherwise, that she had not been murdered. She was stamping up and down the passage, banging at the closed door with her clenched fist, peering into the kitchen, making as much disturbance as was in her power.

"The only thing alive, barring rats, seems to be blackbeetles. We must have slaughtered thousands when we came in. The kitchen's black with them. Come and look." I declined. "But they can hardly have opened that door and shut it with a bang. There's no evidence to show which door it was, but I believe it was one which leads into Bluebeard's chamber."

"Pollie! How can you tell?"

"I can't tell, but I can believe. Can't I believe, my dear? I shall, anyhow. It is my belief"—she spoke with an emphasis which was meant for me—"that the mystery it conceals peeped out, then, fearing discovery, popped back again. It was its hurry to pop back which caused the bang. I wonder, by the way, if it was anyone who made a bolt into the street."

She tried to open the front door, against my wish, and failed. We had opened it from within easily enough before, when we had gone out to interview her Tom; but now it appeared to be as hermetically sealed as the door leading into what she called "Bluebeard's Chamber." It was no use reasoning with her. So soon as she found that it would not open she made up her mind that it should. For a quarter of an hour or twenty minutes she tried everything she could to force it. In vain. By the time we returned to the bedroom she was not in the best of tempers. And I had resolved that nothing should induce me to stay any longer alone with her beneath that roof than I could possibly help.

We had something like a quarrel. She said some very cruel things to me, and, when I told her she was unkind, and that there were aspects in which she reminded me of her Uncle Benjamin, she said crueller things still. I announced my intention to spend the night—what was left of it—upon a chair. She flung herself upon the bed and laughed.

Never shall I forget the remainder of that night, not if I live to be as old as Methuselah. To begin with, that chair was horribly uncomfortable, to speak of physical discomfort only. It was a small, very slippery, wooden Windsor chair; every time I tried to get into an easy position I began to slip off. I wondered more and more how I could ever have been so Quixotic as to have volunteered to become Pollie Blyth's companion. For one thing I had never suspected that she could have been so callous, so careless of the feelings of others, so indifferent to what they suffered on her behalf. Although I was tired out and out I could see that there would be no sleep for me, and no rest either, while I continued where I was. So far as I could judge, so soon as she threw herself upon the bed Pollie was asleep.

It was with quite a sense of shock I realised that this was the case. It seemed so selfish. The feeling of solitude it conveyed was frightful. I could hear her gentle breathing coming from the bed; I myself hardly dared to breathe at all. Half an inch of candle was guttering on the mantelpiece. By its light I could see that she lay on her left side, looking towards the wall, and that she did not appear to have moved since she had first lain down. I called to her:

"Pollie! Pollie! Pollie!" uttering each repetition of her name a little louder.

My voice seemed to ring out with such uncanny clearness I did not venture to really raise it. In consequence my modest tones did not serve to rouse her from her childlike slumber. So sound was her sleep that, all at once, the noise of her breathing ceased. It faded away. She was still, strangely still. So still that in the overwrought condition of my nerves I began to wonder if she was dead. I wished that she would move, do anything, to show she was alive. I tried, once more, to call upon her name. But, this time, my throat was parched; it came as an inarticulate murmur from between my tremulous lips.

I would have given much to have got up and shaken her back to life, and me. But it was as though I was glued to the seat, and that although I was continually slipping off. My body was stiff, my limbs cramped; it was only with an effort I could move them; of that effort I was not capable. I was conscious that I was passing into a waking nightmare. I closed my eyes because I was afraid to keep them open; then opened them again because I was still more afraid to keep them shut.

The house was full of noises. Pollie had not shut the door. It was ajar perhaps an inch or two. I wanted to put a chair in front, to shut it close. Apart, however, from my incapacity to move, I was oppressed by an uncomfortable fancy that someone, something, was peering through the interstice. This fancy became, by rapid degrees, a certainty. That I was overlooked I was sure. By whom, by what, I did not dare to think. How I knew I could not have told. I did know.

My eyes were fixed upon the door. For a moment, now and then, I moved them, with a flicker, to the right or to the left. Only for a moment. Back they went to the door. Once I saw it tremble. I started. It was motionless again. Then I heard a pattering. The rats were audible everywhere—under the floor at my feet, in the walls about me, above the ceiling over my head. The house was full of their clamour. But the pattering I heard was distinct from all the other sounds. It approached the room from without, pausing over the threshold as if in doubt. The door gave a little jerk, ever such a little one, but I saw it. A rat came in.

So it was a rat after all.

It stopped, just inside the door, peering round, as if surprised at the illumination which the candle gave. As if satisfied by what it saw it came in a little further. Close behind it was a second. This was of a more impatient breed; as soon as it appeared, with a little spring it ranged itself beside the other. Immediately there came two more. The four indulged themselves with a feast of observation, as though they were smelling out the land. After a while their eyes seemed to concentrate themselves on me, as if they could not make me out. Perhaps they thought that I was dead, or sleeping. I did not move, because I could not.

On a sudden the four gave a little forward scamper, as if they had been hustled from behind. The door was opened another half-dozen inches. More than a score came in. All at once I became conscious that rats were peeping at me from all about the room; out of holes and crannies of whose existence I had not been aware; above, below, on every side. And I knew that an army waited on the landing, as if waiting for a signal to make a rush. On whom? On me? Or on Pollie, asleep upon the bed? I was paralysed. I wanted to shriek and warn Pollie of what was coming; to let her know that in a second's time the room would be a pandemonium of rats, all of them in search of food. My tongue was tied. I could not speak. I could only wait and watch.

The house was not yet still. Not all had gathered without the door, many were observing me, with teeth sharp set, from hidden cavities. There was continually the clamour of their scurrying to and fro. But some instinct told me that their numbers increased upon the landing. I could hear their squeals, as if they snapped at each other in the press. Another score had harried the first score farther forward. They were so close that where they stood they hid the floor. It seemed so strange to see so many, all with their eyes on me. Yet what were they to those who were without? Something told me that those who watched me in the room had come further out of their holes! that in another instant they would spring down; and that then the rush would come. I think that my heart had nearly ceased to beat; that the blood had turned to water in my veins. I was cold; a chill sweat was on my face. The hand of death had come quite close.

I but waited for its actual touch; for whose approach the rushing of the rats should be the signal; when—what was it fell upon my ear? What sound, coming from below? Not rats? No, not rats. Mechanically I drew breath; I verily believe it was the first time I had breathed for I know not how long. The inflation of my lungs roused me. I listened with keener ears. I knew that what I had heard the rats had also heard; that it was because of it that the rush had not begun; that they attended what was next to come with a sense of expectancy; of doubt; of hesitation.

Moments passed; the sound was not repeated. Had it been a trick of our imagination; mine and the rats'? All was still, even the scurrying of their friends below. If I heard nothing, they did; they retreated. There were fewer within the room; I had not noticed their going, but they had gone. I felt that their unseen comrades, who were about me, had drawn back again into their holes. What was it caused that noise? There was a board that creaked. No rat's foot had caused that. Again. Was that a step upon the stairs?

Someone, something, was ascending from below? Who—what—could it be? An inmate of the Bluebeard's Chamber? What shape of horror would it take? Why did Pollie sleep so soundly? In my awful helplessness inwardly I raged. The rats heard; already they were flying for their lives. Why did she not hear? Would nothing rouse her from her slumbers? Danger, the danger she had herself foretold, was stealing on us. She had boasted of her courage. Why did she not come out of sleep to prove she was no braggart? What was it bound my limbs with chains, and kept me from stretching out my arm to touch her where she lay? What was the choking in my throat, so that when I tried to speak I seemed to strangle?

Silence again. This seemed to be a jest that someone played: the sound, then silence; still silence, long drawn out, then again the sound. If something came, why did it not come quickly? I should not be so fearful of a thing I saw as of a thing that I did not; I could not be.

The steps had reached the staircase which led directly to our room. There were fewer intervals of silence; though, yet, between each, there was a pause, as if to listen. They were very soft; as if someone walked velvet footed, being most unwilling to be heard. If I had sprung to my feet, roused Pollie, rushed to the door, defying all comers to come on, I wondered what would happen; and should have dearly liked to see.

But I was a craven through and through.

The footsteps gained the landing: moved towards the door; stayed without, while their owner listened. It might have been my fancy, but, so acutely was I listening, that I could have declared that I heard a hand placed gently against the panel. An interval. Pollie remained quiet on the bed. She had not moved since first she had lain down. What kind of sleep was this of hers? Did no warning come to her in dreams to tell her that there was something strange without? It was not fair that she should be so utterly at peace, while I had to bear the burden all alone. She was stronger than I. Why did she not wake up?

The door came a little forward; perhaps another half-dozen inches. Again a pause; as if to ascertain if the movement had been observed. Whoever was without was cautious. Then——

Then something appeared at the opening.

What I had expected to see I could not for the life of me have told. Some shape of horror, some monster born of the terror I was in; a diseased imagining of my mental, moral, physical paralysis; a creature, neither human nor inhuman, but wholly horrible, which should come stealing, resistless, in, to force me, in my agony, to welcome death.

What it was I actually saw, at first, I could not tell. It was not what I expected; that I knew. Something more commonplace; yet, considering the hour and the place, almost as strange.

When the mist had cleared from before my vision, I perceived it was a face. What kind of face even yet I could not see; the shock of the unexpected added to my confusion. It was only after it had remained quiescent for perhaps the better part of a minute that I realised it was a woman's.

A woman's face!

But not like any woman's face that I had seen before. As I gazed my fear began to fade; a sense of wonder came instead. Was I asleep or waking? I asked myself the question. Were these things happening to me in a dream? Glancing at me through the partly open door was the kind of face one reads and dreams about; not the kind one meets in daily life. At least, in the daily life which I have led. I was vaguely conscious that it was beautiful; beautiful in so strange a sort; but most clearly present to my mind was the bewildering fact that it had a more wonderful pair of eyes than any I had supposed a woman could have had. It was not only that they were large, nor that they were lovely. They had in them so odd a lustre. It was as though some living thing were in them, which kept coming and going, breaking into light, fading into darkness. They were wild eyes; such as no Englishwoman ever could have had. This face was brown.

For at any rate some minutes it stayed motionless, watching me. Only by degrees did it dawn upon me that possibly its owner was nearly as much startled as I was; that whatever she had anticipated seeing she had not expected to find me sitting on that chair. She kept her glance fixed upon my features; only for a second did it wander towards Pollie sleeping on the bed. I fancy she was endeavouring to determine what it was that I was doing there; why I was on the chair instead of on the bed; whether I was asleep or waking, or even dead. I was so huddled up upon the chair, and remained so very still, that it was quite possible for her, taken unawares, to suppose that I was dead.

"You sleep?"

She spoke to me; in English, which had a quaintly foreign sound; in a bell-like whisper, it was so soft and yet so clear.

I did not answer; the knot in my tongue had not yet come untied. I felt that she did not understand my silence, or the cause of it; and wondered, hesitated too. Presently she ventured on an assertion, uttered with a little cadence of doubt, as if it were a question.

"You do not sleep." Apparently as if still in doubt as to the correctness of the statement, she endeavoured to fortify herself with reasons. "Your eyes are open; you do not sleep. We do not sleep when our eyes are open. Speak to me. Are you afraid?"

Perhaps the suspicion increased in strength that, if I was not stupefied with fear, there was at least something curious in my condition. She opened the door nearly to the full, and she came into the room. I saw that she seemed but a girl, tall above the common, clad in a gown which, while it was loose and seemingly shapeless, and made in a fashion which was altogether strange to me, yet draped itself in graceful folds about her figure. It was made of some stuff which looked to me like silk alpaca; in colour a most assertive, and indeed trying, shade of electric blue. It positively warmed one's eyes to look at it. And it was covered with what looked more like sequins than anything else I could think of; though, with every movement of her body, they gleamed and glittered like no sequins I had ever seen before. Her hair, of which there was an extraordinary quantity, as black as jet, was most beautifully done. Even in my condition of semi-stupor I wondered how she did it. It formed a perfect halo about her face. And on the top was stuck what seemed to be the very double of that queer little thing which Pollie said she found in the scrap of paper which the man had given her. Only, to me, the creature in her hair seemed alive. Its eyes gleamed; its body inclined this way then that, as she stood in the open doorway.

She was covered with jewels; at least, I suppose they were jewels. Though, regarded as ornaments, they were as queer as everything else about her. Her fingers were loaded with rings; funny looking ones they seemed. She stood, bending slightly forward, with her hands in front, so that I could not help but notice them. Bracelets were twined about her arms; of the oddest design. A jewelled snake was about her throat. Another, not only a monster, but a monstrosity, was twisted, girdle fashion, three or four times around her waist. It looked as if it were alive.

When, having, apparently, sufficiently considered the situation, she began to advance towards me, to my amazement and abject horror this creature was set in motion too. It stretched out its evil-looking head in my direction, with an ugly glitter in its eyes; it opened its jaws; its fangs shot out. As they seemed to be extending themselves as far as possible, in order to reach my face, thank God, the guttering half-inch of candle went out upon the mantelpiece. With it my senses seemed to go out too. As they were leaving me I was conscious of the unpleasant odour of a smouldering wick.

CHAPTER XIV
SUSIE

I was lying on the floor. There was a light in the room. A woman was bending over me; the woman with the snake about the waist. The memory of it recurring with a sudden sense of shock, I started up.

"Where is it?"

She looked as if she did not understand.

"Where is what?"

"The snake."

She smiled; why, I do not know.

"The snake? Oh, it is gone."

Apparently it had. In its place was a plain broad band of what seemed gold. I wondered if it was gold. If so, it was worth a great deal. Still wondering, I sank back upon the floor. I saw that beside me was a queer-shaped lamp, which also seemed to be of gold. It was fashioned something like a covered butter-boat, with a handle, the flame coming from the lip. I felt drowsy; the hair seemed to be heavy with perfume; one which was new to me, having a pleasantly soothing effect upon one's nerves. Had it not been for the strangeness of my position I believe that I should then and there have fallen asleep. Turning, I stared at the stranger, who, kneeling on my left, regarded me in turn. Silence; which she broke.

"Are many Englishwomen as beautiful as you?"

I was thinking, lazily, how beautiful she was. The appositeness of the question took me aback; it startled some of the heaviness from my eyelids. I did not know what to reply. My hesitation did not please her. A sudden gleam came into her eyes; as if the wild creature which inhabited them had all at once come to the front.

"Why do you not answer? I am used to being answered. Are many Englishwomen as beautiful as you?"

"They are much more beautiful. I am not beautiful at all."

"You are beautiful. You are a liar."

The plain directness of her speech brought the blood into my cheeks. She marked my change of colour, as if surprised.

"How do you do that?"

"Do what?"

My tone was meek as meek could be.

"You have gone red." I went still redder. "How do you do it? Is it a trick? It becomes you very well; it makes you still more beautiful. Is it the blood shining through your skin? You are so white, the least thing shows. To be white I would give all that I am, all that I have."

She uttered the last words with a simple earnestness which, if she had only known it, became her much more than my blush did me. I ventured on an inquiry.

"Who are you?"

She knelt straight up. There came to her an air of dignity which lent to her a weird and thrilling fascination.

"I am she who inhabits the inner sanctuary of the temple; to whom all men and women bring their supplications, that I may lay them at the feet of the Most High Joss."

I had not the faintest notion what she meant; but her words and manner impressed me none the less on that account. Which fact she observing was good enough not to allow it to displease her. She went on, with the same quaint, yet awe-inspiring simplicity.

"I am she who holds joy and sorrow in the hollow of my hand; ay, life and death. When I lift it the prayers of the faithful may hope for answer; when I do not lift it, their petitions are offered up in vain, for the Great Joss is sleeping; and, when he sleeps, he attends to no one's prayers."

She stopped. I should have liked her to have gone on; or, at least, to have been a trifle more explicit. But, possibly, she was under the impression that she had vouchsafed sufficient information, and, in exchange, would like a little out of me. She put a point blank question.

"Are you Miss Mary Blyth?"

I motioned with my hand towards the bed.

"That's Pollie. She's asleep."

"Pollie? Who is Pollie? I ask, are you Miss Mary Blyth?"

"That is Mary Blyth upon the bed. I'm a friend of hers, so I call her Pollie. She's known to all her friends as Pollie."

She considered, knitting her brows. I half expected her to again roundly call me liar; but, instead, she asked a question, the meaning of which I scarcely grasped.

"Is Susie a name by which one is known unto one's friends?"

"Susie? Isn't that the pet name for Susan?"

For some reason my answer seemed to afford her a singular amount of pleasure. She broke into a soft ripple of laughter; for sheer music I had never heard anything like it before. The sound was so infectious that it actually nearly made me smile—even then! She put her hands before her face, in the enjoyment of some joke which was altogether beyond my comprehension; then, holding out her arms, extended them on either side of her as wide as she possibly could.

"It is a pet name; Susie, a pet name! It is the pet name by which one is known to one's—friends!"

There was a slight pause before "friends"; as if she hesitated whether or not to substitute another word. I should have liked to have inquired what the jest was, but there was something in her bearing which suggested that it was so personal to herself that I did not dare. When she had got out of it what perhaps occurred to her as being sufficient enjoyment, quitting the kneeling posture which she had occupied till then, she rose to her feet and went to the bed.

By now I was wide awake, my perceptions were well on the alert. The sense of terror which had so nearly brought me to a condition of paralysis had grown considerably less. I do not pretend that fear had altogether vanished, nor that with but a little provocation it would not have returned with all its former force. But, for the moment, certainly, curiosity was to the front. My chief anxiety was not to allow one of my mysterious visitor's movements, no matter how insignificant, to escape my notice. I observed with what suppleness she rose to her feet; how, in the noiseless way in which she passed to the bed, there was something which reminded me of wild animals I had seen at the Zoological Gardens. When she bent over the sleeping Pollie there was something in her pose which recalled them again. For some seconds she was still; I had a peculiar feeling, as I watched her from behind, that with those extraordinary eyes of hers she was scorching the sleeper's countenance.

"She is not beautiful. No, she is not beautiful, like you. But there is that in her face which reminds me of another I have seen. She is clever, strong bodied, strong willed, she knows no fear. When she is brought face to face with fear she laughs at it. She sleeps sound. It is like her to sleep sound when no one else could sleep at all." Although I could not see the speaker's face I knew she smiled. "It is funny it should have been given to her. She will never do as she is told; it is because she is told that she will never do it. Obedience is not for her, it is for those with whom she lives to obey." She glanced round. "It is for you."

There was a sting in the little air of malice with which it was said, although the thing was true. It nettled me to think how soon she had found me out. She returned to Pollie without deigning to notice how her words had been received.

"Let her sleep on. So sound a sleep should know no sudden waking." Again there was malice in her tone. She passed her hand two or three times in front of Pollie's face. "Now she'll have no evil dreams. It is funny it should have been given to her; very funny. It should have been given to you; you are different. But it is like that: things happen; the world is crooked."

She had returned towards me.

"Have you a lover?"

Her trick of asking the most delicate questions in the abruptest and baldest fashion I found more than a little disconcerting. Although I tried to keep it back, again the blood flamed to my cheeks, all the more because I half expected to have her repeat her enquiry as to how I got it there. For some ridiculous reason I thought of Mr. Frank Paine. It was too absurd. Of course I had only seen him once, and then I had scarcely looked at him, although I could not help noticing that, though he had not bad eyes, in other respects he was positively ugly, and most stilted in his manners. I might never see the man again, probably never should. I was sure I did not want to. And, anyhow, he was absolutely nothing to me, nor, under any possible circumstances, ever could be. It made me wild to think that I should think of him, especially when I was asked such a question as that.

"No," I stammered.

"No? That is strange. Since you are so beautiful."

"I am not beautiful. Why do you say that I am beautiful?"

"Is it possible that you do not know that you are beautiful? You must be very silly. I knew all about myself long before I was as old as you. You have the kind of face which, when a man sees, he desires; you also have the shape. You are not like her." She jerked her shoulder towards the bed. "You are a woman; and a fool."

I did not like the way she spoke to me at all. She might be a walking mystery—and she certainly was—but that was no reason why she should be impertinent as well.

"Why do you say such things to me? Is a woman of necessity a fool?"

"If she is wise she is. It is a fool that a man desires; if she is a fool she will rule him when he has her. The greater fool is governed by the lesser."

She had a most astonishing way of talking. Considering her age, and, in years, I felt convinced that she was the merest slip of a girl, she professed to have a knowledge of the world which was amazing. I did not know what to say; not being used to carry on a conversation on the lines which she seemed to favour. So she asked another question, with another jerk of her shoulder towards the bed.

"Has she a lover?"

"She has."

"No! That is stranger still! A real lover? What sort of a man is he?"

"He's not a bad sort."

"Not a bad sort? What is that? Is he rich?"

"Rich!" I smiled at the idea of Tom Cooper being rich. "He is very far from being rich, unfortunately for him, and for Pollie too. He is an assistant in a shop."

"A shop? What kind of shop?"

"A draper's."

"A draper's? Isn't that where they sell things for women to wear? What kind of a man is he who is in a shop in which they sell things for women to cover their bodies? Is it his life which he lives there? But, after all, that is the kind of lover one would have supposed she would have had. It is he who must obey." I felt that she was hard on Pollie, and on Mr. Cooper. It seemed to be her way to be hard on everyone. "But you—why have you no lover?"

I really did not know what to answer. It was such a difficult question, to say nothing of its delicacy. Of course I had had lovers, of a sort. One need not give a list, but there had been incidents. At the same time it was not easy to enter into particulars, at a moment's notice, to a perfect stranger, under such conditions as obtained just then.

"I hardly know what to say to you. I suppose I am not too old to have one yet."

It was a silly remark to make. But it was either that or silence. And she did not seem to like me not to answer her.

"One should have a lover when one is still a little young."

"What's your idea of a little young? Are you inferring that I'm a trifle old?"

"The day passes; a lover should come in the morning; when the sun is just lighting the sky."

There was an air of superiority about her which I did not altogether relish. She might be somebody wonderful, and I was quite willing to admit that she was; but one does not care to be snubbed. So far as I could see she was snubbing me all the time. So I asked her a question in my turn.

"You speak as if you had had a great deal of experience. May I ask if you have a lover?"

"Can you not see it in my eyes?"

I could not. Hers were wonderful eyes, especially when the blaze came into them as it did as she spoke. But one required remarkable powers of observation to know that she had a lover merely by looking at her eyes. I hesitated, however, to say as much; and luckily she went on without rendering it necessary for me to say anything at all.

"Can you not see it in my face? my smile? the way I breathe? the joy of life that's in me? Is it that, although you're white, you're stupid? I thought it was plain to all the world; to another woman most of all. One morning I woke; I was what I was; he had not come. He came before the sun set; I was what I am now; there were no shadows that night for me; the sun has not set since."

Her language was really a little above my head. Though I confess that I liked the way in which she spoke. It set my heart all beating. And her words rang like silver trumpets in my ears. And she looked so lovely as she stood with her beautiful head thrown a little back, and her hands held out in front as if her heart was in them. Yet, at the same time, if she had expressed herself in a somewhat different manner, I should have gathered more exactly what it was she meant. She had stopped, as if she thought that it was time for me to speak. So I blundered.

"Was the gentleman a—a countryman of yours?"

"A countryman of mine? What do you mean by a countryman of mine? How do you know what my country is?"

I was sorry I had asked the question directly the words had passed my lips, though I never dreamt that she would take it up in the way she did. She flew at me in a way which gave me quite a start. The wild animal which was in her eyes came to the front with a sudden rush, as if it would spring right out at me.

"I'm sure no offence was intended, and I beg your pardon if any has been given. Because, as you say, I have not the faintest notion what your country is."

"England is my country. I am English—all of me!—to there!"

As she put her hands behind her I suppose she meant that she was English to the backbone. All I could say was that she did not look it, and she did not sound it either. But not for worlds would I have mentioned the fact at that moment. She came closer, eyeing me as if she would have pierced me through and through.

"You think that he is black? You think it? You insult me, the daughter of the gods, in whose hands are life and death! Shall I tear the heart out of your body? Shall I kill you? Tell me!—yes or no!"

"No."

It seemed an unnecessary answer to give, but I felt that I might as well give expression to my sentiments since she was so insistent. Though I thought it quite likely that she might at any moment commence, as she called it, to tear the heart out of my body, while I waited for the moment to arrive I could not but own that, even in her rage, she was the most beautiful woman I had ever seen. But it seemed that she decided that, after all, it would be scarcely worth her while to soil her fingers just for the sake of tearing me to pieces; so she emptied the vials of her scorn on me instead.

"Bah! You are a fool—of the fools! That is all you are. You know nothing, not even what you say. Why should I attend to the witless when they babble? Listen to me—fool!"

She held her finger up close to my nose. I listened with might and main. She spoke as if she intended to lay emphasis upon her every word.

"He is English, my lover, of the English; of the flower of the nation. He is not one who lives in shops which pretend to help ugly women to hide their ugliness; he is not that kind. His home is the wide world. He is tall, and brave, and strong; a ruler of men; handsome beyond any of his fellows." She made that last statement as if she dared me to question it by so much as a movement of my eyelids. "Were you but to see his picture you would faint for love of him." I wondered. "With all women it is so. But, beware! Hide yourself when he is coming; if he but deigns to look on you I'll tear you into pieces. I suffer no woman to stand in his presence, save only I."

Words and manner suggested not only that she was not by any means too sure of the gentleman's affection, but, also, that there was a lively time in store for him. If she wished to be taken literally, and really did mean that no woman was to be allowed to stand in his presence except herself, then the sooner she returned to the particular parts from which, in spite of all that she might say to the contrary, I felt sure she came, then the pleasanter it would be for everyone concerned. I should like to see the man in whose presence I was not to be allowed to stand.

I said nothing when she stopped; I had nothing to say. Or, rather, if I had been allowed a moment or two to think it over, and been given time to get back a little of my breath again, I should have had such a quantity to say that I should have been at a loss as to which end I had better begin. Nor do I fancy that her temper would have been improved wherever I had started.

While she was still glaring as if she would like to eat me, her finger-nails within an inch or two of my face, and I was thinking, in spite of my natural indignation, not to speak of other things, that being in a rage positively suited her, for the second time that night, there came from below what sounded like the opening of a door. On the instant she stood up straight. She looked more than ever like one of the beautiful wild creatures at the Zoo; poised so lightly on her feet, with every sense on the alert, listening as if she did not intend to allow the dropping of a pin to escape her. Suddenly she stooped; waved her hands before my face; caught up the lamp from the floor; vanished from the room.

CHAPTER XV
AN ULTIMATUM

What had happened I could not think, nor where I was. It was pitch dark. I had been roused from sound sleep, as it seemed, by someone falling over me, who was making vigorous efforts at my expense to regain a footing. I remonstrated.

"Who is it? what are you doing?"

"Emily!" returned a voice, in accents of unmistakable surprise.

It was Pollie. She was lying right across me, and, with sundry ejaculations, was using my body as a sort of lever to assist her in regaining her perpendicular. She was plainly as much astonished to find that it was me as I was to find it was her.

"You've been lying on the floor. Why have you been doing that?"

"Because I happen to have been lying on the floor that is no reason why you should tumble over me."

"That's good. How was I to see you in the middle of this brilliant illumination? I called out to you; as you did not answer I was beginning to be half afraid that the black bogies had swallowed you up. Have you been there all night?"

"I don't know." I wondered myself. "I suppose so."

Raising myself to a sitting posture I found that I was stiff all over. I had not been accustomed to quite so hard a mattress. "Have you any idea what time it is?"

"I wish I had. So far as light is concerned all hours seem the same in here, but I'll have that altered before another night comes on. I feel as if I had slept my sleep right out, so I expect that anyhow it's morning."

Her feelings were not mine. My eyelids were heavy. I felt generally dull and stupid, unrefreshed. She gave a little exclamation.

"I touched something with my foot. I believe it's the matches. I thought I put them in my pocket; if so, they've dropped out since; they're not there. Well found! It is!" She struck one. "Hallo, where's the candle?"

I remembered that the one she had left alight had burned right out. But there had been others, three or four pieces of varying length. Every trace of them had vanished.

"Rats," I suggested.

"That's it; the little wretches have devoured them, wicks and tallow and all. When I got off the bed I heard them scurrying in all directions. Did we leave any ends downstairs?"

"I don't think so. We brought up all there was to bring."

"Then that's real nice. For the present we shall have to live by matchlight." As she spoke the one she held went out. "They don't burn long; just long enough to scorch the tips of your fingers. Where's the door?" She moved towards it by the glimmer of a flickering match. She tried the handle. "Why, it seems——" There was a pause. "It does seem——" The match went out, "Emily, it's locked."

"Locked!" I echoed the word.

"Yes, locked; I said locked, or—something. And it wasn't anything last night."

"No; I don't believe it was."

"You don't believe! Don't you remember that because there wasn't a key, and the hasp wouldn't catch, you suggested piling up the furniture to keep it close? What do you mean, then, by saying that you don't believe? you know it wasn't."

"Yes; I do know."

"Well, it's fastened now." I could hear her, in the darkness, trying the handle again. "Sure enough, it's locked; and, from the feel, it's bolted too. Emily, we're locked in."

She was silent. I was silent, too, turning things over in my mind. It seemed, when she spoke again, as if she had been doing the same.

"But—who can have done it? It appears that I was right, that there was someone in those Bluebeard's chambers—perhaps in both, for all we know. If someone could come and lock this door without waking us up, we ran a good risk of having our throats cut, or worse." She lit another match. Apparently my continued silence struck her as peculiar. "Why don't you say something—what's the matter? Don't you understand that we're locked in; prisoners, my dear? Or are you too stupefied with terror to be able to utter a word?"

She held the match in front of her face. It gleamed on something white.

"What's that upon your bodice?"

"My bodice?" She put up her hand. "Why — — it's a piece of paper — — pinned to my bodice! Where on earth — —!" Once more the match went out. "This truly is delightful. Never before did I realise how much we owe to candles. The thing is pinned as if it had been meant never to be unpinned. Where can it have come from? It can't have fallen from the skies. It's plain that there are ghosts about. It's not easy to do a little job like this in the dark, my dear; but I've managed. I've also managed to jab my finger in half-a-dozen places with the pin. Emily, come here; light a match and hold it while I examine this mysterious paper. I can't do everything; and you don't seem disposed to do anything at all."

In endeavouring to do as she requested, I stumbled against her in the darkness.

"That's right; knock me over; you've made me run the pin into my other finger. There, my love, are the matches; what you're grabbing at is my back hair."

Taking a match from the box which she thrust into my hand, I tried to light it at the wrong end; turning it round, a spark leaped into my eye. I dropped it, to rub my eye.

"Clever, aren't you? Just the helpful sort of person one likes to be able to count upon when one is in a bit of a hole. Try again; if at first you don't succeed, perhaps you will next time."

I did. I held the flaming match as conveniently for her as possible; but, at best, it was not much of a light. Every few moments it went out; I had to light another. As I fumbled with them now and then, I was not always so expeditious, perhaps, as I should have been. Pollie grumbled all the while.

"Can't you hold it steady? Who do you suppose can see if your hand keeps shaking?" It was not my hand which shook, it was the flame which flickered. "It's queer paper; sort of cigarette paper, it seems to be; I never saw any like it—at least, so far as I can judge by the light of that match which you won't hold steady. I wonder where it came from, and who it's from. Emily, someone's been playing pranks on us this night; I should like to know just what pranks they were. That's right, let the match go out; can't you keep it alight a little longer?"

"Thank you; it has burned my fingers as it is."

I lit another.

"There is writing on it; I thought there was; I can see it now. Hold that match of yours closer."

In my anxiety to obey her, I gave it too sudden a jerk, the flame was extinguished.

"There! I suppose you'll say that you burned that to an end. If you go on wasting them at this rate we shall be in a fix indeed. How do you know that those aren't all the matches we have got?"

"There are some more upon the mantelpiece—I saw them."

"You saw the boxes; you didn't see the matches; they may be empty. For all you can tell rats may be as fond of matches as they are of candles. Now, do be careful; don't let that go out. Nearer; the way you shiver and shake is trying, my love. I never knew there was so much flicker in a match before. What's it say? Someone's been writing with the point of a pin; you want a microscope to read it. Of course! Let it go out just as I was beginning to see. You are a treasure! This time do try to let us have a light on the subject as long as you can."

She held the paper within an inch of the tip of her nose, and I held a match as close as I dared. She began to decipher the writing.

"'Put the key to the front and the key to the back under the door, and you shall be released. Until you do you will be kept a prisoner. And the fate of the doomed shall be yours. You child of disobedience!' This is pretty; very pretty, on my word. There's a style about the get-up of the thing which suggests that the person who got it up wasn't taught writing in England; but if it wasn't written by a woman, I'm a Dutchman."

"Then it was she."

"She? What do you mean? That's right! By all means let the light go out at the moment it's most wanted. Perhaps you'll tell me what you mean by 'she' in the dark."

"Pollie, after you had gone to sleep I had a visitor."

"A visitor! Emily! And you're alive to tell the tale! And let me sleep on! And never tried to wake me!"

"At the beginning I was too much afraid, and afterwards I couldn't."

"Who was the visitor?"

"Well, that's more than I can tell you, except that it was a woman."

"A woman—Emily—came in here after I had gone to sleep! Don't you see, or if you can't see, can't you feel that I'm on tenterhooks? Will you go on, or must I take you by the shoulders and shake it out of you?"

I told her what there was to tell, in the dark. She stood close up to me. As she said, I could feel she was on tenterhooks. She gripped me with her hands, as if she were unwilling to let there be so much as an inch of space between us, for fear of losing a syllable of what I had to say. As the interest increased her grasp tightened. Yet when I had to stop and tell her that she was pinching me black and blue, she resented my remonstrance as if it had been an unnecessary interruption of my narration. She could not have been more unreasonable had she tried. And to crown it all, so soon as I had finished she professed to doubt me.

"You're sure you've been telling me just exactly what took place. I know your taste for the romantic."

"I've been telling you nothing but the sober facts."

"Sober, you call them? Staggering facts they seem to me. But why didn't you ask the creature who she was?"

"Don't I tell you that I did? And she replied that she was a daughter of the gods, and held life and death in her hand."

"Is that so? She must have been a oner. Emily, I'll never forgive you as long as I live for letting me sleep on."

"Don't! I wish you wouldn't pinch. If you'd been in my place, I don't believe you'd have done anything different—it's all very well for you to talk. Why didn't you wake up on your own accord? Anyone else in your place would have done—I should. The truth is, Pollie, you were sleeping like a grampus."

"Thank you, my pet. I don't quite know how a grampus sleeps, and I don't believe you do either; but I'm obliged for the compliment all the same. I suppose it's meant for a compliment. Of course the thing's as plain as a pikestaff. Your daughter of the gods sneaked out of one of Bluebeard's chambers, where, no doubt, she is at this identical moment. Shouldn't I like to get at her! I will before I'm done. It seems as if she—or somebody— is discontented with the way I've behaved since I came into my fortune, though it's early days to be dissatisfied. And the idea apparently is to get hold of the keys, and then to get rid of me; on the supposition that when I'm once outside I shan't be able, without the keys, to get in again. But I'm not quite so simple as I look. When she went I expect you fell asleep, though why you didn't wake me up, and help chivy her downstairs, is more than I can understand. I'd have daughter-of-the-gods her! Then she sneaked back, searched for the keys. Fortunately, the intricacies of a Christian woman's costume were too many for her. So she jumped to the conclusion that they were concealed in some mysterious hiding-place, quite beyond her finding out, daughter of the gods though she is. She pinned the piece of paper to my bodice, and she locked the door, supposing that we'd the spirits of mice, and that we'd give her what she's no more right to than the man in the moon, just to unlock it again. But you're mistaken, you daughter of the gods! Emily, I can't see your face, and you can't see mine. If you could you'd see determination written on it, and you'd know she was. I don't mean to be kept shut up like a rat in a trap, not much, I don't. Outside there! Are you going to open this door, or am I to open it for you?"

Bang, bang she went with her fists against the panels. The noise she made shook the room.

"One thing's certain, this door's not protected with sheet iron, or any pretty stuff of that kind. If it's not unlocked it won't be long before I'm through it, anyhow. Do you hear, you daughter of the gods?"

Smash, crash went the fists again.

I did not know what to say, still less what to do. It was useless proffering advice. She never was amenable to that. I was sure she would resent it hotly then. Yet what she proposed to gain by going on was beyond my comprehension.

It was becoming pretty plain to me that whatever object her Uncle Benjamin had in view when he made his will it was not his niece's benefit. It seemed as if he had died as he had lived, true to the character which Pollie gave of him. I was beginning to think that he had meant to use her as a catspaw, though why, or in what way, I confess I did not understand. That the house was not a good house I was sure; that it harboured some dreadful characters I felt convinced; perhaps coiners, or forgers, or abandoned creatures of some kind. Pollie might be meant to serve as a sort of cover. Her occupation of the place might be intended to avert suspicion. People seeing her going in and out, and being aware she lived there, would think there was nothing strange about the house. It need not be generally known that she had only access to a part of it. The prohibition against allowing anybody but another girl to cross the threshold was evidently meant as a precaution against allowing that fact to become discovered. Oh yes! nothing could be plainer than that, so far from Pollie's being the lucky heritor of a handsome fortune, she was only the tool of her wicked old uncle; and that, consciously or unconsciously, as such she was to hide from the world some one or other of his nefarious schemes which had to be kept hidden even after he was in his grave.

As such thoughts kept chasing each other through my brain I could keep them to myself no longer.

"Pollie, do you know what I should do if I were you?"

"Break open the door with a chair, or the leg of the bedstead, my dear?"

"I should leave the house this moment."

"Would you indeed? And then?"

"I should go straight to Mr. Paine, and I should renounce the fortune which your wicked old uncle has pretended to leave you, and refuse to fall into the trap which he had laid."

"Emily! Are you insane?"

"No, I'm not insane, and it's because I'm not that I'm advising you. I feel sure that your Uncle Benjamin never meant to do you any good when he made that will of his."

"So far I'm with you. But it's just possible that the niece may prove a match for the uncle; she means to try. This is my house, at present. I'm mistress here, and I mean to play the mistress; not act as if I were afraid to raise my voice above a whisper. So don't you forget it, or we shall quarrel; and, even if things are as bad as you seem to think, I don't see how you'll be better off for that. Light a match, and keep on lighting one till I tell you to stop."

She ordered me as if I were a servant: I obeyed because I could not see my way to refuse. In the match-light she marched to the mantelpiece.

"Here's three boxes of matches for you; I'll take care of the rest. The matches are in them, luckily. Now the question is what is the handiest little article by whose help I can get soonest on the other side of that door. Ah! here's the poker. It is not much use against sheet iron, but I fancy it will work wonders with plain wood."

Brandishing the poker above her head—exactly in the wild way she had done the night before—she strode towards the door. As she did so someone addressed her from without; in a deep rumbling bass, which was more like a growl than a human voice.

"Beware, you fool, beware! Your life's at stake, more than your life. Obey, before it is too late."

In my most natural surprise and agitation, the match, dropping from my fingers, was extinguished as it reached the floor. The room was plunged into darkness. Pollie behaved as if the fault were mine.

"You idiot! Did you do that on purpose?"

She caught me by the arm as if she meant to break it. In her unreasoning rage I quite expected her to strike me with the poker. As I waited for it to fall the voice came again.

"Be warned!—for the last time!—obey!"

CHAPTER XVI
THE NOISE WHICH CAME
FROM THE PASSAGE

Smash, crash, smash! Pollie had thrust me aside. She was battering at the door with her poker, issuing, as she did so, her instructions to me.

"Light a match, you idiot! light a match!"

I did. She paused to enable her to learn, by the aid of its uncertain flicker, what effect her blows had had upon the door.

"Give it to me. Light another! Do as I tell you, keep on lighting one. I'll do all that there is to do; all you have to do is to keep a light upon the scene. Do you hear?—I thought that poker would be equal to a wooden door."

She had broken in one of the panels, leaving a hole almost large enough for her to put her hand through.

"Give me another match; as many as you can; as fast as you can!"

I gave her them as quickly as I could get them lighted. She held half a dozen between her fingers at at a time. Keeping her face close to the break in the panel she endeavoured, by their light, to see what was without.

"Now, Mr. Bogey-man, where are you? Step to the front, don't be shy! Let's see what kind of an article you are. It's only Pollie Blyth, you pretty thing; you're not afraid of Pollie Blyth? Perhaps you're the father of the daughter of the gods; if so, I'm sure I should like to have a peep at you, you must be so good-looking. You see that I'm obeying. When I reach you I'll show you how to do some obeying on your own. I'll thank you properly for treating the mistress of the house as if she were the dirt beneath your feet. Emily, my dear, there's nothing and no one to be seen; move faster with those matches do! I'm afraid Mr. Bogey-man is a cur and a coward. He has a big voice, but that's all that's big about him. Perhaps he suspects that this poker is harder than his head; and, between you, I, and the door post, I shouldn't be surprised if he finds he's right. Keep lively with those matches. I don't fancy there'll be much trouble in dealing with this curiosity in locks; but I should like to have some idea of what I'm doing. Now then, stand clear! Here's to you, Mr. Bogey-man."

She brought down the poker with a force of which I had never supposed her capable; this was a new Pollie, whose existence was becoming for the first time known to me. I wondered what they would have thought of her at Cardew and Slaughter's! The rotten old lock started from its fastenings; the door itself was shaken to its foundations.

"That's one. There's not much about this job to try your strength on. I think we shall manage it in three. Here's to our early meeting, Mr. Bogey-man."

She managed it in three. At the third blow the door was open. I had not expected it so soon. Taken unawares, before I had time to shield the light the draught had blown it out. Of course Pollie turned to rend me.

"That's you all over; such a sensible thing to do. Don't let us have a light when we want it most. How do you suppose that we are going to see Mr. Bogey-man when we can't see anything?"

As it happened, her reproach was premature. Just then we could see a good deal; all that there was to see. As the door swung open the landing was illumined by a faint white light, which was yet strong enough to throw all objects into distinct relief. It seemed to ascend from below. Pollie rushed to the banisters; to discover nothing.

"More tricks, I suppose. What a box of tricks somebody seems to have. Reminds you of the Egyptian Hall, doesn't it, my dear? Thank you, whoever you are, for this magic lantern effect; and for allowing us to see that there is nothing to be seen. It's so good of you to show a trifle of light upon the situation; isn't it, my sweet?"

She paused; as if for an answer. None came. The light continued. She turned to me, speaking at the top of her voice, with the obvious intention of making her words audible to whomsoever the house might contain.

"Tell me, Emily, what you would advise me to do. Shall I go straight away to a police station; say that in two rooms in this house are hidden a pack of thieves; return with an adequate police force, have the rooms broken open and their inmates arrested? or shall I address myself to the persons whom we know are in concealment; tell them that I am Pollie Blyth, the rightful owner of this house; appeal to their better natures; assuring them that if they will trust in me they shall not have cause to complain of misplaced confidence; and that I will do all that an honest woman may to shield them from the consequences of any offences of which they have been guilty. Which of these two courses would you advise me to take?"

I hesitated before replying. When I spoke it was in a voice which was very many tones lower than hers. She objected to its gentleness.

"I would suggest— —"

"Speak up. You're not afraid of being overheard."

I was, though I was not disposed to admit as much. Clearing my throat, I tried to speak a little louder. Although the loudness of my voice startled me, it did not come within miles of her stentorian utterances.

"I think you had better go straight away to the police station; I feel sure you had."

"I believe you are right. But as that would probably mean that anyone found hiding on my premises would be sent to prison for life; and I do not wish to have even the worst characters hauled into jail without giving them a chance to clear themselves, I will listen to the dictates of mercy first of all. Do you understand?"

Going to the closed door which adjoined the bedroom we had just quitted she beat a tattoo on it with the end of the poker.

"You may be sure that what I say I mean, so if you are wise you will be warned in time. Come out, and make a clean breast of why you have been trying to hide in such a ridiculous manner from the rightful owner of these premises, and all may yet be well with you. I'm a forgiving sort of person when I'm taken in the right way. But if you won't come out, I'll have you dragged out by the head and heels, and then all will be ill with you, very ill indeed. For I'm the hardest nut you ever cracked if I'm taken in the wrong way. Do you hear, you daughter of the gods, or whoever you are?"

The inquiry was emphasised by another tattoo with the end of the poker. At its close she paused for a reply. None came. She was evidently dissatisfied that her eloquence should have met with so bald a result.

"Very well, Emily, you will bear me witness that I gave them due and proper warning. It will be all nonsense for them to pretend that they haven't heard. They couldn't help but hear. See how I've shouted. Oh yes, they've all heard right enough! Now they must take the consequences of their own stupidity. Their blood will be on their own heads. They'll have to suffer. Oh, won't you just have to suffer!"

Another salute from the end of the poker. While she was still hammering at the door, the mysterious light which had continued hitherto to illumine the staircase, without any sort of notice died away.

"Emily!—a match!—quick! I think I hear someone moving."

I also had thought that I heard a movement; which was not rats. I struck a light as rapidly as my blundering fingers would permit.

"Come to the banisters, hurry! If anyone is going to act upon my excellent advice, and is coming up the stairs, let's have a chance of seeing who it is."

In my anxiety not to baulk her impatience I hastened towards her before the match had properly ignited; as a result, with a little splutter, it went out.

"You idiot! Don't you know that life and death may hang upon your being able to keep a match alight?"

I knew it as well as she did. The knowledge did not lend to steady my nerves; especially when it was emphasised in such a fashion. I made several ineffectual efforts to induce a match to burn; with one accord they refused to do anything. Uttering an angry ejaculation Pollie struck one of her own.

"Emily, there is someone moving; but they're not coming up, they're going down. Then if they won't come to me I must go to them, that's all. Mr. Bogey-man, or Miss Daughter-of-the-gods, or whoever you are, if you please, I want a word with you."

Without giving me a hint of what she intended to do she rushed down the stairs, half-a-dozen at a time. Of course the match she carried was immediately extinguished. I could hear her, undeterred by its extinction, plunging blindly down through the darkness. I succeeded in getting one of my matches to burn. I leaned over the banisters to let her have the benefit of any radiance it might afford. I could see nothing of her. She was on the flight below.

"Pollie! Pollie!" I cried. "Do be careful what you're doing."

I could not tell if she heard me. The warning went unheeded if she did. My match went out. Before I could strike another there arose, through the darkness, from the passage below, the most dreadful tumult I had ever heard. Shriek after shriek from Pollie; shrieks as of mortal terror. A growling noise, as of some wild animal in sudden rage. The din of a furious struggle. How long the uproar lasted I cannot say. On a sudden there came a wilder, more piercing scream from Pollie than any which had gone before; the growling grew more furious; there was the sound of a closing door, and all was still.

The death-like silence which followed was of evil omen. The contrast to the discord of a moment back was frightfully significant. I clung to the banisters to help me stand. What had happened to Pollie? What, shortly—at any second! might happen to me? I did not dare to try and think. I felt the handrail slipping from my grasp. Merciful oblivion swept over me. I was conscious of nothing more.

BOOK III
THE GOD OF FORTUNE

(MR. FRANK PAINE TELLS THE STORY OF
HIS ASSOCIATION WITH THE TESTAMENTARY
DISPOSITIONS OF MR. BENJAMIN BATTERS.)

CHAPTER XVII
THE AFFAIR OF THE FREAK

I have not yet been able to determine if my connection with the testamentary dispositions of Mr. Benjamin Batters was or was not, in the first place, owing to what I call the Affair of the Freak in the Commercial Road. On no other hypothesis can I understand why the business should have been placed in my hands. While, at the same time, I am willing to admit that the connection, if any, was of so shadowy a nature that I am myself at a loss to perceive where it quite comes in.

What exactly took place was this.

George Kingdon had got his first command. As we have been the friends of a lifetime, and are almost of an age, he being twenty-seven and I twenty-eight, the matter had almost as much interest for me as it had for him. The vessel's name was *The Flying Scud*. It was to leave the West India south dock on Tuesday, April 3. He dined with me the night before. We drank success to the voyage. The following day I went to see him start. All went well; he had a capital send off; was in the highest spirits; and the last I saw of him the ship was going down the river on the tide.

It was, I suppose, about seven o'clock in the evening. It had been a glorious day; promised to be as fine a night. The shadows were only just beginning to lengthen. I had had a drink or two with Kingdon, and felt that a walk would do me good. I strolled along Preston's Road and High Street, into the West India Road, and thence into the Commercial Road. Before I had gone very far I came upon a number of people who were thronging round one of the entrances into Limehouse Basin. They were crowding round some central object which was apparently affording them entertainment of a somewhat equivocal kind. I asked a bystander what was the matter; a man with between his lips a clay pipe turned bowl downwards.

"It's one of Barnum's Freaks. They're giving him what for."

"What's he done?"

"Done?" The fellow shrugged his shoulders. "He ain't done nothing so far as I knows on; what should he 'ave done? They're only 'aving a bit o' fun."

It was fun of a peculiar sort; humorous from the Commercial Road point of view only. I doubted if the "Freak" found it amusing. He was being hustled this way and that; serving as a target for remarks which were, to say the least, unflattering. All at once there came a dent in the crowd. The "Freak" had either tumbled, or been pushed, over. Three or four of his more assiduous admirers had gone down on the top of him. The others roared. Four or five of those in the front rank were shoved upon the rest. The joke expanded. Presently the "Freak" was at the bottom of a writhing heap.

Perceiving that the jest was likely to become a serious one for the point of it, I forced my way into the centre of the crowd.

"Stand back!" I cried. "You ought to be ashamed of yourselves! You ought to pity the man instead of making sport of him. He is as God made him; it is not his fault that he is not like you."

Nor, I felt as I looked at the faces which surrounded me, was it, after all, his serious misfortune either. Unless their looks belied them, in a moral, mental, and physical sense, the majority of them were "freaks," if the word had any meaning. They gave way, however, to let me pass; it seemed that their temper was thoughtless rather than cruel. Soon I had extricated the wretched creature from his ignominious, and even perilous, position. Hailing a passing four-wheeler I put him into it. I slipped some money into the driver's hand, and, bidding him take his fare to Olympia, the man drove off. The crowd booed a little, and then stared at me. Then, seeing that I paid them no sort of heed, they were so good as to suffer me to pursue my way unmolested and alone.

It was only after I had gone some little distance that I realised that I knew nothing whatever about the creature I had put into the cab. I had only the clay-piped gentleman's word for the fact that he, she, or it was a freak at all. The creature—I call it creature for lack of more precise knowledge as to what he, she, or it, really was—was so enveloped in an odd-shaped cloak of some dark brown material, that, practically, so far as I had been able to see, nothing of it was visible. For all that I could tell the creature beneath the cloak might not have been human. There was certainly nothing to show — except the way in which it was shrouded, and that might have been owing to the action of the crowd — that it was what is commonly called a freak. Its connection with the Barnum Show at Olympia might be as remote as mine. If a mistake had been made I wondered what would happen when it was discovered. Playing the Good Samaritan in the London streets is not always a remunerative rôle for any one concerned. In my blundering haste I had probably done at least as much harm as good. I smiled, drily, at the reflection. Anyhow, I had given the cabman a liberal fare. To me, then, as now, a cab fare is a cab fare.

I had turned into Cable Street and was nearing the Tower. By now the night had fallen. In that part of the world, at that hour — I remember that a minute or two before I had heard a clock strike nine, so that either I had been longer on the road, or it had been later at the start, than I imagined — there were not many people in the streets. There seemed to be fewer the further I went. At any rate, ere long, I should have them to myself. I was, therefore, the more surprised when, as I was reaching Tower Hill, without any sort of warning, someone touched me on the shoulder from behind. I turned to see who had accosted me. It was rather dark just there, so that it was a moment or two before I perceived who it was.

It was a woman, and that was about all which, at first, I could make out. She, too, was enveloped in a cloak. It was of such ample dimensions that not only did it conceal her figure, but, drawn over her head, it almost completely concealed her features. Nearly all that I could see was a pair of what seemed unusually bright eyes, gleaming from under its folds. My impulse was to take her for a beggar, or worse, for a woman of the streets.

"What do you want?"

"Take this, it is for helping him just now."

Before I could prevent her she had slipped something into my hand. It felt as if it were something hard, wrapped in a piece of paper.

"For helping whom?"

"The Great God."

She dropped her voice to a whisper. I had not the vaguest inkling of her meaning.

"What do you mean? — What is this you have given me?"

"It is the God of Fortune; it will bring you good luck. Tell me your name."

"My name? What has my name to do with you? Whatever is this? I cannot take it from you; thank you all the same."

I held out to her the little packet she had pressed into my palm. She ignored it; repeating her inquiry.

"Tell me your name, quick!"

There was a curious insistence in her manner which tickled what I, with sufficient egotism, call my sense of humour. She spoke as if she had but to command for me to obey; I obeyed. I furnished her not only with my name, but, also, with my address. There was no harm done. I am a solicitor; figure on the law list; advertisement, of some sort, is to me something very much like bread and cheese. Without thanking me, or dropping a hint to explain her curiosity, so soon as I had supplied her with the information she demanded, turning, she flew off down the street like some wild thing. I doubt if I could have kept pace with her had I tried. I did not try. I let her go.

"This is a night of adventures," I said to myself. "What is the present which the lady's given me; the money which I paid the cabman?—Hallo!—That's queer!"

I was beginning to tear open the piece of paper, and with that intent had already twisted off a corner, when, hey presto! it opened of its own accord, just as if a living thing had been inside, and, with a rapid movement, rent it from top to bottom. I was holding what seemed to be a curiosity in the way of tiny dolls. The toy, if it was a toy, was not so long as my forefinger. It seemed to have been cut out of a piece of wood, and fantastically painted to illustrate some very peculiar original. It had neither feet nor legs, nor hands or arms. Its head, which was set between hunched-up shoulders, was chiefly remarkable for a pair of sparkling eyes, which I concluded to be beads. I turned it over and over without discovering anything which pointed to a hidden spring. It looked as if it had never moved, and never would. There was nothing whatever to show by what means the paper had come open.

"It's odd, and ingenious. I suppose there is a spring of some sort; wood, even when it represents the God of Fortune—I think the lady mentioned the God of Fortune—does not move of its own volition. I'll discover it when I get home."

I slipped the toy into my waistcoat pocket, meaning to subject it to a searching examination later on. However, when I reached my chambers I found letters which demanded immediate attention. They occupied some time. It was only when I was thinking of a nightcap preparatory to turning into bed, and was feeling for a penknife with which to cut a cigar, that I remembered the doll. I tossed it on to the mantelshelf. There it remained.

As I have said, that was the night of April 3. Since nearly a month elapsed before the arrival of Mr. Batters' will, and nothing in any way suggestive occurred in the interval, it would seem as if the connection between the will and the events of that evening was of the slightest. Yet I felt that if it had not been for the Affair of the Freak in the Commercial Road, or if I had afterwards refused to give the woman my name and address, I should have heard nothing of Mr. Batters' will. I do not pretend to be able to explain the feeling, but there it was.

I should, perhaps, in fairness add, that a queer little incident which coincided with the arrival of the will, seemed to point, whimsically enough, in the same direction.

The document came on a Thursday morning. When I entered the room which I used as an office, I found that four communications were awaiting me. The postman had brought them all. The boy I call—to shed dignity on him and on myself—a clerk, had set them out upon the table. Three letters in ordinary envelopes. The fourth was an awkward, bulky, coarse brown paper parcel. On it was the doll which the woman had given me on the night of April 3, in the lonely street near Tower Hill.

I had forgotten its existence. I took it for granted that its presence on that spot was owing to Crumper's sense of humour. I called to him.

"Crumper!" His head appeared at the door. "What do you mean by putting this here?" He stared, as if he did not catch my meaning. There are moments when Crumper finds it convenient to be dull. "You understand me well enough; what do you mean by putting this doll upon my parcel?"

He still looked as if he did not understand. But Crumper had a capacity of being able to handle his face as if it were an indiarubber mask, on which he is able to produce any expression at will.

"Doll, sir? I don't know anything about a doll, sir." He came into the room, pointing with his thumb. "Do you mean that, sir? It wasn't there when I left the room just now; to that I'll take my affidavit."

It is no use arguing with Crumper. The depth of his innocence is not to be easily plumbed. I sent him back to his den; knocked the doll with a fillip of my finger backwards on to the table; opened the brown paper parcel.

Of its contents I was not able, at first, to make head or tail. After prolonged examination, however, I arranged them thus:

(*a*) The Missionary's Letter.

(*b*) The Holograph Will.

(*c*) The Bonds.

(*d*) The Enclosure.

Summed up, the contents of the packet amounted to this.

A certain Benjamin Batters was reported to have died on an island on the other side of the world of which I had never heard; why I was advised of the fact, there was nothing to show. His will was entrusted to my keeping—how my name had travelled through space so as to reach the cognisance of the Mr. Arthur Lennard who had reported the death of the said Benjamin Batters there was not the faintest hint. Bonds—"Goschens"—to the value of £20,000 accompanied the will; since they were payable to bearer this alone suggested profound confidence in an apparently perfect stranger. Finally, there was a smaller parcel which was sealed and endorsed "To be given to my niece, Mary Blyth, and to be opened by her only."

The will—which was almost as rudimentary a document of the kind as I ever lighted on—bequeathed to the said Mary Blyth the income which was derived from the consols. As to the person in whose name the capital was to be vested not a word was said, nor did I perceive anything which would prevent her from dealing with it exactly as she chose. She was also, under curious and stringent conditions, to become the life tenant of a house in Camford Street of which, however, no title-deeds were enclosed, nor was their existence hinted at.

Had it not been for the presence of the bonds I should have set the whole thing down right away as a hoax. The heading on "Arthur Lennard's" letter was "Great Ka Island: Lat. 5° South; Long. 134° East." There might be such a place; the description seemed precise enough, and I had no atlas which would enable me to determine. But, at any rate, the packet in which it came had not been posted there. The postmark was Deptford; the date yesterday's. When I held the paper on which the letter had been written up to the light I found that the watermark was "Spiers and Pond. Freshwater Mill Note. London," which, under the circumstances, seemed odd.

It was, perhaps, nothing that the will was obviously the production of an unlettered person. Such persons do make their own wills, and, probably, will continue to do so to the crack of doom. But it was something that it was both unwitnessed and undated. And when to this was added the fact that the letter which told of Mr. Batters' decease was undated too, the conjunction struck one a trifle forcibly.

Then the conditions under which Mary Blyth was to inherit were so puerile, not to say outrageous. She was never to be out of the precious house in Camford Street after nine at night. She was to receive no visitors; have only a woman as a companion, and if that woman left her, was to occupy the premises alone. After I had read it for the fourth time I threw the paper on to the table.

"Monstrous! monstrous! It consigns the unfortunate woman to an unnatural existence; she cannot marry; is cut off from her fellows; sentenced to lifelong imprisonment. Who would care to become even a millionaire on such conditions? Even if the thing is what it pretends to be, I doubt if it would be upheld by any court in England. I'm inclined to think that someone has been having a little joke at my expense."

But there were the bonds. My experience of such articles is regrettedly small; but, such as it was, it went to show that they were genuine. Bonds for £20,000 are not a joke. They are among the most solemn facts of life. If, then, they were real, the presumption was that the will was not less so. In which case my duty was to have it proved, and to see that its terms were carried out. Anyhow, there were the bonds on which to draw for payment of my fees. Emphatically, my practice was not of sufficient extent to permit me to treat so fat a client with indifferent scorn.

Cogitating such matters, I had been indulging in what is a habit of mine; pacing, with my hands in my pockets, up and down the room. Returning to the table, I prepared to subject the supposititious will to a still more minute examination. It was not till I stretched out my hand that I noticed that, in the centre of the sheet of blue foolscap on which it was inscribed, was—the God of Fortune, the doll in miniature which, once already, I had ejected from a similar position. How it had returned to it was a problem which, just then, was beyond my finding out. I had filliped it right to the extreme edge of the table. No one had been in the room; Crumper had not so much as put up the tip of his nose inside the door. I had not touched the thing. Yet there it was, ostentatiously perched on Mr. Batters' will. I stared at the doll; I had an odd notion that the doll stared at me; a ridiculous feeling, indeed, that the preposterous puppet was alive. I scratched my head.

"I fancy this morning I must be a bit off colour. A penny doll alive, indeed! I shall begin seeing things if I don't look out."

I slipped the doll into my waistcoat pocket; noting, as I did so, that it was ugly enough to startle the most morbid-minded juvenile admirers of its kind. I glanced at the three letters which the morning post had brought me, neither of which proved to be of any account. Slipped the missionary's letter, Mr. Batters' will, and one of the bonds into an envelope. Locked the enclosure to be given to Mary Blyth and the rest of the bonds in a drawer; and, with the envelope in my hand, went to call on Gregory Pryor.

Pryor is a barrister of some years' standing; a "rising junior"; hard-working, hard-headed, a sound lawyer, and a man of the world. What is more, a friend of my father's who has transferred his friendship to me. More than once when I have found myself in a professional quandary I have laid the matter before him; on each occasion he has given me just that help and advice I needed. I felt assured that I should lose nothing by asking for his opinion on the curious case of Mr. Batters' will.

When, however, I reached his chambers the clerk told me he was out, engaged in court. I left word that I would return later in the day. Having nothing on hand of pressing importance, I felt that I could hardly employ the interval better than by finding out all that I could with reference to the house in Camford Street which Mr. Batters claimed as his own. If the claim proved to be well founded, then the document which purported to be his will was probably no hoax.

CHAPTER XVIII
COUNSEL'S OPINION

I should not myself have cared to live in Camford Street, though it had many residents. It was in the heart, if not exactly of a slum, then certainly of an unsavoury district. Its surroundings, residentially speaking, were about as undesirable as they could have been. Camford Street itself was long, dreary, out-at-elbows, old enough to look as if it would be improved by being rebuilt. Painters, whitewashers, people of that kind, had not been down that way for years; that was obvious from the fronts of the houses. Buildings stretched from end to end in one continuous depressing row. Half-a-dozen houses, then a shop; half-a-dozen more, and a blacking manufactory; three more, and a public-house; another six and a "wardrobe dealer's," doubtful third and fourth hand garments dimly visible through dirty panes of glass, and so on, for a good half mile.

Eighty-four looked, what it undoubtedly was, an abode of mystery, as grimy an edifice as the street contained. I know nothing of the value of property thereabouts; whatever it might have been it was not the kind of house I should care to have bequeathed to me. Especially if I had to reside in it. I would rather pass it on to someone who was more deserving. Shutters were up at all the windows. There was not a trace of a blind or curtain. At the front door there was neither bell nor knocker. It seemed deserted. I rapped at the panels with the handle of my stick; once, and then again. An urchin addressed me from the kerb.

"There ain't no one living in that 'ouse, guv'nor."

I thanked him for the information; it never occurred to me to shed a shadow of doubt on it. I felt sure that he was right. I crossed to a general shop on the other side of the way.

"Excuse me," I said to the individual whom I took for the proprietor—"Kennard" was the name over the shop front—"Can you tell me who lives at No. 84?"

"No one."

Mr. Kennard—I was convinced it was he—was a short, paunchy man, with a bald head and a club foot. He pursed his lips and screwed up his eyes in a fashion which struck me as rather comical.

"Who is the landlord?"

"No one knows."

"No one?" I smiled. "I presume you mean that you don't know. Someone must; the local authorities, for instance."

"The local authorities don't. I'm a vestryman myself, so you can take that from me. There's been no rates and taxes paid on that house for twenty years or more; because no one knows to whom to go for them."

He thrust his hands under his white apron, protruding his stomach in a manner which was a little aggressive.

"The last person who lived at Eighty-four was an old gentleman, named Robertson. He was a customer of mine, and owed me three pound seven and four when he was missing. It's on my books to this hour."

"Missing? Did he run away?"

"Not he; he wasn't that sort. Besides, there was no reason. He was a pensioner; he told me so himself. I don't know what he got his pension for, but it must have been a pretty comfortable one, because he paid me regular for over seven years; and I understood at that time, from what he said, that the house was his own. If it wasn't I can't say to whom he paid rent. The last time I saw him was a Friday night. He came in here and bought a pound of bacon—out of the back; twelve eggs—breakfast; five pounds of cheese—I never knew anyone who was fonder of cheese, he liked it good; a pound of best butter—there was no margarine nor Australian either in those days; and a pound of candles. I've never seen or heard anything of him since; and, as I say, that's more than twenty years ago."

"But what became of him?"

"That's more than I can tell you. Perhaps you can tell me. You see, it was this way."

Mr. Kennard was communicative. Business was slack just then. Apparently I had hit upon a favourite theme.

"Mr. Robertson was one of your quiet kind. Kept himself to himself; lived all alone; seemed to know no one; no one ever came to see him. He never even had any letters; because, afterwards, the postman told me so with his own lips; he said he'd never known of his having a letter all the time he was in this district. Sometimes nothing would be seen of him for three weeks together. Whether he went away or simply shut himself up indoors I never could make out. He was the least talkative old chap I ever came across. When you asked him a question which he didn't want to answer, which was pretty well always, he pretended he was silly and couldn't understand. But he was no more silly than I was; eccentric, that was all. Anyhow, when the weeks slipped by, and he wasn't seen about, no one thought it odd, his habits being generally known. When quarter day came round I sent my little girl, Louisa—she's married now, and got a family—across with my bill. She came back saying that she could make no one hear; and, through my window, I could see she couldn't. 'That's all right,' I said, 'There's no fear for Mr. Robertson'—I'd such a respect for the man—'he's sure to pay.' But, if sure, he's been precious slow; for, as I say, that three seven four is on my books to this hour."

"If, as you say, the old gentleman lived alone, he may have been lying dead in the house all the time."

"That's what I've felt. And, what's more, I've felt that his skeleton may be lying there now."

"You suggest some agreeable reflections. Do you mean to say that, during all these years, no one has been in the house to see?"

"No one." He paused; presently adding, in a tone which he intended should be pregnant with meaning, "At least, until shortly before this last Christmas. And I've no certainty about that. A man can only draw his own conclusions."

"What do you mean?"

"You see those shutters? Well, for over twenty years there weren't any shutters hiding those windows. One morning I looked across the street, and there they were."

"Someone had put them up in the night?"

"That was my impression. But Mrs. Varley, who lives next door to this, says that she noticed them coming for about a week. Each morning there was another window shuttered. She never mentioned a word of it to me; so that I can only tell you that when I saw them first they were all up."

"Who was responsible for their appearance?"

"That's what I should like to know. Directly I clapped eyes on them I went straight across the road, and knocked at the door; thinking that if old Robertson had come back—though he'd be pretty ancient if he had—I might get my money after all; and that if he hadn't there'd be no harm done. But no more attention was paid to me than if I hadn't been there. I daresay that if

I've knocked once since I've knocked twenty times; but, though I've always felt as if there was someone inside listening, I've never seen a soul about the place, and no one has ever answered. I tell you what; there's something queer about that house. More than once it's been on the tip of my tongue to warn a policeman to keep an eye on it. It's my opinion that London will hear about it yet."

Mr. Kennard was oracular. When, however, on quitting his establishment I glanced at No. 84, I myself was conscious of a queer feeling that there was an unusual atmosphere about the house, as if something strange was brooding over it. I told myself that I was still a little bilious, and imagined things.

While I had been in conversation with Mr. Kennard I had observed a curious face peering at us through the window of his shop. Now I noticed a man, who struck me as being the owner of the face, loitering a few doors up the street. As I came out, turning, so that his back was towards me, he began to slowly stroll away. Urged by I know not what odd impulse, I moved quickly after him. Immediately, he crossed the street. I crossed at his heels. As if seized with sudden fear, breaking into a run, he tore off down the street at the top of his speed. I was reminded of the behaviour of the woman who had thrust the God of Fortune into my hand.

All the way back to my chambers I was haunted by a disagreeable sense of being followed. I frequently turned in an endeavour to detect my shadower; each time no one suspicious seemed to be in sight. Yet, so persistent was the feeling that, on entering, after lingering for a second or two in the hall, I darted back again into the court; to cannon against the man who had been loitering in Camford Street. Had I not gripped him by the shoulders he would have been bowled over like a ninepin.

There was no mistaking the individual. I had marked his peculiar figure; the nondescript fashion of his dress—a long black coat, made, apparently, of alpaca, reaching to his heels; a soft black felt hat so much too large for his head that it almost covered his eyes. He was a foreigner, undersized, unnaturally thin.

"Well, my man, what can I do for you?" He did not reply. His countenance assumed an expression of vacuous imbecility. I shook him gently, to spur his wits. "Do you hear, what can I do for you? Since you have taken the trouble to follow me all this way, I suppose there is important business which you wish to transact with me."

The fellow said nothing. Whether he understood I could not say. He evidently wished me to believe that he did not, shaking his head, as if he had no tongue. I took him for a Chinaman, though he was darker than I imagine Chinamen are wont to be. His two little bead-like eyes burned out of two small round holes, in circumference scarcely larger than a sixpence. Eyebrows or eyelashes he had none. His skin was scarred by smallpox.

Since, apparently, nothing could be done with him, I let him go. So soon as my hand was off him he darted into the Strand like some eager wild thing. After momentary hesitation I went to see what had become of him. Already the traffic had swallowed him up. He was out of sight.

Gregory Pryor was in when I called the second time. I laid the God of Fortune down before him on the table.

"What's that?" I asked.

"It's a joss."

"A joss?" The promptness of his reply took me aback. "I thought a joss was an idol."

"So it is; what you might call an idol. A symbol some would style it. They're of all sorts, shapes and sizes; that is one of the waistcoat pocket kind. I was once in a case for a Chinaman with an unpronounceable name. He spoke English better than you and I, knew the ropes at least as well, yet he had one of these things in each of about twenty-seven pockets. He was a member of one of the thirteen thousand Taoist sects. He told me that they'd a joss for everything; a joss for the hearth, another for the roof, another for the chimney; three for the beard, whiskers and moustache. In every twig of every tree they saw a joss of some sort. Where did you get yours from?"

I informed him; then spoke of the contents of the parcel which the morning's post had brought.

"I can give you one assurance—this bond's all right. At a shade under the market price, I can do with any number. As for your missionary's letter, let's see if Great Ka Island is on the map."

He got down a gazetteer and an atlas.

"The gazetteer's an old one. There's no mention of it here, so it seems that it was either not known when this was published, or it was too obscure a spot to be worth recording. The atlas is newer. Ah! here we have it. Arafura Sea—New Guinea—Dutch New Guinea. There's a group of Ka Islands—Great Ka, Little Ka, and others. Great Ka's largish, nearly one hundred miles long, but narrow; apparently not ten miles at the broadest part, and tapering to a point. Sort of reef, I fancy. A good deal out of the way, and not in any steamer route I ever heard of. A convenient address for a man who wishes to avoid inquiries."

Leaning back in his chair, pressing the tips of his fingers together, Pryor regarded the ceiling.

"Letter's fishy, and, being undated, no use as evidence. Will's fishy, too. But there are the bonds So long as a lawyer sees his way to his fee, what else matters? I take it that there was a Benjamin Batters, and that there is a Mary Blyth. I also fancy that there's more in the matter than meets the eye. It has come to you in an irregular fashion, and therefore, in the nature of things, it is sniffy. My advice to you is, move warily. Discover Mary Blyth; hand over the estate to her, accepting no responsibility; present your bill, get your money; and, unless you see good reason to the contrary, wipe your hands of her thenceforward. If you do that you won't do very far wrong. Now, good-bye; I've got all this stuff to wade through before I dine."

I left him to the study of his briefs. His advice I turned over in my mind, finally resolving that I would move even more warily than he suggested. Before introducing myself to Mary Blyth, I would spend a day in endeavouring to discover something about the late Benjamin Batters, and, particularly, I would try to learn how it was that, after his death, his affairs had chanced to fall into my hands.

I work, live, eat and sleep in my chambers. As it happens I am the only person on the premises who does so. There used to be others. But now, with the exception of my set, what were living rooms are used as offices, and I am the only actual resident the house contains. After dark—sometimes before—the workers flit away. I have the entire building to myself until they return with the morning.

My rooms are four: bedroom; an apartment in which I am supposed to take my meals; one which I use as an office; and the den, opening immediately on to the staircase, in which Crumper has his being. That night I was roused suddenly from sleep. At first I could not make out what had woke me. Then I heard what was unmistakably the clatter of something falling.

"There's someone in the office."

Slipping out of bed, picking up a hockey stick, making as little noise as possible, I stole officewards. Intuitively I guessed who was there, and proposed to interview my uninvited visitor.

My hasty conclusions proved, however, to be a little out.

CHAPTER XIX
THE RETICENCE OF CAPTAIN LANDER

The office door was ajar. I remembered that I had left it so when I came to bed. Through the opening a dim light was visible. I peeped in.

I had expected to find that my guest would take the shape of the individual who had dogged my footsteps home from Camford Street. I hardly know on what I based my expectation, but there it was. A single glance, however, was sufficient to show that "guest" should read "guests," for they were three. One was the pock-marked gentleman in question; a second was seemingly his brother—they were as alike as two peas; the third was as remarkable a person as I had ever yet beheld. He was of uncommon height and uncommon thinness. I never saw a smaller head set on human shoulders. My impression was that it was a monstrously attenuated monkey, which had thrown a yellow dust sheet about it anyhow. And it was only when I perceived the deftness with which the contents of my drawers were being emptied out upon the table that it occurred to me that, man or monkey, it was advisable I should interfere.

Just as I had decided that it was about time for me to have a finger in the pie, my beady-eyed acquaintance of the afternoon lighted on the God of Fortune, which I had tossed upon the table on my return from Pryor's. Snatching it up with a curious cry, he handed it to his monkey-headed friend. That long-drawn-out gentleman, after a rapid glance at it, held it up with both hands high above his head. At once his two associates threw themselves down flat on their faces, grovelling before the penny doll as if it had been an object too sacred for ordinary eyes to look upon. The man of length without breadth began to say something in a high pitched monotone, which was in a language quite unknown to me, but which sounded as if it were a prayer or invocation. He spoke rapidly, as if he were repeating a form of words which he knew by heart.

I was getting interested. It seemed that I was surreptitiously assisting at some sort of religious service in which the doll played a conspicuous part. As I was momentarily expecting something to happen, something in the Arabian Nights way, as it were, that stupid hockey stick, slipping somehow from my grasp, fell with a bang upon the floor. That concluded the service on the spot. It must needs strike against the door in falling, driving it further open, so that I stood revealed to the trio in plain sight.

My impression is that they took me for something of horror; a demoniacal visitation, for all I know. My costume was weird enough to astonish even the Occidental mind. Anyhow, no sooner did they get a glimpse at me than they stood not on the order of their going, but went at once. Out went the light, and, also, out went they, through the window by which they had entered, and that with a show of agility which did them credit. I caught up that wretched stick, rushed after them in the darkness, and had the satisfaction of giving someone a pretty smart crack upon the head as he dropped from the sill on to the pavement below. I am not sure, but I fancy it was the lengthy one.

Striking a light I looked to see what damage had been done. So far as I could discover the only thing which was missing was the God of Fortune, to which they were entirely welcome. Apparently they prized it more than I did. I had a kind of notion, born of I know not what, that they had been after the Batters' papers. If so, they were disappointed, for I had taken them with me into my bedroom, and at that moment they were reposing on a chair by my bedside.

The greater part of the following day I spent in searching for someone who knew something about Benjamin Batters, or Great Ka Island, or Arthur Lennard, missionary—without result. I learned what I was already aware of, that there were numerous missionary societies, both in England and America; and acquired the additional information that to try to find out something about a particular missionary without knowing by which society he had been accredited, resembled the well-known leading case of the search for the needle in the haystack. At the great shipping office at which I made inquiries no one knew anyone who had ever been to Great Ka Island, or ever wanted to go. And as for Benjamin Batters, the general impression seemed to be that if I wanted to know anything about him I had better put an advertisement in the agony column, and see what came of that.

Altogether, I felt that the day had been pretty well wasted. But as it would probably have been wasted anyhow, I had the consolation of knowing that there had not been so much harm done after all. To the credit side of the account was the fact that I had picked up three or four odds and ends of curious information which had never come my way before. And, as luck would have it, shortly after my return I actually had a client. Or something like one, at any rate.

Crumper was making ready for departure, when he appeared at the door with a face on which was an unmistakable grievance.

"Gentleman wishes to see you, sir. Told him that the office was just closing."

"Did you? Then don't be so liberal with information of the kind. Show the gentleman in."

Crumper showed him in. When I saw him I was not sure that, in the colloquial sense, he was a gentleman. And yet I did not know.

He was a tall, well set-up man of between thirty and forty, distinctly good-looking, with fair hair and beard, and a pair of the bluest eyes I ever saw. He wore a blue serge suit, a turn down collar, and a scarlet tie. I know something of the sea and of sailors, having several of the latter among my closest friends. If he was not a sailor I was no judge of the breed. He brought a whiff of sea air into the room.

I motioned him to a chair, on which he placed himself as if he was not altogether at his ease. He glanced at a piece of paper which he had in his hand.

"You are Mr. Frank Paine?" I inclined my head. "A lawyer?"

I nodded again. He pulled at his beard; observing me with his keen blue eyes, as if he was thinking that for a lawyer I was rather young.

"I want a lawyer, or rather I want advice which I suppose only a lawyer can give me. I was speaking about it to George Gardiner, and he mentioned your name."

"I am obliged to George; he is my very good friend. To whom have I the pleasure of speaking?"

"I'm Max Lander."

"I am pleased to make your acquaintance, as I should any friend of Mr. Gardiner's. You, like him, are connected with the sea."

"How did you find that out? Do I look as if I were?"

"Perhaps only to the instructed eye." I wondered who, with ordinary perception, could associate him with anything else. "I am so fortunate as to have many friends among sailors, therefore I am always on the look-out for one."

"That so?"

He kept trifling with his beard, apparently desirous that the burden of the conversation should rest with me.

"You know Mr. Gardiner well?"

"Not over well."

"He was my schoolfellow, with another man who is now also a sailor—another George; George Kingdon."

"What name?"

"Kingdon. He has lately received his first command; of a ship named *The Flying Scud*."

Mr. Lander ceased to play with his beard. His hands dropped on to his knees. He sat forward on his chair, staring at me as if I were some strange animal.

"Good Lord!"

He seemed agitated. I had no notion why. Something I had said had apparently disturbed him.

"You know Mr. Kingdon?"

"Kingdon? Kingdon? Is that his name? Then devil take him! No, I don't mean that. Perhaps it's not his fault after all; it's the fortune of war. Still—devil take him all the same."

"What has Mr. Kingdon done to you, Mr. Lander?"

"Done!—done!" Apparently his feelings were too strong for words. Rising from his seat he began to stride about the room. Then, resting both hands upon the table, he glared at me. "What has Mr. Kingdon done to me? Did you hear my name?"

"I understood you to say it was Lander."

"That's it, Lander; Max Lander. Now don't you know who I am?"

"It may be my stupidity, but I have not the least idea."

"Do you mean to say that you don't know George Kingdon's taken my ship from me?"

"Taken her from you? I don't understand. I understood that *The Flying Scud* was the property of Messrs. ——"

"Staple, Wainwright and Friscoe; that's so. That's the name and title of the firm; they're the owners. But I was in command of her the last three voyages; and when I brought her home I was hoping it was for the last time."

"It seems that your hope was justified."

"Are you laughing at me, Mr. Paine? Because, if you are, take my tip and don't. I don't mind being laughed at in a general way; but this is a subject on which I bar so much as a smile. I'm too sore, sir, too sore. Do you know the circumstances under which I got chucked from *The Flying Scud*?"

"I do not. May I ask if that is the matter on which you are seeking my advice?"

"Well," he began, pulling at his beard again, hesitating, as if fearing to say too much. "What I want to know is, are your sympathies with the owner, with Kingdon, or with me?"

"Since I know nothing of what you are referring to, what answer do you expect me to give? So far as I am concerned, you are talking in riddles."

"Look here, Mr. Paine, I'll make a clean breast of the whole thing. Gardiner told me you were a decent sort, so I'll take his word for it. You see before you the best done man in London—in England—in the world, for all I know. Done all round! I knew I was taking a certain risk, but I didn't know it was a risk in that particular direction, and that's where I was had. I saw my way to a real big thing. I went for it, shoved on all steam; brought the ship home, pretty well empty as she was; then got diddled. So, when I laid the ship alongside, and the owners found that there was scarcely enough on board to pay expenses, they didn't like it. I got my marching ticket, and Mr. George Kingdon was in command instead. If it hadn't been that I'd got a little money of my own, I should have been on my beam ends before now."

"Do I gather that you complain of the way in which the owners of *The Flying Scud* have treated you?"

"Not a bit of it; nothing of the kind. The only person I complain of is— we'll say a party. If I got that, we'll say, party, alone in a nice quiet little spot for about ten minutes, after that time I wouldn't complain of him. The complaint would be on the other foot."

"Then do you wish me to assist you in a scheme of assault and battery?"

"I don't want that either. The fact is, it's a queer story. You wouldn't believe me if I told it; no one has done yet, so I'm not going to try my luck again with you. What I want to know is this. Suppose I ship, we'll say, a man, and that, we'll say, man, undertakes to hand over certain—well, articles, to pay for passage, and deposits certain other articles by way of earnest money. Before the ship reaches port that, we'll say, man, vanishes into air, the articles which were to have been handed over, vanish with him, and the deposit likewise. What offence has that, we'll say, man, been guilty of against the English law?"

"Your point is a knotty one. Where was the deposit?"

"In a locker in my cabin."

"Secured by lock and key?"

"Secured by lock and key. And the key was in my pocket."

"How was it taken out?"

"That's what I want to know."

"You are sure it was taken out?"

"Dead sure."

"If you have evidence which will show that the person to whom you refer made free with the contents of your locker, then I should say that it was a case of felony. But there may be other points which would have to be considered. I should have to be placed in possession of all the facts of the case before I could pronounce an opinion. The matter may not be so simple as you think."

"Simple! I think it simple! Good Lord!" He held up his hands, as if amazed at the suggestion. "There's another thing I want to know. Suppose on the strength of that, we'll say, man's promises, I make promises on my own account to certain members of the crew. Being done by that, we'll say, man, I was obliged to do them. What is my position, Mr. Paine, toward those members of the crew?"

"That is a question to which I cannot reply off-hand. It would depend on so many circumstances. I am afraid you will have to tell me the whole of your story before I can be of use to you."

"Ah! That so? I was afraid it would be. I said to myself that you can't expect a man, lawyer or no lawyer, to see what's inside a box unless you open the lid. But I can't tell you the story; I can't. I'm too sore, sir, too sore. Smarting almost more than I can bear. I've been done out of a fortune, out of my good name, and out of something I value more than both. That's a fact. I'll look round a bit more, and try to get one of them back, in my own way. Then, if I can't, perhaps I'll come to you again. Sorry to have troubled you, Mr. Paine. What's your fee?"

"For what? I've been of no use to you. For a pleasant conversation with my friend's friend? I charge no fee for that, Mr. Lander."

"You're a lawyer. A lawyer's time is money. I've always understood that a lawyer's fee is six and eightpence. You've found me pretty trying. So I'll make it a pound if you don't mind."

He laid a sovereign on the table. Without another word he left the room. I did not try to stop him. To my thinking the whole interview had verged perilously near to the ridiculous. I took the coin and locked it in a drawer, proposing, with Gardiner's assistance, to hunt up Mr. Lander again. His money should be restored to him, if not in one form, then in another.

I would dine the man, and make him tell his funny tale.

CHAPTER XX
MY CLIENT—AND HER FRIEND

The next day I was engaged. On that following I went up to Fenchurch Street, to the offices of Messrs. Staple, Wainwright and Friscoe. I had ascertained that Gardiner was out of town, and actuated by motives of curiosity thought I would learn where Mr. Lander might be found. As I was going up the steps an old gentleman came down. I knew him pretty well. His name was Curtis. He had been, and, indeed, for all I knew, was still an agent of Lloyd's. For two or three years we had not met. After we had exchanged greetings, I put to him my question.

"Do you know a man named Lander, Max Lander?"

"Late of *The Flying Scud*?"

An odd expression came on his face, as it were the suggestion of a grin.

"That's the man."

"Yes, I know something of Max Lander, Captain Max, as he likes to be called. Though there's not much of the captain about him just at present."

The grin came more to the front.

"He called on me about a matter of which I could make neither head nor tail. I should like to have another talk with him. Can you tell me where he's to be found?"

Mr. Curtis shook his head.

"Just now he's resting. It's been a little too hot for him of late. I fancy he's lying by till it gets a little cooler."

"What's wrong with the man?"

"Nothing exactly wrong, only he's had a little experience. Sorry I can't stay, this cab's waiting for me." He stepped into the hansom which was drawn up by the kerb. "If you want to know what's wrong with Lander, you mention to him the name of Batters—Benjamin Batters."

The cab drove off. Before I had recovered from my astonishment it was beyond recall.

Batters? Benjamin Batters? My Benjamin Batters? There could hardly be two persons possessed of that alliterative name. If I had only guessed that there was any sort of connection between him and Benjamin Batters, Mr. Lander would not have departed till we had arrived at a better understanding. Why had the idiot not dropped a hint? Why had Curtis driven off at that rate at the wrong moment?

I asked at the office for the address of Captain Max Lander. I was snubbed. The name was evidently not a popular one in that establishment. The clerk, having submitted my inquiry to someone elsewhere, informed me curtly that nothing was known of such a person there, and appeared to think that I had been guilty of an impertinence in supposing that anything was. When I followed with a request for information about a Mr. Benjamin Batters, I believe that clerk thought I was having a game with him. Somewhere in the question must have been a sting, with which I was unacquainted; for, with a scowl, he turned his back on me, not deigning to reply.

As I did not want to have an argument with Messrs. Staple, Wainwright and Friscoe's staff, I went away. I pursued my inquiries elsewhere, both for Captain Max Lander and for Mr. Benjamin Batters. But without success. The scent had run to ground. By the evening I concluded that I had had about enough of the job. Instead of trying to find out things about Benjamin Batters, I would seek out Mary Blyth. She should have the good news. I was not sure that I had not already kept them from her longer than I was justified in doing. She should learn that she was the proud possessor of a tumble-down, disreputable house in Camford Street; though, so far as I could see, she had not a shadow of a title to it which would hold good in law; but perhaps she was not a person who would allow herself to be hampered by a trifle of that description; also of a comfortable income derived from consols—conditions being attached to both bequests which were calculated to drive her mad. Having imparted that good news, I would wash my hands of the Batters' family for good and all. There was something about it which was, as Gregory Pryor put it, "sniffy."

With that design I started betimes the next morning. I had no difficulty in finding the establishment of Messrs. Cardew and Slaughter, where Mr. Batters stated in his will that he had last heard of his niece as an assistant. It was an "emporium," where they sold many things you wanted, and more which you did not, from gloves to fire-irons. After being kept waiting an unconscionable length of time, asked many uncalled-for questions, and enduring what I felt to be intentional indignities, I was ushered into the office of Mr. Slaughter.

That gentleman was disposed to mete out to me even more high-handed treatment than Messrs. Staple, Wainwright and Friscoe. Under the circumstances, however, that was more than I was inclined to submit to. He seemed to regard it as sheer insolence that a stranger should venture to speak to him—the great Slaughter!—of such a mere nothing as one of his assistants. As if I had wanted to! We had quite a passage of arms. In the midst who should come running in but the girl herself—Mary Blyth.

She had just been dismissed. I had come in the nick of time to prevent her being thrown—literally thrown—into the street. That was a partial explanation of Mr. Slaughter's haughtiness. Pretty badly she seemed to have been used. And very hot she was with a sense of injury. She had a companion in misfortune; a prettier girl I had never seen. The pair had been sent packing at a moment's notice. If I had been a minute or two later I should have missed them; they would have gone. In which case the most striking chapter in my life's history might have had to be written in a very different fashion.

When it came to paying the two girls the wretched pittance which was due to them as wages, an attempt was made to keep back the larger portion of it under the guise of "fines," that rascally system by means of which so many drapers impose upon the helpless men and women they employ. A few sharp words from me were sufficient to show that this was an occasion on which that method of roguery could hardly be safely practised. I judged that the sum paid them—fifteen shillings—represented their entire fortune. With that capital they were going out to face the world.

In the cab I had an opportunity of forming some idea of what my client was like.

Mary Blyth was big, rawboned, and, I may add, hungry looking. She gave me the impression that she had had a hard life, one in which she had had not seldom to go without enough to eat. In age I set her down as twenty-six or seven. She was not handsome; on the other hand she was not repellent. Her features were homely, but they were not unpleasing, and there was about them more than a suggestion of honesty and shrewdness. Her experience of the rougher side of life had probably given her a readiness of wit, and a coolness of head, which would cause her to find herself but little at a loss in any position in which a changeable fate would place her. That was how she struck me. I liked her clear eyes, her pleasant mouth, her determined nose and chin. Intellectuality might not be her strongest point; obviously, in a scholastic sense, her educational advantages had been but small. Her tongue betrayed her. But, unless I greatly erred, she was a woman of character for all that. Strong, enduring, clear-sighted, within her limits; sure and by no means slow. A little prone to impatience, perhaps; it is a common failing. I am impatient myself at times. Still, on the whole, on her own lines, a good type of an Englishwoman.

My client's appearance pleased me better than I feared would have been the case. I was not so eager to wash my hands of the Batters' connection as I had been.

But it was my client's friend who appealed most strongly to my imagination. She took my faculties by storm. I am not easily disconcerted. Yet, in her presence, I felt ridiculously ill at ease. She was only a girl. I kept telling myself that she was only a girl. I believe that it was because she was only a girl that I was conscious of such curious sensations. She sat opposite me in the cab. Every time her knee brushed against mine, I felt as if I was turning pink and green and yellow. It was not only uncomfortable, it was undignified.

She was just the kind of girl I like to look at; yet, for some reason, I hardly dared allow my eyes to stray in her direction. I could look at Miss Blyth; stare at her, indeed, till further notice, in the most callous, cold-blooded way. But my glances studiously avoided her friend. Her name was Emily Purvis—the friend's name, I mean. I had a general impression that she had big eyes, light brown hair, and a smile which lit up her face like sunshine. I am aware that this sounds slightly drivelling; if it were another man I should say that his language reminded me of a penny novelette. But my mood at the moment was pronouncedly imbecile; I was only capable of drivel. The girl had come upon me with such a shock of surprise. I had never expected to light on anything of that kind when pursuing the niece of Benjamin Batters.

Miss Purvis was small. I like small women. I am aware that this is an age of muscularity, and that athletics do cause women to run to size. But, for my part, I like them little. Bone, muscle, stamina, these things are excellent. From a physical point of view, no doubt, the Amazon, when she is fit, in good condition, is all that she should be. I admire such a one, even when her height is five feet eleven. But I do not like her; I never could. As to having a woman of that description for a wife—the saints forbid!

Miss Purvis was little. Not a dwarf, nor insignificant in any sense, but small enough. I am six foot one, and I judged that the top of her head would just come above my shoulder. Daintily fashioned, curves not angles. Exactly the kind of girl ninety-nine men out of a hundred would feel inclined to take into their arms at sight. The hundredth man would be a sexless idiot; and, also, most probably, stone blind. It was astonishing how afraid I felt of her.

It was an odd drive to my chambers. My client talked, Miss Purvis talked, I only dropped a boobyish remark at intervals. The idea that such a girl as that should only have fifteen shillings between her and starvation, and that to keep herself alive she should have to seek another situation in such a den of roguery, servitude, humiliation, as that from which she had just escaped, was to me most horrible. I was irritated, illogically enough, because Benjamin Batters had not left her a portion of the income which was derived from those bonds of his. I was conscious of the fact that he had had no cognisance of her existence. But, at the moment, that was not the point.

Two incidents marked our progress.

The first was when Miss Blyth, putting her head out of the cab window, recognised, with every appearance of surprise, a man standing on the pavement whom she called Isaac Rudd. I observed that he saw us, and the keenness with which his gaze was fastened on us. There was a seafaring air about the fellow which recalled Max Lander to my mind. Although I said nothing of it to the ladies, I had a shrewd suspicion that he was following us in another cab, which he had hailed as soon as we had passed. Two or three times when I looked out I noticed that a second four-wheeler seemed to be keeping us in sight. In view of my recent experiences, had I been alone I should have lost no time in putting the question to the proof. Not only, however, just then, were my wits a good deal wanting, but I felt a not unnatural disinclination to cause my companions uneasiness. Especially as I more than suspected that Miss Blyth might have enough of that a little later on.

The second incident was a trifle startling.

Shortly after catching sight of the man she called Isaac Rudd, she gave a sudden exclamation. She was staring at something with wide-open eyes. I looked to see what it was.

There, on her knee, was my God of Fortune.

Her surprise at its appearance was unmistakably genuine. How it had come there she was unable to explain. It might have been "materialised," as the Theosophists have it, out of the intangible air. But it seemed that it was not the first time she had encountered it.

It had been slipped into her hand the night before by a fantastically attired individual who was evidently my length without breadth visitor, whom I had interrupted in his pseudo service, and who had dropped out of my office window with my God of Fortune in his hand. Although I made no reference to that occurrence, I was none the less struck by the fashion in which he had chosen to introduce himself to the niece of Mr. Benjamin Batters. The singularity of the thing went further. When the doll was slipped into the lady's hand it was cased in a piece of paper, as it was when it was slipped into mine, from, which, again exactly as had happened with me, it forced itself apparently of its own volition.

I made no comment, but, with Miss Blyth's permission, I put the doll into my waistcoat pocket; concluding that it might prove worthy of more minute examination than I had yet bestowed on it—even to the breaking of it open to discover "the works."

This is a sober chronicle. I trust I am a sober chronicler. I wish to set down nothing which suggests the marvellous. I have an inherent dislike to wonders, being without faith. When men speak of the inexplicable I think of trickery, and of some quality which is not perception. Therefore I desire it to be understood that the following lines are written without prejudice; and that of what happened there may be a perfectly simple explanation which escaped my notice.

I trust that there is.

I had read the missionary's letter, and the will, and had handed to Miss Blyth the sealed enclosure. When she opened it she found that within the packet was a little wooden box. On lifting the lid of this box, the first thing she saw—which we all saw—was my God of Fortune, or its double. It was just inside the box, staring at her, as it lay face upwards. Feeling in my waistcoat pocket for the duplicate, I found that it had gone. It had, apparently, passed into that wooden box, which had, until that moment, remained inviolate within that sealed enclosure. How, I do not pretend to say.

It was but a little thing, yet it affected me more than a greater might have done. A succession of "trifles light as air" may unsettle the best balanced mind. One begins, by degrees, to have a feeling that something is taking place, or is about to take place, of a character to which one is unaccustomed. And under such circumstances the unaccustomed, particularly when one is unable to even dimly apprehend the form which it may take, one instinctively resents.

I decided that, at any rate, that should be the last appearance of the God of Fortune. Taking it from Miss Blyth, who yielded it readily enough, I walked with it to the fire, intending to make an end of it by burning. As I went something pricked my fingers so suddenly, and so sharply, that in my surprise and, I might add, pain, the doll dropped from my hand. When we came to look for it it was not to be found. We searched under tables and chairs in all possible and impossible places, with a degree of eagerness which approached the ludicrous, without success. The God of Fortune had disappeared.

I am reluctant to confess how much I was disconcerted by so trivial an occurrence.

I must have been morbidly disposed; still liverish. That is the only explanation which I can offer why I should all at once have felt so strongly that everything connected with Mr. Benjamin Batters' testamentary dispositions wore a malign aspect. I was even haunted—the word is used advisedly—by a wholly unreasonable conviction that Miss Blyth was being dragged into a position of imminent peril.

This foolishness of mine was rendered more ridiculous by the fact that Miss Blyth's own mood was all the other way. And in this respect Miss Purvis was at one with her. Somewhat to my surprise they seemed to see nothing in the situation but what was pleasant.

Miss Blyth's attitude was one of frank delight. She had never known Mr. Batters' personally; all she knew of him was to the disadvantage of his character. She was enraptured by the prospect of a fortune and a house. It seemed she had a lover. In her mind, fortune, house, and lover were associated in a delightful jumble. She did not appear to realise that the acceptance of the fortune, if the attached conditions were to stand, meant the practical ostracising of the lover. Nor, at the instant, did I feel called upon to go out of the way to make the whole position plain to her understanding. It would have meant the spoiling of the happiest hour she had known.

Miss Purvis enjoyed what she regarded as her friend's good luck to the full as much as if it had been her own. It was delightful to see her. I had plucked up courage enough to observe her so long as she did not know that I was doing so. The moment she became conscious of my scrutiny, my eyes, metaphorically, sank into my boots; actually they wandered round the room, as if the apartment had been strange to me. When she proposed to become Miss Blyth's companion in that horrible house in Camford Street my heart thumped against my ribs in such a manner that I became positively ashamed.

Was I a lawyer, the mere mechanical exponent of an accidental situation, or was I the intimate of a lifetime? I had to ask myself the question. What right had I to throw obstacles in the way, to prevent her doing her friend a service? What right had I to even hint that she might be running a risk in doing her that service? My fears might be—were—purely imaginary. So far they certainly had no foundation in fact. They resembled nothing so much as the nervous fancies of some timorous old woman. It might be ruinous to my professional reputation to breathe a syllable which would point to their existence. People do not want shivery-shakery fools for lawyers. These two young women knew as much—and as little—about the house as I did. If they chose to live in it, let them. It was their affair, not mine. They plainly regarded the prospective tenancy as an excellent jest. I tried to persuade myself that I had no doubt whatever that that was just what they would find it.

So they entered into the occupation of No. 84 Camford Street. I went with them and saw them enter. It was a curious process, that of entry; an unreasonably, unnaturally curious process. It should be necessary to enter no honest house like that. The first step suggested, possibly, that something unsavoury was concealed within, which it was necessary, at all and any cost, to keep hidden from the light of day.

When they were in, and the door was closed, and they had gone from sight, an icy finger seemed to be pressed against my spine. I shivered as with cold. An almost irresistible longing possessed me to batter at the door and compel them to come out. But I had not sufficient courage to write myself down an ass.

Instead, I rode home in the cab which had brought us to the house to which I had taken so cordial a disrelish, oppressed by a sense of horrible foreboding which weighed upon my brain nearly to the point of stupefaction.

"Before I go to bed to-night," I told myself, "I'll take a dozen of somebody or other's antibilious pills. I had no idea I was so liverish."

CHAPTER XXI
THE AGITATION OF MISS PURVIS

That bachelor's balm, a night at a music hall, was of no avail in diverting my mind from the house in Camford Street. In the body I might be present at a vocal rendering of the latest things in comic songs; in the spirit I was the other side of the water. Before the night was over I was there physically, too.

As the ten o'clock "turn" was coming on, and the brilliancy of the entertainment was supposed to have reached high-water mark, I walked down the stairs of the Cerulean and out into the street. I strolled down the Haymarket without any clear idea of where I meant to go.

"You're an ass," I told myself. "An ass, sir! If you'd stopped to see Pollie Floyd she'd have driven the cobwebs out of your head. You pay five shillings for a seat, and when, at last, there is going to be something worth looking at, and listening to, you get out of it, and throw away your money. At this time of night, where do you think you're going?"

I knew all the time, although even to myself I did not choose to confess it—Camford Street. I made for it as straight as I could. It was past half-past ten when I got there. The street was nearly all in darkness. The public-houses were open; but, as they were not of the resplendent order, they were of but little use as illuminants. Mr. Kennard's establishment was shut. Lights were visible in but few of the houses. No. 84, in the prevailing shadows, looked black as pitch. If the two girls had been obedient to the injunctions laid down in Mr. Batters' will—and that first night, at any rate, they would have hardly ventured to contravene them—they were long since within doors. Doing what? Asleep? Were both of them asleep? I wondered, if she was awake, what occupied her thoughts? Was she thinking of—the person in the street?

Too ridiculous! Absurd! It is amazing of what crass stupidity even the wisest men are capable. Why should a girl who was a perfect stranger, be thinking, whether awake or sleeping, at that hour of the night, of an individual who had been brought into accidental business association, on one occasion only, with a friend of hers? I kept on putting such-like brain-splitting questions to myself. Without avail. I simply shirked them. I only hoped. That was all.

I had some nonsensical notion of hammering at the front door to see what would happen. But as I was unable to perceive what could result, except possible scandal—suppose they were in bed! they might think I was burglars, or Mr. Batters' ghost—I held my hand. I was not too far gone to be incapable of realising that frightening a woman into fits was not the best way of winning her trust and confidence. That she was of a nervous temperament I thought probable. I like a woman to be reasonably timorous.

What might have been expected happened. My persistency in strolling about, and behaving as if I were a suspicious character, at last succeeded in arousing the attention of the police. An overcoated constable strode up to me. I stopped him, feeling that it might be better for me to open the ball.

"Officer, do you know anything about the house opposite—No. 84?"

He eyed me; apparently arriving at a conclusion that I bore no conspicuous signs of belonging to the criminal classes.

"We call it the haunted house."

"Haunted? Why haunted?"

It was a horrible idea that she should be sleeping alone, or as good as alone, in a house which bore the reputation of being haunted. Not that I placed any credence in such rubbish myself, but when she was concerned it was a different matter.

"I can't say why; but it's known as such, in the force, and, I believe, among the people in the neighbourhood."

"Ah! Well, officer, two friends of mine—ladies—young ladies—have taken up their residence at No. 84, and as they're all alone I shall be obliged if you'll keep an eye upon the house. If you see any ghosts about the place you run 'em in."

I gave that policeman half-a-crown. I do not know what he thought of me. I was completely conscious that if I continued to placate members of the constabulary force with two-and-sixpence each I should not find the Batters' connection a lucrative one. It was all owing to the state of mind I was in. To have remained in her immediate neighbourhood I would have showered half-crowns.

Yet I tore myself away, and went straight home to bed. Hardly to sleep, for such slumber as visited my eyes was troubled by strange imaginings. It would be incorrect to say that all night I dreamed of her, for most of my dreams took the shape of nightmare visitations; but I do not hesitate to affirm that they were caused by her. I had not been troubled by such things for years. If she was not the cause of them, what was?

I awoke at some most unseemly hour. Since sleep was evidently at an end I concluded that it might be as well to have done with what had been, for the first time for many nights, a bed of discomfort. So I arose and dressed. It was a fine morning. I could see that the sun was shining, even from my window. I concluded that I would put into execution a resolution which I had often formed, and as often broken, of going for a walk before breakfast. One is constantly being told—for the most part by people who know nothing about it—how beautiful London is in the early morning sun.

So soon as I was in Fleet Street I saw something which I had certainly not expected to see, at least, not there, just then—Miss Purvis. Fleet Street was deserted; she was the only living thing to be seen; the sight of her nearly took me off my feet. She had been in my thoughts. Her sudden, instant presence was like the miraculous materialisation of some telepathic vision. I felt as if I had heard her calling me, and had come.

She was distant some fifty yards, and was coming towards me. I was at once struck by the air of wildness which was about her. It moved me strangely. She was not attired for the street, having on neither hat nor bonnet, jacket or gloves. Her hair was in disorder. She looked as if she had been in some singular affray. My heart jumped so within my breast that I had, perforce, to stand as if I had been rooted to the ground. Conscience-stricken, I railed at myself for not having, last night, broken down the door, instead of lounging idly in the street. All the while, I knew that there was something wrong. I owned it now, though I had been reluctant to admit it then.

I think she saw me as soon as I saw her. At sight of me she broke into a little tremulous run, swaying from side to side, as if she was so weak that her feet were not entirely under her own control. It was pitiful to watch. Tearing myself from where I seemed to be rooted, I ran to her. I had reached her in less than half-a-dozen seconds. When I was close, stretching out her hands, she cried, in a faint little voice:—

"It's you! it's you! Oh, Mr. Paine!"

She did not throw herself into my arms, she had not so much strength; she sank into them, and was still. I saw that she had fainted.

I bore her to my rooms. It was the least that I could do. No one was in sight. And though, no doubt, some straggler might have soon appeared, I could not tell what kind of person it might prove to be. I could hardly keep her out there in the street awaiting the advent of some quite possibly undesirable stranger, even had I been willing, which I was not. Lifting her in my arms, I carried her to my chambers.

Not once did she move. She was limp as some lay figure. I laid her on the couch. So far as I could judge, at first she did not breathe. Then, all at once, she sighed; a tremblement seemed to go all over her. I expected her to open her eyes, and see me there. I felt as if I had been guilty of I knew not what, and feared to meet her accusatory glances. But instead she lay quite still, though I could see that her bosom rose and fell, moved by gentle respirations. My blood boiled as I wondered what could have made her cheek so white.

On a sudden her eyes unclosed. For some seconds she looked neither to the right nor left. She seemed to be considering the ceiling. Then, with a start, she turned and saw me.

"Where am I?" she exclaimed.

"You are safe in my chambers. You know who I am, do you not?"

"You are Mr. Paine. Oh, Mr. Paine!"

She began to cry. Turning from me, she buried her face in the cushion.

"Miss Purvis! What is wrong? What is the matter? Tell me what has happened."

She continued to cry, her sobs shaking her whole frame. I was beginning to be conscious that the situation was a more delicate one than had at first appeared. After all, the girl was but a stranger to me. I had not the slightest right to attempt to offer her consolation. I remembered to have read somewhere that you ought to know a man intimately for fifteen years before presuming to poke his fire. If that were the case the imagination failed to picture how long a man ought to be acquainted with a girl before venturing to try, with the aid of a pocket handkerchief, to dry her tears.

She kept on crying. It was a severe trial to one's more or less misty sense of what etiquette demanded. Ought I to remain to be a witness of her tears? She might not like it. She might, very reasonably, resent being practically compelled to exhibit her grief in the presence of a stranger. On the other hand, to leave her alone to, as it were, cry it out, might be regarded, from certain points of view, as the acme of brutality. What I should have liked to have done would have been to take her in my arms, and comfort her as if she had been a child. In the midst of my bewilderment it irritated me to think of the asinine notions which would enter my head. Did I, I inquired of myself, wish to make an enemy, a righteous enemy, of the girl for life?

I tried the effect of another inquiry.

"Miss Purvis, I—I wish you would tell me what has happened."

"Pollie!"

That was all she said; and that utterance was so blurred by a choking gasp as to render it uncertain if that was what she had said.

"Pollie? Who is Pollie?"

Quite possibly my tone was one of dubiety. Either that or the question itself affected her in a fashion which surprised me. She stopped as suddenly as if the fountain of her tears had been worked by some automatic attachment. Raising herself slightly from the couch, she looked at me, her eyes swollen with weeping.

"Pollie? You ask me who is Pollie? And you're her lawyer!"

"Her lawyer?—Pollie's——? You're not referring to Miss——? Of course, how stupid of me! I had forgotten that Miss Blyth's Christian name was Mary. I suppose that by her friends she is known as Pollie. I hope that nothing has happened to Miss Blyth."

"Do you think that I should be here if nothing had happened to Pollie?"

The question was put with an amount of vigour which, in one so fragile, was almost surprising. I was delighted to see in her such a renewal of vigour. It made me feel more at my ease.

"I am only too fortunate, Miss Purvis, whatever the object of your visit. If you will permit me I will get you a cup of tea; that's what you're wanting. I live so much alone I'm accustomed to do all sorts of things for myself. Here's a gas stove; in five minutes the water will be boiling; you shall have your tea. It will do you an immensity of good."

I had always understood that girls liked tea. But, as I moved about the room, preparing to set the kettle on the stove, she stared at me with an apparent want of comprehension.

"Do you suppose that I've come through the streets like this just to get a cup of tea?"

"Never mind for the moment why you've come, Miss Purvis; the great thing is that you have come. Tea first: explanation afterwards. If you take my advice you'll let that be the order of procedure. Nothing like a good brew to promote clarity of exposition."

I lit the stove.

"Mr. Paine! Mr. Paine!"

She jumped off the couch in quite a passion of excitement.

"Now, Miss Purvis, I do beg you will control yourself. I give you my word that in less than five minutes the water will be boiling."

She stamped her foot; rage certainly became her.

"You keep talking about your tea, when Pollie's killed!"

"Killed—Miss Purvis! You don't mean that Miss Blyth is—killed?"

"She is!—or something awful—and worse!"

"But"—I placed the kettle on the stove to free my hand—"let me understand you plainly. Do you wish to be taken literally when you say that Miss Blyth is—killed?"

"If she isn't she will be soon."

"I'm afraid I must ask you to be a little plainer. Where is Miss Blyth?"

"She's in one of Bluebeard's Chambers?"

I began to wonder if her mind was wandering.

"I'm afraid that I still don't——"

"That's the name she gave them. In that dreadful house in Camford Street there are two rooms locked up, and Pollie's in one."

"I see." I did not, though, at the same time, I fancied that I began to perceive a dim glimmer of light. "But if, as you say, the rooms were locked, how did she get in, and what happened to her when she was in?"

In reply Miss Purvis poured out a series of disjointed statements which I experienced some difficulty in following, and more in reconciling. As I listened, in spite of her manifold attractions, I could not but feel that if she should figure in the witness box, in a case in which I was concerned, I would rather that she gave evidence for the other side.

"That house was full of wickedness!"

"Indeed. In what sense?"

"There's a woman in it!"

"A woman? There is a woman? Then that's all right."

"All right?"

"I was afraid there wouldn't be another woman."

"Afraid! Women are ever so much worse than men. And she's—awful. She says she's the daughter of the gods."

"A little wanting, perhaps."

I touched my head. Apparently Miss Purvis did not catch the allusion.

"Wanting! She's wanting in everything she ought to have. She's—she's not to be described. I thought she was rats."

"You thought she was rats?"

"The house is full of them—in swarms! They'd have eaten me—picked the flesh off my bones!—if I'd given them the chance."

I was becoming more and more persuaded that agitation had been too much for her. I had never encountered a case of a person being eaten alive by rats, except the leading one of Bishop Hatto in his rat tower on the Rhine, and that was scarcely quotable.

"Now, Miss Purvis, the kettle is just on the boil. I do beg you'll have a cup of tea before we go any further."

"With Pollie lying dead?"

"But is she lying dead?"

"I believe she's eaten!"

"Eaten?—by rats?"

There was a dryness in my tone which was, perhaps, rather more significant than I had intended.

"Are you laughing at me?—Are you—laughing at me?"

She repeated her inquiry for the second time with a great sob in her voice, which made me realise what a brute I was.

"I am very far from laughing. I am only anxious that you should not make yourself ill."

"You're not! you're not!" She stamped her foot again. I gazed at her with admiration. She was the first beautiful woman I remembered to have seen whose personal appearance was positively improved by getting into a temper.

"You're laughing at me all the time; you haven't a spark of human feeling in you!" This was an outrageous charge. At that moment I would have given a great part of what I possessed to have been able to take her in my arms. "What I've endured this night no tongue can tell, no pen describe. I've gone through enough to make my hair turn white. Hasn't it turned white?"

"It certainly hasn't. It's lovely hair."

"Lovely——?" She stopped, to look at me; seeing something in my countenance—she alone knew what it was—which made her put her hands up to her face, and burst again into tears. "Oh, Mr. Paine!"

My name, as it came from her lips, was a wail which cut me to the heart. Her agitation was making me agitated too. I had only one resource.

"Now, Miss Purvis, this kettle is really boiling."

"If you say another word about that kettle I'll knock it over!"

The small virago was facing me, the tears running down her cheeks, her small fists clenched, as if, on that point at least, she was capable of being as good as her word.

"Knock it over by all means, Miss Purvis, if it pleases you. I—I only want to give you pleasure."

"Mr. Paine!"

Up went her hands again.

"Don't do that. I—I can't bear to see you cry."

"Then why are you so unkind?"

"I don't know; it's my stupidity, I suppose; it's far from my intention to be unkind."

"I know! I know! I'm a nothing and a nobody; an impertinent creature who has come to bother you with a tale which you don't believe, and which wouldn't interest you if you did; and so you just make fun of me."

"Don't say that; not that. Don't say that to me you are a nothing and a nobody."

"I am! I am!"

"You are not."

"Then, why do you treat me as you do?"

"Treat you! How do I treat you? There is nothing I wouldn't do for you—nothing!"

"Mr. Paine!"

"Miss Purvis!"

I do not know how it happened. I protest, in cold blood, and in black and white, that I have no idea. But, on a sudden, I found that I had my arms about her. A moment before I had no intention of doing anything of the kind—that I swear. And I can only suppose that it was because, in her agitation, she really did not know what was happening, that she allowed her head to rest against my breast.

It was while it was there that a voice said, proceeding from the neighbourhood of the door:—

"This is a bit of all right; but where do I come in?"

CHAPTER XXII
LUKE

I have only to point out that, despite the interruption, Miss Purvis continued in the same position, without making the slightest effort to disengage herself, to make it clear that she, to at least a certain extent, was unconscious of her surroundings. For my part I held her somewhat closer, so that I might act as a more efficient protection against I knew not what.

Glancing in the direction from which the voice had come I perceived that a distinctly disreputable individual had intruded himself, uninvited, into the room. He was a tall, shambling fellow, with a chronic stoop, extending even to the neighbourhood of his knees. His attire consisted of a variety of odds and ends, all of them emphatically the worse for wear. A dirty cloth cap, apparently a size too small, was stuck at the back of his head. His black, greasy hair formed a ragged, uneven fringe upon his forehead, reaching in one place nearly to the top of his long, pointed nose. His mouth was too wide for his face, which was narrow. As he stood there with it open, in what I presume he intended for a friendly grin, the fact was revealed that seemingly every alternate tooth in his head was missing. Even in that moment of agitation I could not help mentally noting that I had never seen such a collection of fangs in one man's head before.

"What do you mean, sir, coming in without knocking?"

"What do I mean? That's what I'm here to tell you. And as for knocking, I did knock, with my knuckles; but you was too much engaged to notice my modest knock; so, seeing the door was open, I just come in."

"Then you'll just go out again; and sharp's the word."

While the fellow was speaking, Miss Purvis, awaking, for the first time, to a sense of her delicate position, drew herself away from me. Turning, she stared at the intruder.

"Sharp's the word, is it? That's how it may be. Anyhow, it don't apply to me, because I'm here on business."

"Then come in business hours. I don't receive clients at this time of day. Don't you see that I'm engaged?"

"Engaged, are you? That's as it should be. I congratulate you. Likewise the young lady, for having won so outspoken a young gentleman; and one that's well spoken of, from all I hear."

Whether the fellow was intentionally impertinent I could not tell. It was uncommonly awkward for both of us. Miss Purvis went scarlet. I felt like knocking him down.

"Now, then, out you go!"

"Softly! softly! You listen to me before the band begins to play. I don't allow no one to lay hands on me without laying of 'em back again."

The fellow extended, to ward me off, a pair of enormously long arms. Observing them, I realised that if he would only hold himself upright his height would be gigantic. I am no bantam; yet as I considered his evident suppleness, and sinewy build, I thought it possible that in him I had met my match. Anyhow, I did not wish to indulge in a rough-and-tumble before Miss Purvis.

"Who are you? And what do you want?"

"What I want first of all is to know who you are. Are you Mr. Frank Paine?"

"I am."

"I'm told that you're making inquiries about a party named Batters; now I'm making inquiries about a party named Batters, too; and if you was to tell me what you know, I might tell you what I know."

"You are quite right, I have been inquiring for a person of the name of Batters. And if you will come again, say, between ten and eleven, I shall be glad to hear what you have to say. By that time I shall be disengaged."

"You'll be disengaged, will you? That's hard on the young lady. Engaged to her at seven, and disengaged between ten and eleven, all of the same day."

"Look here, my man!"

"I'm looking, Mr. Paine, I'm looking; and I do hope I'm looking milder nor what you are. May I make so bold as to ask if this young lady's name is Blyth?"

"It is not."

"I thought it couldn't be. It wouldn't hardly seem natural for a beautiful young lady like she is to be grafted from a stock like that. Lovely is what I call her, downright lovely."

"Oh, Mr. Paine!"

Miss Purvis held out her hand. I took it.

"If you suppose because I have borne with you so far I will bear with you much further, you're mistaken. If you take my advice, you'll be careful."

"That's right, sir; that's quite right. Careful's the lay for me."

"If you have anything to say, be quick about it."

"Well, I do happen to have something which I wish to say, and that's a fact; but as for quickness I'm afraid that I'm not naturally so quick as perhaps you might desire." He stopped, to regard me with his bold, yet shifty eyes, as if he were endeavouring to ascertain what sort of person I might be. When he spoke again it was to put a question for which I was unprepared. "Where's Batters?"

"Mr. Batters—if you are referring to the late Mr. Benjamin Batters—is dead."

"Dead? Oh! Late, is he? Ah! He was the sort to die early, was Batters. Where might he happen to have died?"

"On Great Ka Island."

"Great Ka Island? Ah! And where might that be?"

"On the other side of the world."

"That's some way off, isn't it? Most unfortunate. I take it most uncivil of Batters to go and die in a place like that. Especially when I should like to have a look at his grave. You don't happen to know where it is."

"I do not, except that I have been given to understand that he was buried where he died."

"That so? He would be. In the local cemetery, with the flowers growing all around. In a nice deep grave with a stone on top to keep him from getting out of it, and some words cut on it, like 'He lies in peace.' There's no doubt about his lying, anyhow, I'll take my oath to that." He emitted a sound which might have been meant for a chuckle. It startled Miss Purvis. "You don't happen to know when he died?"

"I do not know the precise date, but it was at any rate some three or four months ago."

"That's odd, very. Because, as it happens, I was with him some three or four months ago, and I never saw nothing about him that looked like dying. So far from dying, he was lively, uncommon; fleas wasn't in it with the liveliness of Batters. And to think that he should have died with me looking at him all the time, and yet knowing nothing at all about it. It shows you that there is such things as miracles."

"Do I understand you to say that three months ago you were in the company of Mr. Batters?"

"I was. And likewise four months ago. And I hope to be in his company again before long, dead or alive. It won't be my fault if I'm not; you may go the lot on that."

There was something about the fellow which struck me as peculiar; it was not alone his impudence, which belonged to another sort of singularity. There seemed to be a covert meaning in his manner and his words. I turned to Miss Purvis.

"If you don't mind I think I will hear what this person has to say; it may be of importance to your friend. If you will allow me to leave you here, I think I may arrive quicker at his meaning if I am alone with him."

She signified her consent. I led the way into the office. Without showing in any way that he objected, the stranger followed.

"Now my man, let us understand each other as clearly as we can, and keep to the point as closely as you are able. What's your name?"

"Luke."

"Luke what?"

"Luke nothing. I'm known to those who knew me best as St. Luke, after the apostle, being of saintlike character, but in general Luke's name enough for me. They was modest where I come from."

"What are you?"

"A sailor man, late of the good ship *Flying Scud*."

"*The Flying Scud*?" I stared at him askance, not certain that I had caught the name correctly. That particular ship seemed in the air. "Then do you know Captain Lander?"

As I asked the question his manner changed. It became suspicious. Thrusting his thumbs into his waistcoat armholes he eyed me warily, as if he had all at once been put upon his guard.

"Now how much do you know about it?"

"What do you mean? How much do I know about what?"

"What's Captain Lander told you about me?"

"About you? To me Captain Lander has never so much as mentioned your name."

A sudden wild thought came into my head. "Are you—are you Benjamin Batters?"

The fellow's mouth opened so wide I could see right down his throat.

"Me Benjamin Batters! Good Lord! What made you ask me such a thing as that?"

"Are you? Are you?" As I watched I doubted more and more. "I believe you are."

"I'm not. Good Lord! You ask Captain Lander if I am. You said yourself just now that he was dead and buried."

"And you hinted that he was not, but that he was still alive."

Putting his hand up to his brow he brushed the fringe of hair partially aside, glancing furtively about the room.

"That's as may be; that's another matter altogether. But I don't like your asking me if I was Batters. No man would. Have you ever seen him?"

"Never; unless I see him now."

"Meaning me? I never came across such a man. What do you mean by keeping on asking if I'm Batters? What are you driving at? I won't have it, whatever it is. Why Batters——" He stopped: then second thoughts appearing best, changed from heat to cold. "Batters was not my sort at all."

The man's manner puzzled me.

"What was there about Benjamin Batters which makes you resent any comparison with him?"

He hesitated, putting up his fingers to scratch his head, visibly perturbed.

"Excuse me, but I came here to put a question or two, not to answer any. If you'd told me at the first that Captain Lander was a friend of yours, I should have taken myself off straightway, like as I'm going to now."

I stepped between him and the door.

"No you don't. You stopped at the beginning to please yourself; now you'll remain a little longer to please me. Before you leave this room you'll give me satisfactory answers to one or two questions."

"Who says I will?"

"I do. If you decline I send for a policeman. Then I think you'll find yourself in Queer Street."

His disturbance obviously increased.

"Now, Mr. Paine, I've done nothing to you to make you behave nasty to me. If I made a mistake in coming here to make a few inquiries I apologise, and no man can do more than that, so there's no harm done to either side."

"Was Batters your shipmate?"

"My shipmate?"

"Was he an officer or member of the crew on board *The Flying Scud*?"

"My gracious, no!"

"He was on *The Flying Scud*?"

"He might have been."

"As passenger?"

"*The Flying Scud's* a cargo boat; she don't carry no passengers."

"If he was neither officer, sailor, nor passenger, in what capacity was he there?"

"You ask Captain Lander, he was in command, not me. I've had enough of this bullyragging. You let me go before there's trouble."

"Gently, my man, gently! Now, come, be frank with me. What is the mystery about Benjamin Batters? I see there is one."

"That's more than I can tell you, straight it is. I wish it wasn't. If you was to ask me I should say he was all mystery, Batters was."

"I suppose he was a man?"

"A man?" The inquiry, suggested by the fashion in which he persisted in shuffling with my questions, had an odd effect upon my visitor. He glanced from side to side, and up and down, as if desirous, at any cost, to avoid meeting my eye. "It depends on what you call a man."

"You know very well what I call a man. Was he a man in the sense that you and I are men?"

He shuddered.

"The Lord forbid that I should be in any way like him; the Lord forbid!"

"I observed him narrowly, at a loss to make him out. That there was something very curious about Benjamin Batters I was becoming more and more persuaded. I had as little doubt that my visitor had at least some knowledge of what it was. Equally obvious, however, was the fact that he had reasons of his own for concealing what he knew. How I could compel him to make a confidant of me against his will I failed to see. I tried another tack.

"You say that you were in Batters' company three months ago."

"I might have been."

"How long ago is it since you last saw him?"

"I couldn't exactly say."

"Where did you last see him?"

"Where?" He looked round and round the room, as if seeking for information. Then the fashion of his countenance changed, an ugly look came on it. "I'm not going to tell you when I saw him last, nor where. It's no business of yours. You mind your own business, and leave mine alone. And as for your policeman, I don't care for no policeman. Why should I? I'm an honest man. So you get out of my way and let me pass; and that's all about it."

"Have you seen Benjamin Batters within the month?"

"Never you mind!"

"Your words are a sufficient answer. I believe that you have been conspiring with Benjamin Batters with fraudulent intent. If you do not furnish me with abundant proof that my suspicions are unfounded I shall summon a constable, and give you into custody upon that charge."

It was a piece of pure bluff upon my part, which failed.

"That's the time of the day, is it? I've been conspiring with him, have I? What have I been conspiring about?"

"I have no doubt that that is a point on which Captain Lander will be able to show more than sufficient light."

My words had at last struck home. What lent them especial weight I could not even guess. But that they had moved him more than anything which had gone before his behaviour showed.

"He will, will he? So that's the game you're after. You're a lawyer, and I'm a poor, silly sailor man, so you think you can play just what tricks with me you please. But there's something else Captain Lander can tell you if you ask him, and that's that I can be disagreeable when I'm crossed, and if you don't move away from that door inside a brace of shakes I'm going to be disagreeable now."

"Don't threaten me, my man."

"Threaten?"

His tone suggested that he scorned being thought capable of threatening only, and his action proved it.

He came at me with a suddenness for which I was unprepared. Putting his arms about me while I was still unready he lifted me off my feet. As he was still holding me aloft, crooking my leg inside his, I bore on him with all my might, and brought him with a crash to the floor. Although he lay underneath, his arms still retained their grip.

While I hesitated whether to attack the man in earnest or to remonstrate with him instead—for Miss Purvis might at any moment look in, and then a nice opinion she would have of me—someone standing behind slipped what seemed to be a cord over my head, and drew it so tight about my throat that in an instant I was all but choked. When, gasping for breath, I put up my hand to free myself, it was drawn still tighter. So tight indeed that not only did it cut like a knife, but I felt as if my tongue was being torn out of my mouth, and I lost all consciousness.

CHAPTER XXIII
THE TRIO RETURN

How long I remained unconscious I could not say. When I did come to, during some seconds I was unable to realise my position. It was like waking out of an uncomfortably heavy sleep. Consciousness returned by degrees, and painfully; as it were, by a series of waves, which were like so many shocks. I was oppressed by nausea, my eyes were dim, my brain seemed reeling, as if it were making disconcerting efforts to retain its equilibrium. It was some time before I understood that I was still in my own room; yet, longer before I had some faint comprehension of the situation I was in, and of what was taking place about me.

It was probably some minutes before I completely understood that I was trussed like a fowl, and that the exquisite pain which I was enduring was because of the tightness and ingenuity of my bonds. I was on the floor with my back against the wall. Cords which were about my wrists were attached to my ankles, passed up my back, then round my throat, so that each movement I made I bade fair to choke myself. It was a diabolical contrivance. The cords were thin ones—red-hot wires they seemed to me to be, they cut my wrists like knives, and burned them as with fire. My legs were drawn under my body in an unnatural and uncomfortable position. They were torn by cramp, yet whenever I made the slightest attempt to ease them I dragged at the cord which was about my throat. One thing seemed plain, if the worst came to the worst I should experience no difficulty in committing suicide. Apparently I had only to let my head forward to be strangled.

By way of making the condition of affairs entirely satisfactory something sharp had been forced into my mouth, which not only acted as a gag, effectually preventing my uttering a sound, but which made it difficult for me to breathe. That it was cutting me was made plain by the blood which I was compelled to swallow.

As I have said, it was not at first that I had a clear perception of the personal plight that I was in. When it dawned on me at last I had a morbid satisfaction in learning that I was not alone in it. Someone so close on the left as to be almost touching me was in a similar plight. It was St. Luke. I had mistily imagined that that seafaring associate of the more and more mysterious Benjamin Batters had been in some way responsible for my misadventure. Not a bit of it. I had wronged the honest man. So far as I could perceive, his plight was an exact reproduction of my own. The same attention had been paid to his physical comfort; only apparently the gag had been so placed in his mouth as to leave him more freedom to gasp, and to grunt, and to groan.

Who, then, was responsible for this pretty performance? What man, or men, had I so wronged as to be deserving this return? The problem was a nice one. I looked for the solution.

I found it, and, in doing so, found also something else, which filled me with such a tumult of passion that I actually momentarily forgot the egregious position I was in.

Miss Purvis had been served as I had been.

She had either, wondering at my delay, or startled by the noise, peeped into the office, and so disturbed the ruffians at their work; or the miscreants, penetrating into the inner room, had found her there and dragged her out. However it had been, there she was, trussed and gagged against the wall upon my right. They had shown no respect for a woman, but had handled her precisely as they had done St. Luke and me. My brain felt as if it would have burst as I thought of the indignity with which they must have used her, and of the agony, mental and bodily, she must have endured, and be enduring still. Her face—her pretty face!—was white as the sheet of paper on which I write. Her eyes—her lovely eyes!—were closed. I hoped that she had fainted, and so was oblivious of suffering and shame. Yet, as I watched her utter stillness, I half feared she might be dead.

The gentlemen who were responsible for this pleasant piece of work were three. They were there before me in plain sight. It was with an odd sense that it was just what I had expected that I recognised the trio who had already paid me a visit in the silent watches of the night. There was the imposing, elderly, bald-headed gentleman, who represented length without breadth; there, also, were his two attendant satellites. How to account for their assiduous interest in my unpretending office was beyond my power. Nor did I understand why it should have been necessary to use quite such drastic measures against the lady, St. Luke, and myself. Still less—I admit it frankly—when I observed their conspicuous lack of avoirdupois, did I gather how they had managed to make of us so easy a prey. Under ordinary conditions I should have been quite willing to take the three on single-handed. The truth probably was that St. Luke and I had unwittingly played into their dexterous hands. Had we not been engaged in matching ourselves against each other we should have been more than a match for them. But when they came in, and found the sailor man upon the floor prisoning me close within his arms, all they had to do was to slip one cord round my throat, and another round his. We were at their mercy. No man can show much fight when he is being strangled; especially when the job is in the hands of a skilled practitioner. Never mind what the theory is, that is the teaching of experience.

What they wanted, with so much anxiety, in my office, I was unable to guess. They had already purloined the God of Fortune.

Stay! It had been returned to me again. I had dropped it on the floor; been unable to find it. Could it be that they were after it a second time. I wondered. What peculiar significance, what attribute, could that small plaything have?

Beyond doubt they were treating my belongings with scant regard for the feelings of their owner? If they failed to find what they were seeking it would not be for want of a thorough quest. Pretty well everything the apartment contained they subjected to a minute examination. They allowed nothing to escape them. It was delightful to watch them. If I had been suffering a little less physical inconvenience I should have enjoyed myself immensely. They might be Orientals; but if they were not professional burglars in their own country then they ought to have been. They were artists any way.

To note one point—there was such order in their methods. They began at one corner of the room, and they worked right round it, emptying boxes, turning out drawers, pulling the books out of their covers, and the stuffing out of the chairs, and the furniture to pieces generally, in search of secret hiding-places. Then they began tapping at the walls, tearing off scraps of paper here and there, to see what was behind. It beat me to imagine what it was that they were after, though it was flattering to think what a first-rate hand at concealment they must be taking me to be. Apparently they were under the impression that a solicitor had plenty of waste time which he occupied by secreting odds and ends in solid walls. The rapidity with which they did all they did do was simply astonishing, particularly when one had to admit with what thoroughness it was done. But when they came to dragging the carpet up, and tearing boards from the floor, I began to wonder if they were going through the house piecemeal.

The litter was beyond description. My practice might not have been a large one, but my papers were many. When a large number of documents are thrown down anywhere, anyhow, they are apt to look untidy. Even in that moment of martyrdom I groaned in spirit as I thought of the labour which their rearrangement would involve.

One mental note I did take; that, despite the eagerness with which they turned out papers from every possible receptacle, they seemed to attach to them but scant importance. That they were after something connected with Mr. Benjamin Batters I had no doubt. Yet they unearthed the Batters' papers among the rest—even the Batters' bonds!—and tossed them on one side as if they contained nothing which was of interest to them. If they were able to read English I could not tell, but every now and then the tall, thin party glanced at a paper as if it was not altogether Double Dutch to him.

At last, short of pulling the room itself down about their ears, they had, apparently to their own entire dissatisfaction, exhausted its resources. There was a pause in the operations. There ensued a conclave. The elderly gentleman spoke, while, for the most part, the others listened. What was being said I had no notion. They were sparing of gesture, so no meaning was conveyed through the eye to the brain. I am no linguist. My knowledge of Eastern tongues is nil. I did not know what language they were speaking; had I known I should have been no wiser. One fact, however, was unmistakable; their words were accompanied by glances in my direction, which I did not altogether relish. If ever I saw cruelty written on a human countenance it was on the faces of those three gentlemen. Theirs was the love of it for its own sake. Their faces were rather inhuman masks, expressionless, impassive, unfeeling. It was not difficult to conceive with what ingenuity they could contrive tortures with which to rack the nerves of some promising subject. It was easy to believe that they would put them into practice with the same composure with which they would observe the sensations of the object of their curious experiments.

I had already had some experience of their skill in more than one direction, and I did not desire a practical demonstration of it in yet another.

And for the present I was to be spared the exhibition. It seemed that they all at once bethought themselves that there were other apartments of mine which still remained unsearched. Whereupon off they went to search them. To us they paid no need. Plainly they were sufficiently acquainted with the good qualities of their handiwork to be aware that from us they need fear nothing. That we might be able to free ourselves without assistance was a million to one chance which it was unnecessary to consider. Until some one came to loose us we were bound. Of that they were absolutely sure. So they left us there to keep each other company, and to console each other if we could, while they went to overhaul the rest of my establishment. It was a pleasant thought for me to dwell upon.

Miss Purvis' eyes were open, but that was about the only sign of life she showed. They wandered once or twice towards me; wandered was just the word which expressed the look which was in them. Her face was white and drawn. There was that about it which made me doubt if even yet she was conscious of what was being done; I wondered if the pain which she was suffering had taken effect upon her brain. It would not have been surprising if it had. It was only by dint of a violent and continued exercise of will that I myself was able to retain, as it were, a hold upon my senses. There was, first of all, the torture of the cramped position. Then there was the way in which the cords cut into the flesh—what particular kind of cords had been used I could not make out, but I suspected fiddle-strings. Then there was the fact that the slightest movement made with a view of obtaining relief threatened not only strangulation but decapitation too.

I wondered what the time was. A laundress, one Mrs. Parsons, was supposed to arrive at eight. It must be nearly that. I had been up for hours; I was convinced that it was hours. It must be after eight. If the woman had any regard for punctuality, at any moment she might appear. If she did not arrive within five minutes she should be dismissed. How could she expect to keep my rooms in proper order if her habits were irregular? I had long wondered how it was my chambers did not do me so much credit as they might have done; I had an eye for such things although she might not think it. Now I understood. If Mrs. Parsons would only have the sense, the honesty, the decency, to keep to her engagements and come at once, while those scoundrels were engaged elsewhere, in a moment I should be free. Then I would show them.

A clock struck seven. It must be wrong. There was a second, third, fourth, all striking seven. An hour yet before the woman was even due! And whoever heard of a laundress who was punctual? Before she came what might not happen? For another hour, at least, we were at the mercy of these ingenious adventurers.

They reappeared. What havoc they had wrought in the rooms in which I lived, and moved, and had my being, I could only guess. Either, from their point of view, they had not done mischief enough, or the result of what they had done had not been satisfactory. Plainly, they were discontented. Their manner showed it. The tall gentleman spoke to his two associates in a tone which suggested disapprobation of their conduct. They seemed, with all possible humility, to be endeavouring to show that the fault was not entirely theirs. This he appeared unwilling to concede. Finally, flopping down on to their knees, touching the floor with their foreheads, they grovelled at his feet. So far from being appeased by this show of penitence, putting out his right foot, he gave each of them a hearty kick. The effect this had on them was comical. They sprang upright like a pair of automata, endeavouring to carry themselves as if they had been the recipient of the highest honours.

The tall gentleman moved towards Miss Purvis. They meekly hung on his heels. He addressed to them remarks to which they scarcely ventured to reply. He eyed the lady. Then glanced towards me. I wondered what was the connection which he supposed existed between us. Something menacing was in his air. He hovered above the helpless girl as a hawk might above a pigeon. Stretching out his cruel-looking hand he thrust it almost in her face. I expected to see her subjected to some fresh indignity, and felt that, if she were, then rage might give me strength to break the bonds which shackled me.

If such had been his intention, it was either deferred, or he changed his mind. He gave a gesture in my direction. Immediately one of his familiars, advancing, tilted me back with no more compunction than if I had been an empty beer cask. Thrusting his filthy fingers into my mouth he dragged out the gag with so much roughness that it tore my tongue and palate as it passed. Returning me to the position which suited him best, out of simple wantonness, with the hand which held the gag he struck me a vigorous blow upon the cheek; so vigorous that, as it jerked my head on one side it seemed to cause the thong which was about my throat to nearly sever my head from my shoulders. Even as he struck me I recognised in my assailant the individual who had dogged my steps from Camford Street, and whom afterwards I had treated to a shaking. This was his idea of crying quits. While the blood still seemed to be whirling before my eyes I said to myself that, if all went well, to his quittance I would add another score. The last blow should not be his.

The removal of the gag did not at once restore to me the faculty of speech. My mouth was bleeding, I was nearly choked by blood. My tongue was torn, and sore, and swollen. It felt ridiculously large for the place it was supposed to occupy. Evidently the attenuated gentleman understood that there were reasons why I should not be expected to join in conversation until I had been afforded an opportunity to get the better of my feelings. He stood regarding me, his parchment-like visage perfectly expressionless, as if he were awaiting the period when I might be reasonably required to give voice to my emotions.

When, as I take it, he supposed such a time to have arrived, he addressed me, to my surprise, in English, which was not bad of its kind.

"Where is the Great Joss?"

I had no notion what he meant. Had I understood him perfectly I should have been unable to give him the information he required. So soon as I attempted to speak I found that my tongue refused, literally, to do its office. I could only produce those mumbling sounds which proceed, sometimes, from the mouths of those who are dumb.

In his judgment, however, it seemed that I ought already to have advanced to perfect clarity of utterance. He repeated his inquiry.

"Where is the Great Joss? I am in haste. Tell me quick."

"Untie my hands and throat."

That was my reply. The words, as they came from my lips, assumed a guise in which they could hardly have been recognisable for what they were meant to be, so inarticulately were they spoken. Whether he understood them I could not say, he ignored their meaning if he did. One of his satellites—the one who had struck me—hazarded an observation, with a deep inclination of his head, but his superior paid no heed to him whatever. He persisted in his previous inquiry.

"Tell me, where is the Great Joss?"

With an effort I mumbled an answer.

"I don't know what you mean."

Evidently the reply did not fall in with his view at all; he disbelieved it utterly.

"Tell me where is the Great Joss, or the woman shall die."

His meaning was unmistakable. He stretched out his finger towards Miss Purvis with a gesture. That he was capable of murder I had not the slightest doubt. That he would make nothing of having an innocent, unoffending girl tortured to death before my eyes I believed. Fleet Street might be within a hop, skip, and a jump; but, for the present, this spot in its immediate neighbourhood was delivered over to the methods of the East. If I could not afford this monster, who had sprung from some unknown oriental haunt of merciless fiends, the satisfaction he demanded, I might expect the worst to happen before help could come. With him I felt assured that in such matters one could rely upon the word being followed by the blow.

I made an effort to appease him.

"I don't know where your Joss is. It dropped upon the floor."

My reference, of course, was to the toy which Miss Blyth had given me, and which, when I had let it fall, I was unable to find. Still my answer did not seem to be the one he wanted. He scrutinised me in silence for some seconds before he gave me to understand as much.

"You play with me?"

There was that in his tone which was anything but playful. I made all possible haste to deny the soft impeachment.

"I don't. Is it the God of Fortune you are after?"

"The God of Fortune? What do you know about the God of Fortune?"

"It was given to me. I let it drop. When I came to look for it I couldn't find it anywhere."

There was something about my reply which he did not like. I was sure of it by the way in which he spoke, in that unknown tongue, to his associates. Instantly they approached Miss Purvis, standing one on either side of her. Their attitude was ominous.

"Do you wish that she shall die?"

I did not. I could scarcely have more strenuously desired that she should live. As I told him with such clearness of language as I could muster. Considering all things I was eloquent.

"What it is you want from me I don't know; consciously I have nothing which is yours. But you had better understand this, if you are able to understand anything at all, that only for a minute or two at most are we in your power. If you want to be let off lightly you will loose that lady at once; if you harm so much as a hair of her head the law of England will make you pay for it dearly."

In reply the fellow was arrogance itself.

"What do we care for your law? What has your law to do with us? Are we dogs that you should use us as you choose? You have stolen, and have hidden, the Great Joss. Return him to us; or as you have shamed us so we will shame you."

"Not only have I not stolen the Great Joss, but I don't even know what the Great Joss is. The only Joss I've seen was one about the size of my finger, which, as I've told you already, I dropped on the floor, and couldn't find."

"You laugh at us."

"I do not laugh. I am speaking the simple, absolute truth."

"You lie. The gods have told us that the secret of the hiding-place of the Great Joss is here. Show it to us quickly, or the woman shall die."

"It is your gods who lie, not I."

The fellow said something to his colleagues. At once, whipping Miss Purvis from off the floor, just for all the world as if she were a trussed fowl, they placed her on the table.

"Be careful what you do!" I shouted.

"It is for you to be careful. We come from far across the sea to look for the Great Joss, which you and yours have stolen, and you make a mock of us. We are not children that we may be mocked. Give us what is ours, or we will take what is yours, though we desire it not, and the woman shall die."

"I tell you, man, that if anyone has robbed you it isn't I. I have not the faintest notion who you are, or what you're after; and as for your Great Joss, I've not the least idea what a Great Joss is. What I say is a simple statement of fact; and what reason you suppose yourself to have for doubting me is beyond my comprehension."

"That is your answer?"

"Don't speak as if you suspected me of a deliberate intention to deceive. What other answer can I give? If, as is possible, you are suffering from a genuine grievance, I shall be glad to be of any assistance I can. But you must first give me clearly to understand what it is you're after. At present I am completely in the dark."

"The woman must die."

The fellow was impervious to reason. He repeated the words with a passionless calm which added to their significance. Again I screamed at him:

"You had better be careful!"

He ignored me utterly. Turning to his collaborators he issued an order which was promptly obeyed. Loosing Miss Purvis' bonds they stretched her out upon the table, and tied her on it with a dexterous rapidity which denoted considerable practice in similar operations. I observed the proceedings with sensations which are not to be described. I had hoped that at the last extremity rage would supply me with strength with which to burst the cords which prevented me from going to her assistance. I had hoped in vain. The only result of my frenzied struggles was to increase the tension, and to make my helplessness, if possible, still clearer.

"Help! help!" I yelled. "Help!"

I was aware that I was the only person who lived in the house, and that the hour was yet too early for the occupants of offices to have arrived. But I was actuated by a forlorn hope that my voice might reach someone who was in a position to render aid. None came. What I had endured, and was enduring, had robbed my voice of more than half its power. And though I shouted with what, at the moment, was the full force of my lungs, I was only too conscious that my utterance was too inarticulate, too feeble, to allow my words to travel far.

As for that attenuated fiend, who, it was clear, was not by any means so long as he was wicked, he regarded my maniacal contortions with a degree of imperturbability which seemed to me to be the climax of inhumanity. Although it was certain that he both saw and heard me, since it was impossible that it could be otherwise, not by so much as the movement of a muscle did he betray the fact. He suffered me to writhe and scream to my heart's content. He simply took no notice; that was all. When the process of tying down Miss Purvis had been completed, being informed of the fact by one of his assistants, he turned to examine, with a critical eye, how the work had been done. Moving round the table, he tried each ligature with his finger as he passed. Since he found no fault, apparently the way in which the woman had been laid out for slaughter met with his complete approval.

He condescended once more to bestow his attention upon me.

"For the last time—where is the Great Joss?"

"I can't tell you—how can I tell you if I don't know what the Great Joss is? For God's sake, man, tell me what it is you're really after before you go too far. If you want my help, give me a chance to offer it. Explain to me what the Great Joss is. It is possible, since you appear to be so positive, that I do know something of its whereabouts. Tell me, clearly, what it is, and all I know is at your service. Put my words to the test, and you will find that they are true ones."

To me it seemed impossible that even such an addle-headed idiot as the individual in front of me could fail to see that I was speaking the truth. But he did, he failed entirely. He had convictions of his own, of which he was not to be disabused.

"You lie again, making a mock of the gods. To the gods the woman shall be offered as a sacrifice."

He spoke with a passionless calm which denoted a set purpose from which there was no turning him.

I raved, I screamed myself hoarse. He paid no heed. I could do no more. I could either keep my eyes open and watch what went on, or close them, and my imagination would present me with pictures more lurid still. The situation was not rendered more agreeable by the fact that, although they had not given her back the power of speech, as they had done me, by the removal of the gag, I was conscious that she was perfectly cognisant of all that was being said, and especially of the frenzied appeals which I made on her behalf—in vain.

During the minutes which followed I was as one distraught. Now I watched, with wide open staring eyes; now I shut them, in a sudden paroxysm of doubt as to what horror I might be compelled to be an unwilling witness; then, being haunted by frightful imaginings of what might be transpiring without my knowledge—for she could make no sound—I opened them again to see.

The three scoundrels set about their hideous business with a matter of fact air which suggested that, in their opinion, they were doing nothing out of the common. And perhaps, in that genial portion of the world from which they came, such butcheries were the everyday events of their lives.

The tall man issued some curt instructions. The two shorter ones set about gathering the papers which were scattered about the room, and piling them in a heap beneath the table. On these they placed more or less inflammable fragments of my solider belongings. It seemed to be their intention to have a bonfire on lines of their own. Unless they were acquainted with a trick or two in that direction, as well as in others, how they proposed to keep it alight, after ignition, one was at a loss to understand.

About the procedure of the principal villain there was no such room for doubt. There was a frankness in his proceedings which caused me now to shriek at him in half imbecile, because wholly impotent, rage; and now to shut my eyes in terror of what he might be doing next.

By way of a commencement he took from some receptacle in his clothing what turned out to be a curiously shaped lamp. This he placed on the table at Miss Purvis' feet. Having lit it by the commonplace means of a match from a box of mine which was on the mantelpiece, he threw on it, at short intervals, what was probably some variation of what firework vendors describe as "coloured fire." The result was that surrounding objects assumed unusual hues, and the room was filled with a vapour, which was not only obscuring, but malodorous. From his bosom he produced an evil-looking knife. Laying a defiling hand upon his victim's throat, partly by sheer force, partly by the aid of his knife, he tore her garments open nearly to the waist. Bending over her, he seemed to be marking out some sort of design with the point of his blade on the bare skin, in the region of the heart. Drawing himself upright he suffered his voluminous sleeves to fall back, and bared his arms, as a surgeon might do prior to commencing an operation.

Then he leaned over her again; his knife held out.

CHAPTER XXIV
THE GOD OUT OF THE MACHINE

How it all happened I have but a misty notion.

My eyelids were twitching; my eyes were neither shut nor open. I could not look, nor hide from myself the knowledge of what was being done. I saw the silent woman, the whiteness of her flesh, the gleam of steel, the tall figure stooping over her. There were the attendant demons, one on either side. All was still. My voice had perished, I could no longer utter a sound. And all that was done by the man with the knife was done in silence.

So acute was the stillness I listened for the entry of the steel into the flesh—as if that were audible!

Then, on a sudden, all was pandemonium. Of the exact sequence in which events occurred, I have, as I have said, but a shadowy impression.

Something struck the fellow with the knife full in the face. What it was at the moment I could not tell. I learnt afterwards that it was a soft, peaked sailor's cap, thrown by a strong wrist, with unerring aim. The impact was not a slight one. Taken unawares the tall man staggered; he had been hit clean between the eyes. He put his hand up to his face, as if bewildered. Before he had it down again he had been seized by the shoulders, flung to the ground, and the knife wrenched from him.

His assailant was Captain Lander.

"Lander!" I gasped.

The captain glanced in my direction, then at the woman stretched upon the table, then at the gentleman upon the floor. Him he appeared to recognise.

"So it's you, is it? What devil's work have you been up to now? This is not Tongkin! Look out there—stop 'em, my lads!"

The attendant demons, perceiving that a change had come o'er the spirit of the scene, were making for the window, judging, doubtless, discretion to be the better part of valour. I then learned that Captain Lander was not alone. He had three companions. These made short work of stopping the flight of the ingenuous colleagues. One of the captain's companions, a man of somewhat remarkable build, gripping the pair by the nape of the neck by either hand, banged their heads together. It was a spectacle which I found agreeable to behold.

The long gentleman was rising from the ground. The captain assisted him by dragging him up by the shoulder. They observed each other with looks which were not looks of love. The captain jeered.

"So we've met again, have we? It seems as if you and I were bound to meet. We must be fond of one another."

The other replied with the retort discourteous.

"You dog! You thief! You accursed!"

He seemed to be nearly beside himself with rage, which under the circumstances, perhaps, was not surprising.

The words apparently conveyed a taunt which drove the man to madness. Forgetful of the disparity which existed between them and how little he was the captain's match, he flung himself at him with the unreflecting frenzy of some wild cat. Lander laughed. Putting his arms about the frantic man, with a grin he compressed them tighter and tighter till I half expected to see him squeeze the life right out. When he relaxed his hold the other had had enough. Tottering back against the wall, he leaned against it, breathless. I had supposed his face to be a mask, incapable of expression, but perceived my error when I noted the glances with which he regarded his late antagonist.

Careless of how the other might be observing him, Lander, with a few quick touches of the tall gentleman's own knife, released the girl who had already, in very truth, tasted of the bitterness of death. Seeing the gag, he withdrew it with a tenderness which was almost feminine. His own coat he threw over her shoulders. A tremor passed all over her; she raised herself a little; then, with a sigh, sank back upon the table.

As if satisfied that with her all would now be well, Lander turned to me. In a moment my bonds were severed.

"Why, Mr. Paine, how come you in this galley?"

"That is more than I can tell. Is the lady badly hurt?"

"Not she. She'll be all right in a minute. I came just in time." He uttered an exclamation on perceiving the sailor man, Luke, bound, at my side. "Why, it's the Apostle! Lads, here's our friend, Luke! The trusty soul! Tied hand and foot, just like a common cur—and gagged as well! Mr. Luke, this is an unexpected pleasure! We'll have the gag out at any rate, if only for the sake of hearing your dear old tongue start wagging. I hope that didn't hurt you; you must excuse a little roughness, for old acquaintance, but I think we'll leave you tied."

Mr. Luke seemed to experience as much difficulty in recovering the faculty of speech as I had done. Stammering words came from his bleeding lips.

"Then—in that case—you'd better—kill me."

"No: we won't kill you, not just yet; though I would have killed you out of hand, if I could have got within reach of you—you know when. On second thoughts I fancy we'll untie you. Pray tell us, Mr. Luke, where's the Great Joss now?"

Mr. Luke was stretching his limbs, gingerly, apparently finding the process anything but an agreeable one.

"That's—what I—want to know," he mumbled.

"No? Is that so? you done too? Poor Luke! how sad to think your confidence should have been misplaced. It's a treacherous world." The captain turned to me. "Mr. Paine, I believe you are the only person who can give us precise information as to the present whereabouts of the Great Joss."

"I?"

I stared at him amazed.

"Yes, you. I'll tell you why I think so."

BOOK IV
THE JOSS

(CAPTAIN MAX LANDER SETS FORTH THE
CURIOUS ADVENTURE WHICH MARKED THE
VOYAGE OF THE "FLYING SCUD.")

CHAPTER XXV
LUKE'S SUGGESTION

I've no faith in your old wives' tales. Not I. But the luck was against us. Everything went wrong from the first. And there's no getting away from the fact that we sailed on a Friday.

The weather in the Bay was filthy. Our engines went wrong in the Red Sea. We lay up at Aden for a week. There was a bill as long as my arm to pay. Then when we got out into the open the weather began again. Never had such a run! It was touch and go for our lives. One night, half-way between Ceylon and Sumatra, I thought it was the end. We had more than another touch off the Philippines. By the time we reached Yokohama we were a wreck—nothing less.

The ship ought to have been overhauled before we started. But the owners wouldn't see it. They insisted that a patch here, and a coat of paint there, would meet the case. But it didn't. Not by a deal. As we soon found. At Aden, after all, the engines had only been tinkered. They went wrong again before we had been three days out. The weather we had would have tried the best work that ever came out of an engineer's shop. Those nailed together pieces of rusty scrap iron worried the lives right out of us. If we had gone to the bottom they would have been to blame.

We were late at Yokohama. A lot. The agents didn't like it, nor the consignees either. There were words. After all I'd gone through I wasn't in a mood to take a jacketing for what wasn't any fault of mine. So I let them see. The result was that there were all round ructions. I admit that, under severe provocation, I did go farther than I intended. And I did not mean to knock old Lawrence down. But it was only by the mercy of God I had brought the ship into port at all. And it was hard lines to meet nothing but black looks, and words, because I hadn't performed the impossible.

Lawrence resented my knocking him down. David Lawrence was our agent; a close-fisted, cantankerous Scotchman. I own I ought to have kept my hands off him. But when he started bullyragging me on my own deck, before the crew, as if I was something lower than a cabin boy, when I had had about enough of it, which wasn't long, I let fly, and over he went.

I was sorry directly afterwards. And when he gave me to understand that not a ha'porth of stuff should come aboard that boat while I was in command, I swallowed the bile and started to apologise. Not much good came of that. As soon as my nose was inside his office he began rubbing me the wrong way. The end of it was that I nearly knocked him down again. And should have quite if his clerks hadn't kept me off him. After that I knew the game was up. I knew that nothing worth having would come my way at Yokohama. I got drunk for the first time in my life. The ship was eating her head off for port dues. I slipped her moorings and ran out to sea.

What I was to do I had not the faintest notion. I was perfectly well aware that I might as well sink her where she was as to take her back as good as empty. If I didn't lose my certificate it would be no further use to me, because that would be the last command that I should ever have. I took her to Hong Kong on the off chance of picking something up. But, as I had half expected, news of *The Flying Scud* had travelled ahead. There was nothing but the cold shoulder waiting for me all along the line. I did get a few odds and ends, but nothing worth speaking of, and I cleared out of Hong Kong for the same reason I had cleared out of Yokohama.

Yet, though I should scarcely have thought it possible, there was worse to follow.

The men, like their captain, were in a bad temper. Which was not to be wondered at. They were pretty near to mutiny. If they got all the way I should be landed indeed. Not that I minded. I was beyond that. I slept with one loaded revolver under my head, and another in my hand. Possibly a bit of a scrimmage would have had the same effect on me as a little blood-letting. I should have been the better for it afterwards.

I confess I did not know where I was going. I crawled along the Chinese coast with some dim idea of gaining time. Given time I might be able to form some sort of reasonable plan. One thing was sure, I had no intention of going home to be ruined. If that was to be the way of it, I could be ruined just as well where I was. Better perhaps. I sneaked through the Hainan Strait. A day or two after we ran out of water.

Just where we were I am not prepared to say. That's the truth. No lies! The coast was strange to me. I know the China Seas perhaps as well as a good many men, but I had never been in the Gulf of Tongkin before. I will say this, we were not a thousand miles from Lienchow.

We were still hugging the coast when they told me the stores were out. I ordered them to take her in as close as she could be got. A little delay more or less didn't matter a snap of the fingers to me. I had got as far that. Considering we weren't over-coaled it was pretty far. It was a lovely evening, a Friday as it happened—I must have been born on a Friday! In about a couple of hours the sun would be setting, so, if we were quick, there would be time to get something aboard before the night was on us. And quick would have to be the word, because, in the forecastle they had reached pretty nearly their last biscuit.

I am not excusing myself. I own I could not have managed worse if I had tried. I knew all along the stores were running short. I had refused to refit at Hong Kong out of pure cussedness. What I said was that if the lubbers wouldn't ship their cargo, I wouldn't buy their stores. And I didn't. I meant to take in fresh supplies when we had a chance. We had not had a chance as yet. But now that we had come down to nothing it was clear that we must get something, if it was only enough to take us along for a day or two.

Fortunately the sea was calm, the anchorage good. We were able to run close in. Directly a boat was lowered the men started off as if they were rowing for grub-stakes. Which they were.

So far as I could see the country thereabouts was uninhabited. If that was the case, it was a poor look out for us. But as it was a shelving shore, with trees crowning the crest as far as the eye could reach, it was possible that both houses and people might be close at hand though hidden from sight. Which, if I wished to avoid further trouble, was a state of things devoutly to be desired.

I saw the boat reach land, men get out of it, climb the slope, disappear from view. And then, for more than three mortal hours, I saw no more of them. It was pretty tedious waiting. Every man-jack on board kept a keen look-out. Discipline was not so good as it might have been—for reasons. There was no conspicuous attempt, as the minutes crept slowly by, to conceal the apparently general impression that it was a case of bunk; that those sailor men had thought it better to throw in their lot with the natives of those parts, rather than to continue the voyage with me. At the bottom of my boots I felt that if such was the fact it was not for me to say that they were fools.

However, it proved not to be the fact. Sometime after darkness had fallen, just as I was concluding that it would perhaps be as well to send a second boat in search of the first, and take command of it myself, boat No. 1 returned. It was greeted with language which might be described as hearty. They had had some luck, brought something in the victual line. Without any reference to my authority a raid was made on what they had brought. I said nothing, not caring what they did. If they wanted to keep themselves alive, what did it matter to me?

The boat had been in command of a man named Luke. At Yokohama I had had a few words with the first mate, and sent him packing. At Hong Kong there was a difference of opinion with the second, he went after the first. As the third fancied himself ill, and thought he'd try the hospital ashore for a change, it looked as if we were going to be under officered. There was a handy man aboard who called himself Luke. Just Luke. I didn't know much about him, what I did know I didn't altogether like. But, as I say, he was a handy man. One of those chaps who can drive an engine or trim a sail. He knew something about navigation. Said he had a mate's certificate, but I never saw it, and never had any reason to believe anything he said. Anyhow, being in a bit of a hole I took his word for it, and first mate he was appointed.

Some little time after he'd come aboard I was sitting in my cabin, feeling, as usual, like murder or suicide, when there was a tapping at the door. It was Luke.

"Beggin' pardon, captin, but can I have a word with you?"

"Have two."

He had three—and more. He stood, looking at me in the furtive, sneaking way he always had, twiddling his cap with his fingers like a forecastle hand.

"Excuse me, captain, but I don't fancy as how you've been overmuch in luck this trip."

"My dear Mr. Luke, whatever can have caused you to imagine a thing like that?"

"Well—it's pretty obvious, ain't it?"

He grinned. I could have broken his head.

"Is it for the purpose of imparting that information that I am indebted to the pleasure of your presence here?"

"Well no; it ain't." He scraped his jaw with his hand, as if to feel if it wanted shaving, which it did. "The fact is, I shouldn't be surprised if you chanced upon a bit of luck still, if you liked."

"If I liked! You're a man of humour."

"It's this way." He hesitated, as if doubtful as to the advisability of telling me which way it was. "It all depends upon whether you'd care to run a trifle of risk."

"After what I've gone through it'd have to be a pretty big trifle of risk which would prevent me snatching a chestnut out of the fire."

"That's what I thought."

He cleared his throat.

"Get on, man, get on!"

"It's this way."

"You've said it's this way, but you haven't said which way."

"There's a—we'll say party, as wants a passage to England, bad."

"Where is this party?"

"Over there."

He nodded his head in the direction of the shore.

"Who is this party?"

"That's where it is; he's a Joss."

"A Joss? What do you mean? What are you grinning at? Don't try to play any of your damfool jokes with me, I'm not taking any."

"It's no joke, captain; it's dead earnest. The party is a Joss, and that's where it is."

"What do you mean by a Joss?"

"It seems that a Joss is a sort of a kind of a god of the country, as it were."

Luke's grin became more cavernous.

"Are you suggesting that we should raid a temple; is that what you're after?"

"Well, no, not quite that. This party, although a Joss, is an Englishman."

"An Englishman!"

"Yes, an Englishman; and having had enough of being a Joss he wants to get back to his native land, 'England, home and beauty,' and that kind of thing, and he's willing to pay high for getting there."

"Where's the risk?"

"Well, it seems that the people in these parts think a good deal of him, and they don't care to have their gods and such-like cut their lucky whenever they think they will. Besides, he wouldn't want to come empty-handed."

"How do you mean?"

Luke glanced round, as if searching for unseen listeners. His voice sank.

"I didn't manage to get more than half-a-dozen words, as it might be, with the party in question— —"

"How did you manage to get those?"

The dear man's face assumed a crafty look.

"Well, it was a kind of accident, as it were; but that is neither here nor there. From what I'm told there's a slap-up temple on the other side of the hill, what's crammed with the offerings of the faithful. This here party's been a good time in the neighbourhood, and through their thinking a lot of him, as I've said, they've brought him heaps and heaps of presents. It's them he wants to take away with him."

"If they're his who's to say him no?"

"Well, there's a lot of other coves about the temple, and they won't allow they are his. Anyhow, they'd raise hell-and-Tommy if they knew he thought of taking them to England."

"I see. As I supposed at first, it's a big steal you're after."

"It's hardly fair to call it that, captain. The things are his. It's only those other blokes' cussed greediness."

"It is that way sometimes. One man says things are his which other people claim; then, poor beggar, he gets locked up because they are so grasping. What is he disposed to pay for taking him and his belongings?"

"Just whatever you choose to ask."

In Luke's eyes, as they met mine, there was a peculiar meaning.

"Then he'll find his passage an expensive one."

"I don't think you'll find there'll be any trouble about that. You get him and his safe to England, and I shouldn't be surprised but what you'd find, captain, that you'd made a good voyage after all. The only thing is, there's no time to be lost. He's in a hurry. He's not so young as he was, and he's about as sick of this neighbourhood as he can be."

"He can come aboard at once if he likes."

"Well, that would be sharp work, wouldn't it? But I don't know that it can be done quite so quick as that. You see, there's a good deal of stuff, and it's got to be got away, and without any fuss. But I tell you what, captain, he would like to have a word with you, if so be as you wouldn't mind."

"Where is he? Did you bring him with you in the boat?"

"No, I didn't do that. He ain't a party as can go where, when, and how he likes. There's eyes upon him all the time, and there's other things. But I do know where he's to be found, and I did go so far as to say that if so be you was willin' I'd bring you straight back to him right away, and then you might talk things over; I did make so bold as to go as far as that."

"Do you wish me to understand that he's waiting for me now?"

"Well, that's about the size of it."

"I'll come."

I went.

CHAPTER XXVI
THE THRONE IN THE CENTRE

Never shall I forget that row in the moonlight. It was one of those clear, soft, mysterious nights, which one sometimes gets in those latitudes, when the air seems alive with unseen things. One's half shy of talking for fear of being overheard. I'm no hand at description, but those who have been in those parts know the sort of night I mean. I was not in a romantic mood, God knows. Nor, so far as I could see, was there much of romance about the expedition. But I had been brooding, brooding, brooding, till things had got into my blood. As I sat there in the boat I felt as if I were moving through a world of dream.

We had brought a funny crowd. At the back of my mind, and I felt sure at the back of Luke's, was the feeling that if the thing had to be done at all then the quicker it was done the better. It was a case of taking time by the forelock. *The Flying Scud* had a ragged crew. The Lord alone could tell what was the nationality of most of them. Out of the bunch we had picked the best. There was the chief engineer, Isaac Rudd. He had shipped with me before. I knew him, and that he wouldn't stick at a trifle. A man who had had to wrestle with such engines as ours wasn't likely to. In a manner of speaking he was as deep in the ditch as I was; because if things had gone wrong his share of the blame was certainly equal to mine. If there was a chance of levelling up then we were both about as eager to snatch at it. Then there was Holley, Sam Holley, whom I had made second mate. Though he was a fat man, with a squeaky voice, I was hoping there were not too many soft streaks in him. There was his chum, Bill Cox, the very antipodes of himself. A shrivelled-up little fellow, with a voice like a big bassoon. Those two always went together.

Lord knows who the rest were. Though I had a kind of an inkling that Luke had done his best to see there were no shirkers, I had not breathed a syllable about the game we were after. But Luke might have dropped a hint. There was that about the fellows which to me smelt like business. And I felt sure that each man had about him somewhere something which would come in handy to fight with.

Still, I knew nothing about that. The impression I had wished to convey was that we were enjoying a little moonlight excursion, and that if anything was about, it was peace and mercy.

We reached shore. I spoke to them as Luke and I were getting out.

"You chaps will stay here. Mr. Holley, you'll be in command and see that there's no roving. Mr. Rudd, you will come with us to the top of the hill. Mr. Luke and I are going to see a friend on a little matter of business. If you hear a double catcall, or the sound of firearms, or anything that makes you think that we're not altogether enjoying ourselves, you pass the word at once. Then you chaps will come on for all you're worth. Leave one man in charge of the boat; that's all."

We then went up the slope. At the top we left Rudd, with a final tip from me to keep his eyes skinned, and his ears open. Luke and I plunged right away into what seemed to me to be a trackless forest. How he could find his way in it, considering he had only been there once in his life before, and then in broad daylight, was beyond my understanding. But there were one or two things about St. Luke which I couldn't make out, either then or afterwards. Anyhow he forged his way ahead as if he had been used to the place from his cradle up. Never seemed puzzled for a moment.

Presently we reached an open space. The moon shone down so that it was as light as day. Only there was a fringe of outer darkness all around. Luke made a queer noise with his lips. I suppose it was some sort of bird he was imitating. He repeated it three times; with an interval between each. Then something came out of the darkness which took me all aback.

It was a woman.

When she first appeared she had something white over her, head and all. Coming close up to us, drawing the covering aside with a dexterous switch, she stood bareheaded. I stared in amazement. I had not known there were such women in the world. I stammered to Luke—

"Who's this?"

To my astonishment she answered—in English a thousand times better than mine. It was a treat to listen to her.

"It is I."

Off came my cap in a twinkling.

"I beg your pardon. I had no idea I was to meet a lady."

"A lady? Am I a lady? Yes?" She laughed. She alone knew what at. Such laughter! "I am Susan."

Susan! She was as much a Susan as I was a Jupiter. I said then, and I say now, and I shall keep on saying, she was the loveliest creature I had ever seen even in—I won't say dreams, because I don't dream—but in pictures. She was straight as a mast. Carried herself as if she were queen of the earth; which she was. Yet with a dainty grace which for bewitching charm was beyond anything I had ever imagined. And her eyes! They were like twin moons in a summer sky. As I looked at her every nerve in my body tingled.

She added, since she saw me speechless:

"I am the daughter of the gods."

That was better. She was that. The daughter of the gods—as she put it herself. I could have dropped at her feet and worshipped. But she went on:

"You are from the ship? You are the captain?"

"I am Max Lander."

"Max Lander?" She repeated my name in a sort of a kind of a way which made everything seem to swim before my eyes. "It is a good name. We shall be friends."

"Friends!"

She held out her hands to me. As I took them into mine, Lord! how I shivered. I fancy she felt me shaking by the way she smiled. It made me worse, her smile did. She kept cool through it all.

"Shall we not be friends?"

"My dear lady, I—I hope we shall."

Talk about being at a loss for words! I could have poured out thousands. Only just then my dictionary had all its pages torn out, and I didn't know where to lay my hand upon one of them.

"It is my father you have come to see."

"Your father?"

I had forgotten what had brought me. Everything but the fact that she was standing there, in the moonlight, within reach of me, had passed from my mind. Her words brought me back to earth with a bang. Her father? Was it possible that I had come to see her father? She, the daughter of the gods; what manner of man must be her sire? I stuttered and I stammered.

"I—I didn't understand I'd come to see your father."

"He is the Great Joss."

"The Great Joss?"

What on earth did she mean? What was a Joss, anyhow, great or little? I had heard of joss-sticks, though I only had a hazy notion what they were. But a real live Joss, who could be the father of such a daughter, was a new kind of creature altogether. She offered no explanation.

"He waits for you. I am here to bring you to him. Come."

She fluttered off among the trees.

"Luke," I whispered as we followed, "this is not at all the sort of thing I was prepared for."

"She's a fine piece, ain't she?"

A "fine piece!" To apply his coarse Whitechapel slang to such a being! It was unendurable. I could have knocked him down. Only I thought that, just then, I had better not. I preserved silence instead.

It was like a page out of a fairy tale; we followed the enchanted princess through the wood of wonders. The gleaming of her snow-white robes was all we had to guide us. Shafts of light shot down upon her through the trees. When they struck her she shone like silver. She moved swiftly through the forest; out of the darkness into the light, then into the dark again. No sound marked her passing. She sped on noiseless feet. While Luke struggled clumsily after her.

She took us perhaps a quarter of a mile. Even as we went I wondered if Isaac Rudd upon the hill-top would hear us should we find ourselves in want of aid. How help would reach us if he did. One would need to be highly endowed with the instinct of locality to follow us by the way which we had come. A rendezvous hidden in a primeval forest, as this one seemed to be, might not be found easy of access by any sailor man.

She stopped; waiting till we came close up to her.

"It is here. Be careful; there is a step."

It was only when she opened a door, and I perceived the shimmer of a dim light beyond, that I realised that we were standing in the shadow of some kind of building. The darkness had seemed to be growing more opaque. Here was the explanation. If it had not been for her we should have knocked our heads against the wall. Nothing betrayed its neighbourhood; not a light, not a sound. If it had been placed there, cheek by jowl with the towering trees, with the intent of concealing its existence as much as possible from the eyes of men, the design had been well conceived and carried out. At night no one would suspect its presence. How it would be by day I could not tell. I doubted if it would be much more obvious then. It was no hut. As I glanced above me it seemed to be of huge proportions. Its blackness soared up and up like some grim nightmare. What could it be?

Our guide entered. I followed; Luke brought up the rear. It was some seconds before I began to even faintly understand what kind of place it was which we were in. Then I commenced to realise that it must be some kind of heathen temple. Its vastness amazed me. Whether it was or was not exaggerated by the prevailing semi-darkness I could not positively determine. To me it seemed to be monstrous. Height, breadth, length, all were lost in shadows. Wherever I looked I could not see the end. Only a haunting impression of illimitable distance.

The door by which we had entered was evidently a private one. There was only space for one at a time to pass. To such an edifice there must have been another entrance, to permit of the passage of large crowds. Though I could not guess in which direction it might be. Columns rose on every hand. I had a notion that they were of varied colours; covered with painted carvings. But whether they were of wood, stone, or metal I could not say. Their number added an extra touch of bewilderment. One gazed through serried lines and lines of columns which seemed to bridge the gathering shadows with the outer darkness which was beyond.

Until our guide moved more towards the centre of the building, with us at her heels, I did not understand where the light which illumined the place came from. It proceeded from what I suppose was the altar. The high altar. A queer one it was. And imposing to boot. Anyhow, seen in that half light, with us coming on it unprepared, and not expecting anything of the kind, it was imposing, and something more. I don't mind owning that I had a queer feeling about my back. Just as if someone had squeezed an unexpected drop of water out of a sponge, and it was going trickling down my spine.

There was some fascinating representations of what one could only trust were not common objects of the seashore. These were of all sizes. Some several times as large as life, and, one fervently hoped, a hundred times less natural. They stood for originals which, so far as my knowledge of physiology goes, are to be found neither in the sea, or under it; on the earth, or over it; or anywhere adjacent. The powers be thanked! They were monsters; just that, and would have been excellent items in a raving madman's ideal freak museum. Anywhere else they were out of place. There was one sweet creature which particularly struck my fancy. It was some fourteen or fifteen feet high, and was about all mouth. Its mouth was pretty wide open. It would have made nothing of swallowing a Jonah. And was fitted with a set of teeth which were just the thing to scrunch his bones.

These pretty dears were arranged in a semicircle, each on a stand of its own. The small ones were outside. They grew bigger as they went on, until, by the time you reached the biggest in the middle, if you were a drinking man you were ready to turn teetotaler at sight. The hues they were decked in were enough to make you envy the colour blind. Coming on this livening collection without the slightest notice, in that great black mystery of a place, with just light enough to let them hit you in the eye, and hidden in the darkness you knew not what besides, was a bit trying to the nerves. At least it was to mine. And I'm not generally accounted a nervous subject.

The strangest thing of all was in the centre. I stared at it, and stared; yet I couldn't make out what it was.

It was on a throne; if it wasn't gold it looked like it. It was large enough for half-a-dozen men. Standing high. Right in the middle, flanked by the biggest pair of monsters, the seat was on a level with the tops of their heads. It was approached by a flight of steps, each step apparently of different coloured stone. Coloured lamps were hung above and about it. One noticed how, in the draughty air, they were swinging to and fro. From these proceeded all the light that was in the place, except that here and there upon the steps were queer-shaped vessels, seemingly of copper, in which something burned, flashing up now and then in changing hues, like Bengal lights. From them, I judged, proceeded the sickly smell which made the whole place like a pest-house. And the smoke was horrid.

In the very centre of the throne was something, though what I could not make out. It seemed immobile; yet there was that about it which suggested life. The face and head were as hideous as any of the horrors round about, and yet—could the thing be human? Long parti-coloured hair—scarlet, yellow, green, all sorts of unnatural colours—descending from the scalp nearly obscured the visage. There seemed to be only one eye and no nose. If there were ears they were hidden. Was it some obscene creature or the mockery of a man? There were no signs of legs. The thing was scarcely more than three feet high. Being clad in a sort of close-fitting tunic, which was ablaze with what seemed diamonds, legs, if there had been any, could scarcely have been hidden. There was certainly nothing in the way of breeches. Arms, on the other hand, there were and to spare. A pair dangled at the sides which were longer than the entire creature. Huge hands were at the ends.

While I gazed at this nightmare creation of some delirious showman's fancy, wondering if such a creature by any possibility could ever have had actual existence, that most beautiful woman in the world who had brought us there turned to me and said, as simply and as naturally as if she were remarking that she'd take another lump of sugar in her tea:—

"This is the Great Joss—my father."

And Luke, clearing his throat, with an air half apologetic and half familiar, observed, in a sort of husky groan, which I daresay he meant for a whisper,

"Hallo, Ben, my cockalorum bird, how goes it along with you, old son?"

CHAPTER XXVII
THE OFFERINGS OF THE FAITHFUL

No notice was taken of Luke's inquiry. Instead, the whole place was filled all at once with a variety of discordant sounds. They seemed to proceed from the monsters which were ranged about the central figure. At the same time their arms began to move, their heads to waggle, their mouths to open and shut, their eyes to roll. Possibly, to the untaught savage, such an exhibition might have appeared impressive. It reminded me too much of the penny-in-the-slot figures whose limbs are set in motion by the insertion of a coin. The slight awe which I had felt for the figures vanished for good and all.

"That's enough of it," I observed. "I like them better when they're still. Would whoever's pulling the strings mind taking a rest?"

I had a sort of a kind of an idea that by someone or other my remark was not relished so much as it deserved. A suspicion that in some quarter there was a feeling of resentment that what had been intended to confound me should have ended in a fizzle. The noises stopped; the figures ceased to move; it was as if the coin-in-the-slot had given us our pennyworth. Instead, something which, from my point of view, was very much more objectionable began to happen.

From the immediate neighbourhood of the figure on the throne snakes' heads began to peep. There was no mistake that they were all alive—oh! The evil-looking brutes began to slither over the sides. I never could abide snakes, either in a figurative or a literal sense. The mere sight of one puts my dander up. Whipping up a couple of revolvers out of my coat pockets, I headed the muzzles straight for them.

"Someone had better call those pretty darlings off before I shoot the eyes clean out of their heads!"

To my surprise the warning was immediately answered.

"You'd better not shoot at them, my lad, or you'll be sorry."

The words came from the creature on the throne.

"So you are alive, are you? You'd better call them off, or I'll shoot first, and be sorry after."

"They're not touching you, you fool!"

"No, and I'm not going to wait until they are."

The things were coming unpleasantly close—their approach setting every nerve in my body on edge. In another second or two I would have fired. Luke caught me by the arm.

"Gently, captain, gently. The snakes won't hurt you; our friend won't let them. It's only his way. Captain, let me introduce you to my old friend, Mr. Benjamin Batters. My friend and me haven't seen each other for years, have we, Ben?"

"Can't say I ever wanted to see you."

"Just so, just so; still friends do meet again. Ben, this is Captain Lander."

"He doesn't seem to know his proper place."

"When I glance in your direction, Mr. Batters, I'm inclined to make the same remark of you."

"Damn the man!"

The creature proved himself to be very much alive by seizing one of the serpents in his huge hands and whirling it above his head as if it had been a club.

Luke played the part of peacemaker.

"Now, gentlemen! Come, Ben, no offence was meant, I'm sure. Tell the captain what you want. He's in rather a hurry, Captain Lander is."

"Then let him go to the devil, and take his hurry with him."

"By all means. I wish you good evening, Mr. Batters."

I swung round on my heels. The creature screamed after me.

"Stop, you fool, stop! I'm the Joss—the Great Joss; the greatest god this country's ever known. In my presence all men fall upon their knees and worship me."

"Let 'em. Tastes differ. I like my gods to be built on other lines."

I expected to be attacked by a shower of execration. But the creature changed his mood.

"And I'm sick of being a god—sick of it—dead sick! Curse your josses, is what I say—damn 'em!" There followed a flood of adjectives. "I want to get out of the place, to turn my back upon the whole infernal land, to never set eyes on it again. I'm an Englishman, that's what I am—an Englishman, British born and British bred. I want to get back to my native land. Captain Lander, or whatever your cursed name is, will you take me back to England?"

"When?"

"Now—at once—to-night!"

"I do not carry passengers. I doubt if I have proper accommodation. What will you give me for taking you?"

"I'll show you what I'll give you."

The creature scrambled off his throne by means of his arms and hands, like some huge baboon. As I had suspected, he appeared to have no legs. Reaching the ground he moved at what, under the circumstances, was an extraordinary pace. Wheels had been attached to the stumps of his legs. Using his hands as a monkey does its forearms, he advanced upon these wheels as if they had been castors. As we followed him Luke whispered in my ear:—

"You mustn't mind what he says; he's a bit off his chump, poor chap."

"From what I can see there seems to be a bit off him elsewhere besides the chump."

"Oh, he's lived a queer life. Been cut to pieces, stewed in oil, and I don't know what. He's a tough 'un. It's a miracle he's alive. I thought he was dead years ago. When I first knew him he was a finer man than me."

Mr. Batters had brought us to an apartment which seemed to be used as a repository for the treasures of the temple. The room was not a large one, but it was as full as it could hold. Curios were on every hand. Trading in Eastern seas I had seen something of things of the kind; I knew that those I saw there had value. There were images, ornaments, vessels of all sorts, and shapes, and sizes, apparently of solid gold. He lifted the lid of a lacquered case.

"You see that? That's dust—gold dust. There are more than twenty cases full of it, worth at least a thousand pounds apiece. You see those?" He was holding up another box for my inspection. "Those are diamonds, rubies, pearls, sapphires, opals, and turquoises."

"Real?"

"Real!" he screamed. "They're priceless! unique! They're offerings which the faithful have made to me, the Great Joss. They come from men and women who are the greatest and the richest in the land. Do you think they would dare to offer me imitations? If they were guilty of such sacrilege

I would destroy them root and branch. And they know it!" The creature snarled like some great cat. "I know something of stones, and I tell you you won't find finer gems in any jeweller's shop in London—nor any as fine." He waved his arms. "You won't match the things you see here in all Europe—not in kings' palaces nor in national museums. I know, and I tell you. If all the things you see in this place were put up in a London auction room for sale to-morrow, they'd fetch more than a million pounds—down on the nail! I swear they would! If you'll take me with you to England to-night—me and my daughter here; this is my daughter, Susan. She's her father's only child." The irony of it! My stars! A shudder went all over me as I thought of her being connected by ties of blood with such an object. "If you'll give the pair of us ship-room, and all these things—they're all my property, every pin's worth, all offerings to the Great Joss—you and your crew shall have half of everything you see. That shall be in payment of our passage."

Half!

My mouth watered. His appraisement of the value of the things I saw about me went to all intents and purposes unheeded. Divide his figures by twenty. Say their worth was £50,000. Half of that, even after I, and Luke, and Rudd, and the rest of them had had their pickings—and out of a venture of this sort pickings there would have to be—the remnant would still leave a handsome profit for the owners. I knew the kind of men with whom I had to deal. Only give them a sufficient profit, I need not fear being placed in their black books. However it might have come. And then there was half that collection of gems—I would have that too. And half the gold dust. Ye whales and little fishes! this might yet turn out the most profitable voyage I'd ever made.

Yet I easily perceived that there might be breakers ahead.

"You say that all these things are yours?"

"Every one—every speck of gold dust. All! all! I am the only Great Joss; they have been given to me."

"Then, in that case, there will be no difficulty in removing them."

The response came brusquely enough, and to the point.

"That's where you're a fool. Do you suppose I'd share the plunder if there weren't? If it was known that I was going to make myself scarce, let alone hooking off with this lot of goods, there'd be hell to pay. I haven't stayed here all this time because I wanted; I had to. They made of me the thing you see; cut me to pieces; boiled, burned, and baked me; skinned me alive. Then they dipped me in a paint-pot and made of me a god. The next thing they'll make of me'll be a corpse; I can't stand being pulled about with red-hot pincers like I used to. There's a hundred adjectived priests about this adjectived show. They all want to have a finger in my pie. When I had a word with Luke here, and arranged with him to have a word with you, I sent the whole damned pack off miracle working at a place half-a-dozen miles away from here. We'll have to be cleared off before they're back or there'll be fighting; they can fight! And the man who falls into their hands alive before they've done with him will curse his mother for ever having borne him."

"How do you propose to go—walk?"

"Walk!" He laughed—a laugh which wasn't nice to hear. "I haven't walked for twenty years—since they burned my legs off so that I shouldn't. When the Great Joss goes abroad he travels in his palanquin—there it is. And as he passes the people throw themselves on to the ground and hide their faces in the dust, lest, at the sight of his godlike form, they should fall dead. You'll have to fetch your chaps, and be quick about it! They'll have to carry me, and I'll stuff the palanquin as full as it will hold with the things which are best worth taking. I know 'em!"

I reflected for a moment. Then turned to Luke.

"Do you think you can find your way to Rudd?"

The girl interposed.

"Let me go; I shall be surer—and quicker."

"You can't go alone; they won't take their orders from you." An idea occurred to me. "I'll come with you, and we'll take as many things with us as we can carry. Luke, you stay behind and help Mr. Batters put the things together in convenient parcels. I doubt if there'll be enough of us to take everything. Pick out the best. As time's precious, what we can't take we shall have to leave behind."

I crammed my pockets with the smaller odds and ends, none the less valuable, perhaps, because they were small. I packed a lot of other things into a sort of sheet which I slung over my shoulder. The girl stowed as much as she could carry into the skirt of her queer fashioned gown. She held it up as children do their pinafores. Out we went into the night.

As we hurried along my breath came faster even than the pace warranted at the thought of being alone in the darkness with her.

We went some way before a word was spoken. Then I asked a question.

"Do you want to go to England?"

"Want!" She gave a sigh, as of longing. "I have wanted ever since I was born."

"Then you shall go whoever has to stay behind."

"Stay behind—how do you mean?" She seemed to read in my words a hidden significance. "My father must go. If he stays I stay also."

"Is he really your father?"

"Of course he is my father. My mother was one of the women of the country. They burned her when I was born."

"Burned her?"

"As a thank offering for having borne unto the Great Joss a child."

She spoke in the most matter-of-fact tone. I wondered what sort of place this was I had got into, whether the people hereabouts were men or demons. She went on quietly.

"My father is the Great Joss. It was a great thing to the people that a woman should have borne to him a child."

"A child who was a goddess."

I was ashamed of myself directly the words were uttered. It seemed to be taking an unfair advantage to say things to her like that. But she didn't seem to mind.

"A goddess? That is what men worship."

"Just so. That is what men worship."

She laughed to herself softly, so that only I, who was close at her side, could hear. There was that in the sound which set my blood on fire.

"If I am a goddess, whom you worship, then you must be god, and I must worship you. Shall it be?"

I did not answer. Whether she was playing with me I could not tell. I knew all the while that it was just as likely. But there was something in the question, and in the way in which she asked it, which put all my senses in confusion. It was a wonder I didn't come a dozen times to the ground. My wits were wandering. We exchanged not another syllable. I had lost my tongue.

As we neared Rudd he challenged us.

"Who comes there?"

"It's all right, Rudd; it's I." He was plainly surprised at the sight of my companion. But, being a discreet soul, asked no questions. Perhaps he had already concluded—being quite capable of drawing deductions on his own account—that queer things were in the air. "Stay where you are. I shall be back in a minute and shall want you. I'm going to fetch the men out of the boat. There's a job of work on hand."

We ran down the slope. Found the boat where I had left it. Deposited in it the things which we had brought away with us; no one offering a comment. As I unloaded I gave hurried instructions. In certainly not much more that the minute of which I had spoken to Rudd we were starting back to him. One man we left in the boat; five we took with us. Of their quality in a scrimmage I knew nothing; but, as I had suspected, each had brought with him something with which to make his mark in case of ructions. If one might judge from their demeanour the suggestion that there might be friction ahead seemed to give them satisfaction rather than otherwise. Especially when I added a hint that there was plunder to be got by those who cared to get it. They put no inconvenient inquiries. Whose property it might chance to be was their captain's affair not theirs. For once in a way they recognised the force of the fact that it was theirs only to obey.

All they wanted was a share of the spoil.

CHAPTER XXVIII
THE JOSS REVERTS

We passed through the forest in single file; the girl first, I next; the men hard upon each other's heels. We found Luke apparently alone. I thought that the Joss had returned for some purpose to the temple.

"What's he gone for?" I asked.

Luke made a movement with his forefinger, suggesting caution. He spoke in a hoarse whisper.

"He's not gone; he's there—in the palanquin." His voice sank lower. "I rather fancy that he don't want to be looked at more than he can help. Poor chap! he feels that, to look at, he ain't the man as once he was."

Luke grinned. Sympathy did not go very deep with him.

The palanquin was drawn out upon the floor. The girl stooped over it.

"Father!" A voice proceeded from within—a surly voice:—

"I'm here all right; don't let's have any nonsense. Tell 'em to be careful how they carry me; I don't want to be jolted to bits by a lot of awkward fools. They're to hurry for all that; those devils may be back at any minute. We've arranged the things as best we can; Luke will tell them what's to be taken first."

Luke volunteered to be one of the palanquin bearers, suggesting that Isaac Rudd should be the other. Isaac glanced doubtfully towards me.

"It's all right, Mr. Rudd. There's a friend of mine in there, an invalid, who is not able to walk very well over uneven ground. If you will assist Mr. Luke, I'll be obliged. You'll find that you'll be able to carry him very easily between you."

Isaac expressed his willingness to lend a hand, though I could see that he still had his doubts as to what was in the palanquin. To be frank, I was doubtful too. I wondered what it contained besides Benjamin Batters.

Luke and his friend, considering the short time they had had at their disposal, had put the goods into convenient form for transit. Some had been packed in wooden cases, some in bundles, some in sacks. Each man took as much as he could carry—inquiring of himself, I make no doubt, what it was that he was bearing. I took my share. The girl took hers. Luke and Rudd shouldered the palanquin; the second in front, the first behind—Luke taking up his position in the rear, so that he might the more easily, if necessary, hold communication with its occupant.

The procession started. The girl was its guide, now in advance, now at the palanquin side holding converse with her father. I gathered from what I heard that he was not in the sweetest temper. Luke and Rudd were not practised bearers. The way was difficult. The light trying. Now and then one or the other would stumble. The palanquin was jolted. From its interior issued a curse which, if not loud, was deep and strong.

We reached the open on the crest of the slope without interruption. I was beginning to conclude that, consciously or unconsciously, Batters had exaggerated the danger which would attend his attempt at flight. We had borne him away if not in triumph, at least with impunity; looted the temple of its best belongings; no one had endeavoured to say us nay. It might be almost worth our while to return for what we had left behind. Actual peril there appeared to be none. No one seemed cognisant of what was going on, or seemed to care. If the temple itself had been portable, we might have carried it away entire; the result apparently would have been the same.

Thinking such thoughts I watched Luke and Rudd go swinging down the slope in the moonlight. I almost suspected them of intentional awkwardness; they treated that palanquin to such a continuous shaking. Its occupant must have been gripping the sides with his huge hands, or surely he would have been dislodged and shot on to the ground. With a stream of adjectives he enlivened the proceedings.

"Small blame to him," said I to myself. "If jolting's good for the liver, as I've heard, he'll have had a good dose of the medicine before he's through. If swearing 'll make it easier, for the Lord's sake let him swear."

And he swore. And right in the middle of about as full flavoured a string of observations as I had ever heard there arose a wild cry from the forest behind us. In a second the Joss' head appeared between the curtains.

"Quick! quick! It's the devils—the devils!"

It needed no urging from me—or from him either—to induce everyone concerned to quicken his pace. On a sudden the forest where, a moment back, had reigned the silence of the grave, was now alive with shouts and noises. People were shrieking. What sounded like drums were being banged. Guns were being fired. The Great Joss' absence was discovered. Possibly the absence of a good deal of valuable property had been discovered too. The alarm was being given. The priests—those pious souls who had burned the girl's mother alive as a reward for having borne the Great Joss a child!—were warning the country far and wide of what had happened. In a few minutes the whole countryside would be upon us.

I don't fancy the fighting instinct was very hot in any of us just then. There was something ominous about that din. We were few. The proceedings on which we were engaged might appear odd regarded from a certain point of view. Fortunately, we were near the boat.

As luck would have it, when he was within a dozen paces of the water's edge, Luke, tripping over a bush, or something, dropped on to his knee. The palanquin, torn from Isaac's shoulders, descended to the ground with a crash. What were Mr. Batters' feelings I am unable to say. I expected to see him shot through the roof, like a jack-in-the-box. But he wasn't. So far as I could tell in the haste and confusion he was silent. Which was ominous. The girl sank down beside the fallen palanquin with the evident intention of offering words of comfort to her revered, though maltreated, parent.

Before she had a chance of saying a word Luke had righted himself. Rudd had regained possession of the end which he had lost. Mr. Batters inside might be dead. That was a matter of comparative indifference. No inquiries were made. Somehow the palanquin was being borne towards the boat. Of exactly what took place during the next few minutes I have only vague impressions. I know that the palanquin was got into the boat somehow, with the Great Joss, or what was left of him, still inside. The men, disposing of their burdens anywhere or anyhow, began to get out their oars. I dropped my loot somewhere aft. The boat was got afloat. The girl—who had all at once got as frightened of the sea as a two-year-old child—I lifted in my arms, carried through three feet of water, and put aboard. I followed.

A wild-looking figure came tearing after us down the slope. There were others, but he was in front, and I noticed him particularly. He was a tall, thin old party, dressed in yellow, with a bald head, and a face that looked like a corpse's in the moonlight. It was yellow, like his dress. As wicked a physiognomy as ever I set eyes upon. He was in a towering rage. When he got down to the shore we were in deep water, perhaps twenty yards away. He seemed so anxious to get at us I expected to see him start swimming after us. Not a bit of it. I rather imagine that the people just thereabouts were not fond of water in any form. He refused to allow the sea to damp so much as the tips of his toes. He screamed at us instead—to my surprise, in English—not bad English either.

"The Joss! The Great Joss! Give us back our Joss!"

"Wouldn't you like it?" I returned.

I wasn't over civil, not liking his looks. I wondered if he had had a hand in burning the girl's mother. He looked that sort of man.

He raised his hands above his head and cursed us. He looked a quaint figure, standing there in the moon's white rays. And ugly too. Dangerous if he had a chance. His voice was not a loud one, but he had a trick of getting it to travel.

"You dog! you thief! you accursed! you have stolen from us the Great Joss! But do not think that you can keep him. Wherever you may take him, though it be across the black water, to the land beyond the sun, we will follow. He shall be ours again. As for you, the flesh shall fall from off you; the foul waters shall rot your bones; you shall stink! Mocker of the gods!"

There was a good deal more of it. He continued his observations till we were out of hearing. Repeating that he would follow us pretty well everywhere before he would allow that Great Joss to be a bad debt. Though he was a barbarian and loose in his geography, it struck me that he meant what he said. If he could have laid his hands on me, and have had me in a position where I couldn't have laid mine on him, I should have had a nice little experience before he'd done. That was the kind of mood he was in.

Long before he had said all that he had to say he was joined by quite a crowd. When he had about cursed himself out, he started on a funny little entertainment of another kind. He made a fire close down by the sea. His friends formed about it in a circle. He stood in the centre. As the flames rose and fell he dropped things on them, stuff which smoked and burned in different colours. The sort of rubbish which boys in England buy in ha'porths and penn'orths, and make themselves a nuisance with. Possibly, out there it costs more, so is thought a lot of. As he put his rubbish on his fire, his friends moved round first one way and then the other, behaving themselves generally like fantastic idiots. And he threw himself into attitudes which would have been a photographer's joy. I had an impression that he was calling down the wrath of the gods upon our heads, and doing it in style.

Our return to the ship created a good deal of excitement. One might lay long odds that every man on board had been watching, for all that he was worth, whatever there was to watch, without being able to make head or tail of what he had seen. So that our arrival just gave the final touch to the general curiosity.

The things, whose departure those gentlemen on shore were weeping for, were got on board. The Great Joss wanted to be hoisted up in his palanquin. When I pointed out that there were obstacles in the way, he came out of it with a rush and shinned up the ship's side like a monkey. His appearance on deck made things lively. The men took him for the devil, and shrank from him as such. Not wanting any more fuss than might be helped, I led the way down the companion as fast as I could. He came after me. Goodness alone knows how. It seemed to me he was as handy on no legs as some people upon two. His daughter followed.

I had been turning matters over in my mind coming along. There had never been such a thing as a passenger known on *The Flying Scud*. At that moment there was a vacant two-berth cabin suited to people who might not be over and above particular. The Great Joss and his friend Luke should have it. The Great Joss' daughter should have Luke's quarters.

When Luke appeared he professed himself agreeable. Indeed, too agreeable. There was an eagerness about the way in which he snatched at my suggestion which made me thoughtful even in that first moment. It was against nature that a man should be half beside himself with delight at the prospect of being berthed with such a monster. As I eyed Luke, noting the satisfaction which he was unable to conceal, I wondered what was at the back of it.

However, so things were settled. Mr. Batters and the first mate were placed together. Miss Batters had the first mate's quarters.

When I got on deck again land was out of sight: I was disposed for solitude and a quiet think. But I wasn't to have them. I soon became conscious that Isaac Rudd was taking peeps at me. He kept coming up out of the engine room, an oily rag in his hand, and a sort of air about him as if he wondered when I proposed to speak to him. At last I took the hint.

"Well, Mr. Rudd, what is it?"

He came up, wiping his paws with his oily rag. His manner was sententious.

"I thought, sir, that you might have something which you wished to say to me."

"About what?"

"This little game."

"What little game?"

"The one we've just been playing. You see we've all been taking a hand in it, and there's a kind of feeling aboard this ship that there might be something a little delicate about it, which might bring us into trouble before we've done. And no man likes to take a risk—for nothing."

"I see. That's it. You know me, and you know that I'm as good as my word. You may tell the men from me that if the venture is brought safely into port, and turns out what I expect, it will be twenty-five pounds in the pockets of every man on board this ship, and a hundred for each officer."

"And what for the first engineer?" With that confounded oil rag of his he wiped his scrubby chin. "I'm thinking that, under the circumstances, I shouldn't like to guarantee that the engines 'll last out for a hundred pounds. They're just a lot of bits of iron tied together with scraps of string. To keep them going will mean sleepless nights."

I laughed.

"Are they so bad as that? I'm sorry to hear it, Mr. Rudd. Rudd, you're a blackguard. You want to rob your captain—and the owners."

"Damn the owners!"

"That's against Scripture. An owner's always blessed."

"He'll never be upon the other side if he sends a ship to sea with such engines as we have."

"They are a trial, aren't they, Rudd?"

"They're that."

"So I think we may say that, under the circumstances, if the engines do last out, it will mean five hundred pounds in the pocket of the chief engineer."

"Five hundred pounds? I'm not denying it's an agreeable sum. I'd like to handle it. And it'll be no fault of mine if the machine blows up before it's just convenient. There's just one other question I'd like to put to you. Is it the devil that we've took aboard?"

"It's not. But it's something that's seen the devil face to face, and tasted of hell fire."

Turning on my heel I left Isaac to make of my words what he could. A variety of matters demanded my immediate consideration. I had pledged my word that every man on board that ship should, in case of a certain eventuality, receive a definite sum of money. The promise was perhaps a rash one. But there was reason behind it. It would have to be kept. Then there were the owners to be considered—and myself.

Where were the funds to come from with which to do these things? What would they amount to, leaving fancy figures out. I should have to have a clear understanding with the Great Joss. The sooner the better, while I still, as it were, had a pull on him. Isaac Rudd had lost no time. Neither would I.

I went down the companion ladder to have that understanding.

CHAPTER XXIX
THE FATHER—AND HIS CHILD

The cabin door was fastened. I rapped. Luke inquired from within—

"Who's there?"

"I! Open the door." So far as I could judge no attempt was made to do as I requested. There were whispers instead. The voices were audible though the words were not. I rapped again. "Do you hear? open this door!"

Luke replied.

"Beggin' your pardon, captain, but Mr. Batters isn't feeling very well. He hopes that you'll excuse him."

A louder rapping.

"Open this door."

There were sounds which suggested that something was being done in a hurry; an exchange of what were apparently expostulatory murmurs. Then the Great Joss spoke.

"This is my cabin, Captain Lander——"

I cut him short.

"Your cabin!" I brought my fist against the door with a bang. "If you don't open at once, I'll have the ship put about, take you back from where you came, and dump you on shore. I'm in command here, and all the cabins in this ship are mine. Now, which is it to be—open?—or back?"

Luke began to mutter excuses.

"If you'll just wait five minutes, captain——"

I felt convinced that they were doing something they didn't wish me to see, and which was highly desirable that I should see. I didn't wait for Luke to finish. I just planted my shoulder against the door, and heaved. It leaped open. I had counted on the fastenings being rickety. There was Luke and the Great Joss with their hands full of papers and things which they had evidently just been attempting to conceal. The girl stood looking on. I took off my cap to her.

"Miss Batters, I wish to speak to your father in private. Might I ask you to leave us." She went without a word. I turned to Luke. "Mr. Luke, go up on deck, and wait there till I come."

There was an ugly look on his face.

"If you don't mind, captain, I should just like——"

"Do as I tell you, sir or you cease to be an officer on board this ship." He saw that I meant business; moved towards the door. "You needn't trouble to take those things with you."

"Put them down, you fool," growled Mr. Batters.

Luke put them down, and departed, not looking exactly pretty. When he had gone, pushing the door to I stood with my back against it. The Great Joss and I exchanged glances. He spoke first.

"You've a queer way of doing things."

"I have. Of which fact your presence here is an illustration."

"I've not shipped as one of your crew. I'm a passenger."

"At present. Whether you continue to be so depends on one or two things. One is that you behave. You come from a place where there are some queer customs."

"What do you mean by that?"

"What I say." He winced in a fashion I did not understand, causing me to surmise that the customs in question might be even queerer than I supposed. "The first time, Mr. Batters, you show disrespect for any orders I may give, or wishes I may express, the ship goes round—you go back. I fancy your friends will be glad to receive you back among them."

He glared at me with his one eye in a manner I did not altogether relish. There was an uncanniness about his looks, his ways, his every movement. As he confronted me, squatted on the floor, he was the most repulsive-looking object I had ever seen. It was hard to believe that such a creature could be human. And English! The sight of him filled me with a sense of nausea. I hastened to go on.

"There is another point on which your continuance as a passenger depends. What do you propose to pay for your passage?"

"I've told you—halves."

"That is too indefinite. I want something more definite. Moreover, it is the rule for passage money to be paid in advance."

"If you prefer that way of doing business you shall have a hundred pounds apiece for us, and I'll give you the money now."

"Is that all? Then the ship goes round."

"You shall have more if you'll only wait."

"How long?"

"Till I've had time to look about me. You can't expect me to have everything cut and dried before I've been on board ten minutes. You see these things?" I did. They were everywhere. I wondered where Luke and he proposed to sleep. "They're worth a million pounds."

"Nonsense!"

"It's not nonsense, you——fool."

The opprobrious epithet was seasoned with a profusion of adjectives.

"Mr. Batters, that is not the way in which to address the commander of a ship. As I see that you and I are not likely to understand each other I will give instructions to put the ship about at once, and take you back. It's plain I made a mistake in having anything to do with you."

I made as if to go.

"Stop, you idiot!"

"Mr. Batters? What did you observe?"

"I apologise! I apologise! What you say is right. I have been used to rummy ways. I can't slough 'em at sight. Even a snake takes time to change its skin. But when you talk about the value I set on the things I've got here being nonsense, it's you who're mistaken, not me. Look at that!"

He held up a hideous-looking image. I took it from him, to find it heavier than I had expected.

"That's gold—solid. Weighs every bit of twenty pounds, sixteen ounces to the pound. It's got diamonds for eyes, twenty-five or thirty carats apiece; pearls for teeth, and its forehead is studded with opals. The stones in the rings, bracelets, and bangles are all real. I tell you what you're holding in your hands is not worth far short of fifty thousand pounds."

"It may be so. I'm no judge of such things. But what proof have I of the correctness of your statements?"

"That's it; what proof have you? You've only my word. You may cut my heart out if I'm wrong. And what I say is this. When we get to London we'll have them all sold, or else valued—whichever you please. You shall either have half the things—toss for first choice, then choose turn and turn about; or half of whatever they fetch."

"You'll give me a written undertaking to that effect?"

"I will."

"And I can take an inventory of everything you have?"

"If you like."

"And remove them to my cabin for safer custody?"

"If you think that they will be safer there. You can stow 'em in the hold for all I mind. All I want is for them to be safe, and have my fair half. Only I don't see what harm they'll do in here, except that you've bursted off the lock, which is a thing as can be replaced. I'm not likely to leave the ship, and I'll watch it that they don't go without me."

There seemed reason in what he said. It sounded fair; above-board enough. Though every pulse shrunk from his near neighbourhood, crying out that there was that about him which was good neither for man nor beast, I could not but admit to myself that this was so.

I was still holding in my hand the obscene image which, according to him, was worth fifty thousand pounds. I had been watching Mr. Batters. Glancing from him to it I saw that, perched upon its head, was a little doll-like looking figure, as long, perhaps, as my middle finger. It was not there a second before. I wondered whence it came, how it retained its place.

"What's this?" I asked.

"That?" There was a curious something in Mr. Batters' tone which set my nerves all jangling. "Where I've been they call that the God of Fortune. It's my very own god. It watches over me. When you see it I'm never far away."

I reached out my disengaged hand to take hold of it for examination. But I seemed to have grown dizzy all of a sudden, and clumsy. It must have been because I was clumsy that, instead of grasping it, I knocked it off its perch. It fell to the floor. I stooped to pick it up.

"I don't think you'll find it. I expect it's gone."

It did seem to have gone. Or perhaps my sudden dizziness prevented my seeing so small an object in the imperfect light. I certainly did feel strangely giddy. So overpowered was I by most unusual sensations that, yielding the £50,000 horror into Mr. Batters' outstretched hand, almost before I knew I found myself on the other side of the cabin door.

I staggered up on deck. The night air did me good. I drew great breaths. The giddiness passed. I began to ask myself what could have caused it. Had Mr. Batters been practising a little hocus pocus? Playing up to the part of the

Great Joss? If I had been sure, I would have put the ship about right there and then. Back he should have gone, to play the part out to the end.

Luke hailed me.

"Beggin' pardon, captain, but may I go below? Mine's the next watch. I should like a wink of sleep."

"You may. A word with you before you go. You got me into this business. I'm not sure I thank you. What do you know about this man Batters?"

He looked up at the stars, as if for an answer to my question.

"Him and me was boys together."

"And since?"

"We've come across each other once or twice. But it's half a lifetime since we met."

"You seem to have recognised each other pretty quickly when you did meet."

"He knew me. I didn't know him. And never should have done—never. I can't hardly believe now it's the Ben Batters I used to know. Only he's proved it."

"How came he to be what he is?"

"That's more than I can say. He hasn't told me no more than he's told you. He always was a hot 'un, Ben was. Bound to get into a mess before he'd done. Always a-fightin'. But I never thought he'd have come to this. Fine figure of a man he used to be. They must have took the skin right off him—used him something cruel."

I shuddered at the thought. Better to have died a dozen deaths.

"Do you think he's to be trusted?"

"Well—as for trustin'—that depends. Seems to me no one's to be trusted more than you can help."

I felt, as he went, that he had summed up his own philosophy. He trusted no one. It was the part of wisdom for no one to trust him. I wished that, in my haste, I hadn't berthed the two together. The first excuse which offered Luke should be shifted. I did not like the notion of such a pair hobnobbing. The stake was too big.

Someone touched me on the arm. It was the girl.

"Miss Batters! You ought to be in your berth. It's late."

Her answer surprised me.

"I'm afraid."

She stood so close that I could hear a little fluttering noise in her throat, as if she found it hard to breathe. I wondered if she was affected by the motion. She did not look as if she were. She was straight as a dart. And beautiful.

"Afraid? Of what?"

"Of the water. There is trouble on the sea. Evil spirits live on it."

"You needn't be afraid of evil spirits while you're with me. Who's put such notions into your head? English girls aren't afraid of the sea. And you are English."

"Is it alive?"

"Is what alive?"

"The ship?"

"The ship!"

"What makes it go? It rushes through the water; it trembles, I feel it trembling beneath my feet; it makes a noise."

"Those are the engines."

"The engines? Are they alive?"

"Alive? Yes, while Mr. Rudd and his friends keep feeding them they're alive. Come and have a look at them."

"No. I dare not. I'm afraid."

"There's nothing to be afraid of. This is a steamer. The engines drive it along. Don't you know what a steamer is? Haven't you ever heard of one?"

She shook her head. I didn't know what to make of her. Her ignorance was something beyond my experience. Presently she was off on a fresh tack.

"Is England far?"

"Pretty well. If we've luck we shall get there in about a month."

"A month?—four weeks?" I nodded. "I cannot live—four weeks—upon the sea!"

She gave what seemed to me to be a gasp of horror.

"Oh, yes, you can. You'll get to love it before you've done."

"Love it! Love the sea! No one ever loves the sea."

"Don't they? That's where you're wrong. I do, for one."

"My lord!"

All in a second down she flopped upon the deck. I was never so flummoxed in my life. I couldn't think what was wrong.

"Miss Batters! What is wrong?"

She turned her lovely face up to me—still on her knees.

"Are you the lord of the sea?"

"The lord of the sea! For goodness sake get up. The watch 'll think you're mad. Or that I'm threatening to murder you." I had to lift her before she'd move. Then she seemed reluctant to stand upright in my august presence. I tried my best to disabuse her mind of some of her wild notions. "I'm a plain sailor man, I am. I've sailed the sea, boy and man, the best part of my life; east and west, north and south. And though I don't mind owning I like a spell of dry land for a change, it would be strange if I hadn't grown to love it. I'm ready to grumble at it with any man. I'm no more lord of the sea than you are. I'm just captain of this ship. That's all."

"You are the captain of this ship."

"That's it, Miss Batters."

"Why do you call me that?"

"Call you what?"

"Miss Batters. I am not Miss Batters. I am Susan."

I had been looking away. When she said that I looked at her. I wished I hadn't. There was something on her face—in her eyes—which set me all of a flutter. Something had come to me since I had entered those waters. I didn't use to be easily upset. I couldn't make it out at all. I couldn't meet her glance, but looked down, smoothing the deck with the toe of my shoe, not recognising the sound of my own voice when I heard it.

"I don't know that I quite care for the name of Susan. I think I prefer—Susie."

"Susie? What is that?"

"That—that's the name your friends will call you."

"My friends?" She gave another little gasp. "Susie?" To hear her say it! "But I have no friends."

"You will have; heaps."

"But I have none now. Not one."

"Well——"

I cleared my throat. I had never been so stuck for a word before. Could have kicked myself for being such a fool. She took my clownishness as implying a reproach. I could tell it from her tone.

"No. I have no friend. Not one."

I made another effort. I wasn't lacking as a rule. I couldn't understand what ailed me then.

"Well, it's early days for me to speak of friendship, since I've only known you for an hour or two; but if I might make so bold, Miss Batters— —"

"Miss Batters!" She stamped her foot, her little bare foot. "I am not Miss Batters. I am Susie." Her tone had changed with a vengeance. Her manner too. She was every inch a queen. A few feet more. "Can I not be Susie to you?"

I turned away. I only wanted to get hold of myself. She put my head in such a whirl. But before I had a chance of finding out whereabouts I was her voice rang out like a boatswain's whistle.

"I hate sailor men." I turned again to stare. "And I hate the sea!"

Before I could slip a word in edgeways she had swung herself round and vanished down the companion ladder. I took off my cap to wipe my forehead. Though the night was cool my brow was damp with sweat.

"This is going to be a lively voyage, on my word!"

I had never said a truer thing since the day that I was born.

CHAPTER XXX
THE MORNING'S NEWS

It was a lively voyage! Oh, yes! For those who like that kind of liveliness.

Everything went wrong, just in the old sweet way. Rudd had to sleep with his engines. As sure as he turned his back on them for five consecutive minutes something happened. I began to wonder if we shouldn't have got on faster if we had had sweeps aboard. You don't often see hands starting to row a steamer along. But anything was better than standing still; or being blown back—which was worse. It was no use rigging a sail against the winds we had, or we might have tried that. But the wind was against us, like everything else.

The weather seemed to have cleared on purpose to give us a chance of getting the Great Joss aboard. It broke again directly afterwards. More than once, and more than twice, I wished it hadn't. Then perhaps we shouldn't have been favoured with the company of Mr. Batters. In shipping him we'd shipped a Tartar. I became inclined to the belief that we owed half of our bad luck to him. The crew was dead sure that at his door could be laid the lot of it. They swore he was the devil himself, or his brother.

I wasn't sure they were far out. Either what he had gone through had affected his brain, or he was possessed by the spirit of mischief, or there was something uncanny about him. I never knew anything like the tricks he was up to. Weather had no effect on him. As for decent hours, he scorned them. It's my belief that what sleep he had was in the day. I know he was awake pretty well all night.

Once I was dragged out of my berth in the middle of the night because he was frightening the watch out of their senses. When I got on deck I found a heavy sea. Everything sopping. The seas breaking over the scuppers. Pitch darkness. And Mr. Batters up in the tops. The crew were of opinion that he was holding communion with his friends in hell. I shouldn't have been surprised. He looked as if he was at something of the kind.

How he kept his place was a wonder. Although he had no legs he seemed to have a knack of gluing himself to whatever he pleased. Up there he had an illumination all on his own. It must have been visible for miles across the sea. He had smeared himself and everything about him with something shiny, phosphorus or something. He always was playing tricks with stuffs of the kind. It made him look as if he was covered with flames. He was waving his arms and going through an acrobatic performance. Snakes were twining themselves about the illuminated rigging. The old villain had smuggled a heap of them in his palanquin. He lived with them as if they were members of his family. They seemed to regard him as akin. Talk about snake charming! I believe that at a word from him they would have flown at anyone just as certainly as a dog would have done.

No wonder the watch didn't altogether relish his proceedings. I sang out:

"Come down out of that, Mr. Batters, before there's trouble."

I did put a bullet into one of his precious snakes. It was this way.

I had a revolver in my hand. The boat gave a lurch. The trigger must have caught my coat sleeve. It snapped. There was a flash. A report. One of his snakes straightened itself out against the blackness like a streaming ribbon. You could see it gleam for a moment. Then it vanished. I suppose it dropped into the sea. A good thing too. The idea was that it had been hit by that unintentional shot. I can only say that if that was the case it was the victim of something very like a miracle.

Old Batters understood what had happened long before I did. He came down that rigging like ten mad monkeys. And he went for me like twenty. If the watch hadn't been there he'd have sent me after that snake. It took the lot of us to get the best of him. If the men had had their way they'd have dropped him overboard.

I wished I had let them before I finished.

A more artful old dodger never breathed. I drew up the agreement of the spoils; but it was days before I could get him to set his hand to it. At first he pretended he couldn't write. As it happened I had seen him write. It seemed to me he was always writing. When at last I had induced him to sign, in the presence of Luke, Rudd, and Holley, he eluded me on the subject of the inventory. I could not get one. His stock of excuses was inexhaustible. And they were all so plausible. It is true that I made notes of a good many things without his knowledge. But a formal inventory I never had. As to my suggestion that at least the more valuable things should be removed to my cabin for safe custody, when I renewed it he expressed his willingness on conditions that he went with them, and his snakes. I declined. On those terms I preferred that he should remain custodian.

Then there was his intimacy with Luke. That continued, in spite of my attempts to stop it. Though they grew slacker when I began to suspect that after all Mr. Luke might not be on such good terms with his boyhood's friend as he perhaps desired.

I got my first hint in this direction when, one afternoon, someone was heard bellowing in Mr. Batters' cabin like a bull. I made for it. I found Mr. Luke upon the floor; his friend upon his chest; his friend's hands about his throat. He was not bellowing just then. Mr. Batters had squeezed the grip right out of him. He was purple. In about another minute he would have known what death by strangulation meant. We got his dear friend off him. The dear friend said unkind things about Mr. Luke.

By the time we had brought the first mate round he was about as limp a man as you might wish to see. He made one remark, which was unprintable. He turned round in his bunk, where we had laid him, and for all I know he went to sleep.

Since, before that, I had taken care to see that he was berthed apart from Mr. Batters, there was nothing to disturb his slumber.

After that I did not feel it necessary to keep quite so sharp an eye on the attentions which he paid our passenger. They did not seem to be so friendly as they had been before.

As if I hadn't enough to plague me, there was the girl. When I begin to write of her my language becomes mixed. As were my feelings at the time. And there were moments when she got me into such a state that I didn't know if I was standing on my head or heels.

She was her father's own child, though it seemed like sacrilege to connect the two. Insubordination wasn't in it along with her. She twisted me round her finger. Except when I stiffened my back, and felt like stowing her in the long-boat, and cutting it adrift, with a bag of biscuit and a can of water. And then five minutes afterwards I'd feel like suicide for ever having thought of such a thing.

She wore me to a shadow.

The sea agreed with her far better than I had expected, or she either, especially considering the weather we had. She was all over the boat. All questions, like a child. There was nothing you could tell her enough about. It was extraordinary how the taste for imparting information grew on one. If you didn't explain everything that could be explained, and a good deal that couldn't, it wasn't for want of trying. She had got together a mixed up lot of facts before she had been upon that vessel long. Because when you begin to look into things you find that there are a good many you think you know all about till a sharp-witted young woman starts you on to telling her all you do know. Then, before you've time to wriggle, you are stuck. There are men who sooner than get that will say anything.

It is bad enough to feel you are making a fool of yourself when the subject is why steamers don't sink when they're floating, or why engines shove them along, or that kind of thing. But when the question's what love is, and you feel but can't tell, it's worse.

"Why do you say you love me?"

I had mentioned to her casually that I did, being driven clean off my balance before I knew it, though I meant every word I had said. And about two hundred thousand more. In spite of my having had more trouble with her old villain of a father that very afternoon. And being full of hope that when it came to hanging him I should be there to see.

"Because I do."

"But what is love?"

"Love? Why, love!"

It was evening. The wind had been falling away all day. Now it was dead calm, the first we had had since shipping Batters. We were something over twelve hundred miles from Aden. There's the exact spot marked on my chart. But I should never forget it if it wasn't. That mark means adjectives. I had had it all out with Batters about our route. The short cut was what he wanted. It was what I wanted too. But what I did not want was to pay the Canal dues. In fact I couldn't. There was not enough money belonging to the ship on board. I hadn't told Batters as much as that, but I had made it clear to him that he'd have to pay. So the arrangement stood that we were to come home by Suez; and he was to hand me over the coin to take us through. We should have to coal at Aden. How we had managed so far was beyond my understanding. Rudd was a marvel. He would make a skip of coal go as far as some men would a ton. Stores we had taken in here a little, and there a little, living from hand to mouth. But we had bought no coal. I had said to Rudd:

"Shall we run into Colombo and have some put into our bunkers there?"

He pondered—it was his way to ponder—then shook his head.

"I'm thinking we'll last to Aden. I'm thinking it. And I don't seem to fancy a stop at Colombo with Mr. Batters aboard."

I looked to see from his face if his words had any hidden meaning. There seemed to be something behind everything he said, till you grew tired of trying to find out what it was. He was always dropping hints, was

Rudd. There appeared to be nothing unusual about his wooden-looking countenance. So I concluded to give his words their dictionary meaning.

"If you think we can last to Aden, we will. It will save time. And coal's cheaper there."

So it was settled. And now we were heading straight for Aden. The weather had cleared. I had told that girl I loved her. Every vein in my body was on fire because of it. Luke was on the bridge. I felt that in spite of the darkness, and it was pretty dark—as well I remember!—his eye was on us as much as on the ship's course. We had been walking up and down for exercise. She was leaning over the taffrail apparently preparing to enter on a kind of philosophical discussion about what love was.

"Is it good to love?"

"That depends."

My tone was grim.

"Do I love you?"

"I should like to hear you say so."

"I love you."

I thought that was what she said. But she was leaning so far over, seeming to be watching the smudge of soapsuds we were leaving behind us, that I couldn't quite catch her words. Though I was all of a quiver to.

"What do you say?"

"I say I love you."

"Susie! Do you mean it?"

"I don't know. I don't know what love is. How should I? I'm only a savage. You said so the other day. I want telling things."

"You don't want telling what love is."

"Do you mean that you don't want to tell me? You never will tell me what I really want to know. I'll ask one of the men. I'll ask Luke. He tells me things."

"Susie! Luke's too fond of interfering in matters which are no business of his. He'll get himself into trouble before he's done."

"Why?"

"Don't you dare to ask Luke what love is!"

"Dare! I dare do anything. I'll go and ask him now."

She'd have been off if I hadn't caught her arm.

"Susie! Don't! For my sake!"

"Then tell me!—tell me yourself!"

Stamp went her foot. It was one of her favourite tricks. Directly she lost patience down it went.

"I'll tell you, if you'll give me time." I tried to find the words, but couldn't. I held out my arms instead. "It's this."

"What?"

"Don't you understand?"

"What am I to understand?"

"Don't you understand that I want you to be my wife?"

"Your wife! Your wife!" She spoke in a crescendo scale, as if I had insulted her. "You said you were my friend!"

"Don't you understand that I want to be something more than your friend?"

"You want to beat me! to use me like a dog! to have me burned!"

"Susie!"

"My father said in England there were no wives."

"No wives in England? He—he was making fun of you."

"He was not making fun of me. He has told me all my life. When I asked him why they burned my mother, he said because she was his wife. He is an Englishman. In England they have no wives."

I had a glimpse of the confusion which was in her mind. But at that moment I was incapable of straightening out the evil.

"Your—your father's was a peculiar case. There are wives in England."

"Is that true?"

She thrust her face close to mine. She was terrifically in earnest.

"It is perfectly true. They abound."

"Then I will not go to England."

"But—Susie!—you've got hold of the wrong end of the stick. In—in England a wife's the man's superior."

"It's a lie. See how you stammer. You cannot lie like my father with an even tongue. A wife is her husband's slave. At his bidding she fetches and she carries. He beats her as he beats his dog. When she grows old he takes another. And she dies."

"My—my dear Susie, I assure you that that description doesn't apply to England. There, unless she's a wife, a woman isn't happy."

"Then in England women are more unhappy than in the country from which I come. I will not go there. I will not go to any place where there are wives."

She strode past me as I stared at her, thunderstruck. I continued thunderstruck when she had gone.

She had a deal to learn.

That night I slept badly. In the morning I was roused by someone hammering at the door.

"Who's there?"

"It's me, sir; Holley. The cutter's gone."

"What!"

"The cutter's gone. And the watch is hocussed."

I was standing at the door in my nightshirt.

"What the devil do you mean? Where's Mr. Luke?"

"He had the morning watch. He's gone too. It's his chaps as is hocussed. Leastways, they're lying on the deck like logs. And Mr. Batters, he's gone. And his things. His cabin's stripped clean. And his daughter, she's gone."

"Holley!"

I was thrusting myself into a pair of trousers. All of a sudden the ship stopped dead, with an unpleasant shock.

"What's that? She can't have struck!"

I rushed up. Rudd met me.

"I have to report to you, sir, that the engine's ceased to work."

"Very well. Patch it up and start it again as soon as you can. It's not the first time it's stopped."

"But I'm thinking it'll be the last. Someone's been playing tricks with the machine. I'm fearing it's Mr. Luke."

CHAPTER XXXI
THE TERMINATION OF THE VOYAGE
OF "THE FLYING SCUD"

We had been completely done. So completely that it was some time before I was able to realise that I had been diddled quite to that extent. Not a detail had been overlooked. Mr. Batters and Mr. Luke had gone conscientiously to work. They had been thorough. They had left us the ship. That was about all. They would probably have taken that if they had had any use for it. It seemed they hadn't. If I could only have laid hands on that latest thing in freaks, there would have been one Joss less. I would willingly have made a Joss of Luke if I had only had a chance. To have boiled, burned, and skinned him would have been a pleasure. He should not only have been legless, he should have been armless too. As for that girl, who didn't want to go to a place where there were any wives, she should have become acquainted with a climate where there was something less agreeable.

That was how I felt towards her at first. But after a while I came to the conclusion that she had been under the domination of her father. Hadn't dared to call her soul her own. So anger turned to pity. I would just simply take her to a place where there were wives. I'd let her know what it felt like to be one. That would be punishment enough for her.

As for Luke and Batters! What wouldn't I have given for a quiet half hour with the pair, with boiling oil, branding irons, and everything just handy.

Mr. Luke must have stowed pretty well all our eatable stores inside that cutter. As first mate, under peculiar circumstances, I had let him do, in some respects, a good deal as he pleased. He had had the run of the stores. He had not gone far from collaring the lot. It seemed that certain of the hands had noticed him fiddling a good deal with the cutter of late. Especially when he had been in charge of either of the night watches. But, of course, they had said nothing to me till it was too late, which was a pity.

Mr. Batters had taken with him all the treasures of the temple. Those offerings of the faithful, half of which were to have been mine. No wonder he had not been of opinion that they would have been safer in my cabin. And he pledged his word that he would make it his especial business to see that not one of them left the ship until he did. That elegant monster which he valued at £50,000 had gone. Even the palanquin. Oh, it was pretty!

Mr. Luke had made everything snug by generously treating the members of the morning watch to a little drink directly they came on duty. That drink was no doubt one of Mr. Batters' concoctions. They remembered no more so soon as they swallowed it. So for four hours Mr. Luke had the deck to himself. No watch was kept. The wheel was lashed. The cutter was filled with the treasures of the temple, then lowered. Goodness and Mr. Luke alone know how. And it must be remembered that Mr. Batters was an ingenious man.

It was reported from the engine room that the order was received to "Go slow." Probably while *The Flying Scud* went slow the cutter was cast loose, with Mr. Batters and the girl inside it. Shortly afterwards the order was changed to "Full steam ahead." The inference seems to be that immediately after giving that order the ingenious Mr. Luke went overboard to join the cutter. And *The Flying Scud* went full steam ahead, with no one on the look-out. Under the circumstances, it was, perhaps, just as well that the engines did break down.

It's an elegant story for the commander of a ship to have to write. Especially one with a clean certificate, and of sober habits. There we were, without engines, without coal, without stores, without enough cargo to act as ballast, about half-way between Aden and Colombo. We were a mad ship's company. For my own part I felt like cutting any man's throat, including my own. All that day we hung about, doing nothing, except cursing.

Towards night, the engines proving hopeless, we rigged a sail. There was just about enough wind to laugh at us. So we let it laugh us along. There was no Canal for us. The man who was to have paid our shot had gone—the shot with him. So we headed for the Cape. The long way round was the only way for us. Engineless, the prospect was inviting.

There is no need to speak in detail of the remainder of that voyage, no need at all. In one sense it was over—quite. In another it was only just beginning. I won't say how long it took us to reach home or what we suffered before we got there. And will only hint that by the time we sighted English waters, I felt as if I was a twin brother of Methuselah's. We hadn't walked the entire distance, but we might almost just as well have done.

It was evening when I landed. There was a mist in the river. A drizzling rain was falling. Appropriate weather with which to bid us welcome home. The lights of London gleamed dimly through the fog and wet. So soon as

I had set foot on land I saw, coming at me through the uncertain light, the individual who, as he stood with his friends upon that moonlit shore, had cursed us for bearing the Great Joss to the ship across the motionless waters of the Gulf of Tongking.

Since that night we had ourselves anathematised someone else for serving us as we had served him.

I had only seen him once, and then from some little distance in the moonshine, but there was no possibility of mistaken identity. This was the man. He was dressed in the same fantastic garb, and came at me like a ghost out of shadowland. He took me by the shoulders, and he cried—as he had done upon that moon-kissed shore:—

"The Great Joss! The Great Joss! Give us back the Great Joss!"

Exactly what took place I cannot say. I was so taken aback by the unexpectedness of the encounter—having never dreamed that I should set eyes upon the man again—that, for some moments, sheer surprise robbed me of my faculties. Before I was myself again, the man had gone. Others had thrust him from me. Although I rushed here and there among the people who stood about I could not find him. He had vanished.

I had swallowed a good many bitter pills since last I left that wharf—the bitterest was still to come. I had to pay my visit to the owners. On the night of my arrival it was too late to see them. The pleasure was postponed to the morning. It was a pleasure!

I came out from their presence a disgraced man. Which was no more than I had expected, though it was no easier to bear on that account. The blame was wholly mine. So they would have it. For some of the language which they used to me I found it hard to keep my hands from off them. My tale of the Great Joss, and of all that I had hoped to gain for them by that adventure, they received with something more than incredulity. If the thing had resulted as I had hoped, that they would have pocketed their share of the spoils, and betrayed no scruples, I knew them too well to doubt. But because, as I held, through no fault of mine, the affair had miscarried, there was no epithet too opprobrious for them to bestow on me. By their showing I had been guilty of all sorts of crimes of which I had never heard. I had betrayed their trust; smirched their good name—as if in the eyes of those who knew them it could be smirched; been guilty of piracy; acted like a common thief; offended against the law of nations; brought shame on England's mercantile marine.

Oh, it was grand to hear them talking! They might have been saints from whose brows I had plucked the halos. They were good enough to explain that it was only because they disbelieved my entire story, and placed no credence in any part of it whatever, that they refrained from handing me over to the properly constituted authorities, to be by them passed on to the Chinese Government, to be dealt with as my offences merited. They took me for a jay. And were so kind as to add that they looked upon the tale as a clumsy, dishonest, and disingenuous attempt to draw a red herring across their track—the phrase was theirs!—and so prevented them from taking proper and adequate notice of the scandalous neglect of duty, and of their interests, of which, to my lasting shame, I had been guilty.

It was a rare wigging that I had. And, to the best of their ability, they included in it everyone who had been with me on board *The Flying Scud*. There were four of us, at least, who swore that we'd be even for it with someone somehow. Isaac Rudd, Sam Holley, his chum, Bill Cox, and I; we were the four.

And all we had to go upon, to help us towards getting even, was a scrap of paper. Half a sheet of common note.

It was the only thing Mr. Batters had left behind him. I had found it in a corner of his cabin, crumpled up into a sort of ball, as though he had thrown it there and forgotten all about it. On it this was written:

"To my niece, Miss Mary Blyth, care of Messrs. Martin and Branxon, Drapers, Shoreditch."

We would look the lady up. Where the niece was the uncle might not be far away. At least she might have some knowledge of his whereabouts. If she had we would have it too, or know the reason why. I still had the written undertaking, which he had signed, by which he was to divide with me equally, as a consideration for services rendered, the treasures of the temple. I had handed this to the owners as proof of the truth of my statements. They had thrown it back to me with a sneer. And something worse than a sneer.

That act amounted to a renunciation of all interest in any property which the document conveyed, or so it seemed to me. Good! They might smart for their scepticism yet. Let us find the niece; then the uncle. If Miss Blyth could only give us a hint as to where he might be found, though it was on the other side of the world, we'd find him. He had valued his belongings at a million. We might be snatched out of the gutter yet.

The search began badly. They knew nothing of a Miss Blyth at Messrs. Martin and Branxon's, or so I was informed by an official individual in the counting-house. That was a facer. It looked as if Mr. Batters, at his tricks again, had purposely placed in our way what seemed like a clue to his lair for the sake of having still another game with us. But a night or two afterwards I tackled a young fellow as he was coming out of the shop after closing hours, and put my question to him. He turned it over in his mind before he answered.

"There's no Miss Blyth here now, but there was. I believe her name was Mary. I could soon find out. She's left some time; directly after I came. I can't think where she went. I've heard the name, but I can't remember. I might inquire if you like, and let you know to-morrow night."

I agreed. He did inquire. The next night he let me know. Miss Blyth had gone to a big shop, which he named, at Clapham. The next day, being engaged, I let Rudd go over to Clapham to see what he could do.

He made a mess of things. The lady was pointed out to him by one of her fellow assistants. Before he could get within hail of her, she slipped round a corner and was out of sight. Came across her again in a restaurant where she couldn't pay her bill. Paid it for her. Then, as he was about to follow her, with a view of pursuing his inquiries, he saw, standing on the pavement in front of the place, the individual who had cursed us on that moonlit shore.

The sight of him struck Rudd all of a heap. By the time he recovered his presence of mind, the lady had vanished, and the gentleman too.

The juxtaposition of Miss Blyth and that cursing gentleman seemed to suggest that we were on the track of the retiring Mr. Batters. What is more, that the scent was getting hot.

The evening after I called at that Clapham establishment, just as the premises were being closed, and asked to see Miss Blyth. Some jackanapes informed me that the young woman had been dismissed that very day. He didn't know what her address was, but had heard that she had gone off with a party who called himself Frank Paine, and who said he was a lawyer.

At that it was my turn to be struck all of a heap. A short time previously I had called upon Mr. Frank Paine, intending to ask his opinion as to the validity of the document which had Mr. Batters' name attached. But, somehow, the conversation got into other channels. I came away without it. Not by so much as a word had he hinted that he knew anything about Mr. Batters or his niece.

As I walked along, pondering these things, Rudd, at my side, suddenly exclaimed:

"Captain, there she is! that's Miss Blyth! the young lady for whom I paid the bill!"

He was pointing towards two young women who were advancing in our direction, on the opposite side of the road. Having got it clear to which of the pair he referred, I sailed across to meet them. She was Miss Blyth. She admitted as much. But that was all the satisfaction I received. She staggered me with the information that her uncle, Mr. Benjamin Batters, was dead. As I was trying to understand how he had come to his death, and when, and where, she took umbrage at my curiosity, or manner, or something. She and her friend jumped into a hansom cab, which dashed off at the rate of about twenty miles, leaving Rudd and I on the kerbstone, staring after it like moonstruck gabies.

CHAPTER XXXII
THE LITTLE DISCUSSION BETWEEN
THE SEVERAL PARTIES

That night we held a consultation. We four. It was getting dead low tide with us. If we didn't light upon those treasures of the temple, we should have to find a ship instead. And that before long. If we had to go aboard of her as cabin boys.

It seemed to me that something might be got out of Mr. Paine. In the way of information. Things pointed that way. The more I thought, the more they seemed to point. I told the others. We decided to wait upon him in a body. And man the pumps for all we were worth. If he proved dry, if nothing could be got out of him, then we should have to admit that the tide was low. And that we were stranded. But we had hopes.

The morning after we were in Mitre Court, where his rooms were, betimes. The idea was that he shouldn't escape us, that we should see him as soon as he was visible, and so play the part of the early bird that catches the worm. But when we found that the door into the street was open, I, knowing the lay of the land, without any parley, led the way upstairs. And it was well for him we did. For we came upon as lively a little scene as ever we'd encountered.

There was a larger company assembled than we had expected. Quite what was happening we couldn't at once make out. The first thing I saw was a girl tied down upon a table, and—of all people in the world—that cursing gentleman leaning over her with a knife in his hand. Having torn her clothes open at the throat, he looked as if he was going to write his name on her nice white skin with the point of his blade. He got no farther than the start. I introduced myself. And landed him one. He didn't seem to know whether he was glad or sorry to meet me. I loosed the girl. When I looked round I saw the room was in a mess, and on the floor, trussed like a fowl, was Mr. Paine. But what made me almost jump out of skin for joy, was the sight of our dear friend Luke tied up beside him.

I released that excellent first officer. Then things were said. When he understood that we were spoiling to cut him up into little pieces, and that it seemed likely that he had fallen from the frying-pan into the fire, he explained. What we wanted to know was the present address at which Mr. Batters could be found. It seemed, according to him, that he was aching to know it too.

"Bless my beautiful eyes!" He spat upon the floor. "Do you think if I knew where the hearty was that I'd be here? He used me shameful, he did that."

"It seems incredible that he should have used you badly, Mr. Luke."

"It does. After all I'd done for him. But he did. After we— —"

He coughed. I finished his sentence.

"Had taken such a ceremonious leave of us all on board *The Flying Scud*. Yes? Go on."

"We got picked up by a liner as was making Suez."

"As you anticipated you would be. I see. You're a far-sighted person, Mr. Luke."

"They landed us at Suez. We stopped there two or three days getting packing-cases to—to— —"

"To pack the treasures of the temple in. They must have been rather conspicuous objects to carry about with you anyhow. Go on."

"Then hang me if one evening I didn't wake up and find that I'd been senseless for close on two days. The devil had hocussed me."

"Hocussed you? Impossible!"

"He had. Then he'd slipped away, him and his blessed daughter, while I was more dead than alive, leaving me with as good as nothing in my pockets. What I had to go through no one knows. If I ever do set eyes on him again, I'll— —"

The peroration was a study of adjectives.

"Then it appears that you are just as eager to have another interview with Mr. Benjamin Batters as we are. I am sorry your venture was not attended with better fortune. It deserved success. Pray what were you to have had out of it?"

"I was to have had half the blooming lot. And the girl— —"

"And the girl! Indeed? And the girl! Mr. Luke, I should dearly like— —"

Mr. Paine interposed.

"Excuse me, Captain Lander, but if it is of Mr. Benjamin Batters you are speaking, if it is to him so many mysterious references have been made as the Great Joss, then I may state that, to the best of my knowledge and belief, that gentleman is dead."

"Dead?—to the best of your knowledge and belief?—what do you mean?"

As I stared at him, a remark was made by the young lady who so narrowly escaped being made the subject of an experiment in carving. Although evidently very far from being as much herself as she might have been, she had pulled herself together a little, and was holding both hands up to her throat.

"You're forgetting that Pollie's lying perhaps worse than dead in Camford Street."

Mr. Paine gave a jump.

"I had forgotten it!—upon my honour!"

"What's that?" I asked.

"Miss Blyth—to whom Miss Purvis refers as Pollie—is the niece of the Mr. Batters of whom we have been speaking. She's his heiress, in fact."

"His heiress?"

"Yes; his sole residuary legatee. Among other things he left her a house in Camford Street—No. 84—on somewhat mysterious conditions. For instance, she was to allow no man to enter it."

"No man?"

"No; only she and one feminine friend were ever to be allowed to put their feet inside the door."

"Oh?"

I began to smell a rat. Mr. Paine waved his hand towards the young lady the cursing gentleman had been about to practise on.

"This is Miss Purvis, the feminine friend whom Miss Blyth chose to be her sole companion. Other conditions were attached to the bequest equally mysterious. Indeed, it would really seem as if there was something in that house in Camford Street the existence of which the late Mr. Batters was particularly anxious should be concealed from the world. Miss Blyth only entered on the occupation of her property yesterday. Yet Miss Purvis came at an early hour this morning to tell me that something extraordinary had happened in the middle of the night. Something, she doesn't quite know what, but fancies it was some wild animal, made a savage attack upon Miss

Blyth without the slightest provocation. And when Miss Purvis recovered from the shock which the occurrence gave her, she found that she herself had been thrown into the street."

"Mr. Paine!" I laid my hand upon the lawyer's shoulder. "Do you know what's inside that house?"

"I haven't the faintest notion. How should I have?"

"It's the late Mr. Batters!"

"The late Mr. Batters?"

"The thing the existence of which Mr. Batters was most anxious to keep concealed, was Mr. Batters himself—for reasons. So he's put about a cock and bull story making out he's dead, and then hidden himself in this house of which you're talking."

"Captain Lander!"

"Mind, it's only my guess, as yet. But I don't think you'll find that I'm sailing very wide of the wind. The more I turn things over, after listening to what you've said, the more likely it seems to me that the Great Joss, whom we've all been on tiptoe to get a peep at, has hidden himself in that house which he pretends to have left to his niece, and is waiting there for us to find him. And I'm off to do it!"

"Someone's had the start of you."

The interruption came from Rudd. The absence of the cursing gentleman, and his two friends, explained his meaning.

"They've gone hot-foot after him," I cried. "What's good enough for them is good enough for me!"

We journeyed in three cabs. Speed was a consideration. So we chartered hansoms. I went in front with Luke. He didn't seem over and above anxious for my society. But I didn't feel as if I could be comfortable without him. So we went together. Though I am bound to admit that I'm inclined to think that I enjoyed that ride more than he did. Rudd, Holley, and his chum came next. Mr. Paine and the young lady last. I liked his manner towards that young lady. In a lawyer, whom one naturally looks upon as the most hard-hearted of human creatures, it was beautiful. He could not have treated her more tenderly if she had been a queen. And, though she was still in a very sad condition, I have a sort of idea that, when they were once inside that cab, speed with them wasn't much of a consideration.

And though those hansoms did rattle us along in style, we found that someone had got to that house in Camford Street in front of us.

CHAPTER XXXIII
IN THE PRESENCE

The cursing gentleman and his two friends were awaiting us upon the pavement. I said a word of a kind to the long 'un.

"Look here, my bald-headed friend, I don't quite know who you are, or what you want, but I've seen enough of your little ways to know they're funny; so if you take my advice you'll make yourself scarce before there's trouble."

He held out his hands. Looking, on the dirty pavement of that shabby street, like a fish out of water.

"The Great Joss! The Great Joss! He is in there—give him back to us—then we go."

I reflected. After all there was some reason in the creature. He was almost as much interested in Mr. Batters as I was. Considering how Mr. Batters had treated me I didn't see why he shouldn't learn what an object of interest he really was. It might occasion him agreeable surprise. The fellow was in such dead earnest. It beat me how he and his friends had got where they were. Reminding me of the flocks of migratory birds which one meets far out at sea. Goodness only knows by what instinct they pursue the objects of their search. I turned to Mr. Paine.

"This gentleman was high priest, or something of the kind, in the temple in which Mr. Batters was Number One God."

"Number One God?"

"That's about the size of it. He was a god when I first made his acquaintance. This gentleman's own particular. Since he and his friends have come a good many thousand miles to get another peep at him, I don't think there'll be much harm in letting him have one if it's to be got. So, so far as I'm concerned, right reverend sir, you can stop and see the fun."

Mr. Paine stared. He didn't understand. The look with which he regarded the foreign gentleman wasn't friendly. The experience he had had of his peculiar methods was a trifle recent. Perhaps it rankled.

I turned my attention to the house in front of which the lot of us were standing, cabs and all.

"The question is, since no one seems inclined to open the door, how we are going to get in to enable us to pay our little morning call."

Rudd practically suggested one way by hurling himself against the door as if he had been a battering ram. He might as well have tried his luck against a stone wall. As much impression would have been made. When I ran my stick over it, it sounded to me like a sheet of metal.

Luke proffered his opinion.

"You'll want a long chisel for this job. Or a pair. Nothing else 'll do it. That door's been put there to keep people out. Not to let 'em in. It'll be like breaking into a strong room."

Luke proved right. All our efforts were unavailing. That door had been built to keep folks out.

"If this is going to be a case for chisels," said Rudd, "we'd better start on it at once, before those police come interfering."

We were already centres of attraction to a rapidly increasing crowd. Our goings-on provided entertainment of a kind they didn't care to miss. Long before we had put that job through the police did come. What is more, we were glad to see them.

Rudd fetched a pair of crowbars from an ironmonger's shop close by. With his assistance, and acting under his instructions, we started to shift that door. We never got beyond the starting. We might as well have tried to shift the monument. He rigged up contrivances; tried dodges. There was the door just as tight as ever. And just as we were thinking of breaking the heads of some of the members of that interested crowd, up the police did come.

Mr. Paine explained to them what we were after. Then he and the young lady and Rudd went off with one of them to the station, while another stayed behind. In course of time they returned, together with an inspector, three more policemen, and two specimens of the British working man, who were wheeling something on a barrow. The interest of the crowd increased. The new arrivals were received with cheers.

Those workmen, in conjunction with Isaac Rudd, fitted up a machine upon the pavement. It was some kind of a drill I believe. Presently not one but half a dozen holes had been cut right through that door. Into these were inserted crowbars of a different construction to those we had been using. We all lent a hand. And the door was open.

The crowd pressed forward.

"Keep back!" cried the inspector.

And the police kept them back.

The inspector entered, with the young lady, Mr. Paine, Rudd and I. The rest were kept out, including the cursing gentleman and his two friends, which seemed hard on them after all they must have gone through. But it was little that they lost. At the beginning anyhow.

For as soon as we set foot inside the passage we found that there was another door defying us. It seemed to lead into a room upon our left. Rudd called one of the workmen in to consult with him. They sounded the door, they sounded the wall, and concluded that the shortest way into the room was through the wall. So soon the house was being knocked to pieces before our eyes. There was sheet iron on the other side of that wall. But they were through it in what seemed no time. And there was a great hole, large enough to admit of the passage of a man.

And on the other side of this hole stood Susie.

She stared at us, and we stared at her, neither understanding who the other was. But when I did understand I felt as if my legs were giving way. And something inside me set up a clamour which was deafening. And when she saw it was me she called out:

"Max!"

She was through that wall like a flash of lightning. I had her in my arms almost before I knew it.

"Susie!" I said. "My sweet!"

I could tell by the way of her that she knew more about wives than she did when I saw her last. And that she had grown reconciled to the idea of being one. And perhaps a bit more than reconciled. The fates be thanked.

Miss Blyth was in the room with her. Alive and sound, and, indeed, unhurt. They had been frightened out of their wits when they heard us, and at the noise we made, thinking they were going to be murdered, at the least.

"Where's your father?" I asked.

"When he brought her in," she answered—meaning Miss Blyth—"he went out, shutting the door behind him, taking the key. He left us prisoners. We've been prisoners ever since. We've heard and seen nothing of him. Where he is I don't know. Unless he's above."

He was above. In a room at the top of the house. With another door to it. So that we had to get through the wall again.

He had had a sort of throne rigged up. Intending, maybe, to have an imitation of the one which he had occupied when I had first come upon him in the temple. If that was so the imitation was a precious poor one. But he was on it. Dead. And cold. He had been gone some hours.

Whether he had committed suicide, or whether the end had come to him in the ordinary course of nature, there was nothing to show.

A colony of snakes was in the room. Those favourites of his. One shared the throne with the Great Joss. It was on the seat, in front of him, where his legs ought to have been. My idea was that the thing had killed him. But it seemed that that was not the case. The creatures were declared not to be venomous. And there was no mark of a snake-bite about him anyhow.

While we stood looking at the throne, and what was on it, there was a movement behind. The cursing gentleman and his two friends came in. At sight of the Great Joss they threw themselves on their faces, and bit the floor. I never saw men so scared. Or so surprised. I had a sort of notion that they had supposed him to be immortal, and that he couldn't die. When the body came to be examined, and it was discovered what a torso it really was, and to what prolonged and hideous tortures the man must have been subjected, one began to understand that they might have had reasons of their own for thinking so. It might very well have been incomprehensible to them why, if he could die, he hadn't died.

At the foot of the throne was the little doll-like thing which I had seen perched on the head of the fifty thousand pound monstrosity. He had called it the God of Fortune. Saying that where it was he was not far away.

The case seemed to present an illustration of the truth of his words. The doll was broken to atoms. The Great Joss and the God of Fortune seemed to have come to an end together.

BOOK V
AUTHOR'S POSTSCRIPT

CHAPTER XXXIV
HOW MATTERS STAND TO-DAY

I should have preferred that the close of Captain Max Lander's statement should have been the conclusion of this strange history. But for the satisfaction of any reader who may desire to know what became of A, B, C, or D, these following lines are added.

What have been described by Captain Lander as "the treasures of the temple" were found in the house in Camford Street. So far as could be ascertained, intact. The question of ownership involved a nice legal problem. The native attendants of the temple vanished almost as soon as they appeared. No one knew where they went to. Nothing has been seen or heard of them since. It seemed, therefore, that they put forward no claims. There remained the girl, Susan, presumably the dead man's daughter, though there was no legal proof of the fact; Mary Blyth, who had claims under her uncle's will; Captain Lander, who held the document entitling him to a half share; and the owners and crew of *The Flying Scud*. All these had claims which required consideration. In the end, by great good fortune, an amicable settlement was arrived at, which gave satisfaction to all parties concerned.

As might have been expected, the value set on the property by Mr. Batters proved to be an exaggeration. It was worth nothing like a million. Still, it fetched a considerable amount when realised, and after the owners and crew of *The Flying Scud* had been appeased—excepting Mr. Luke, who was markedly dissatisfied because he only received an ordinary seaman's share—an appreciable sum remained as surplus. To this was added the cash which had been bequeathed to Miss Blyth by the will whose validity was, at best, extremely doubtful; the whole being divided, in equal portions, between the niece and the daughter. As Miss Batters immediately afterwards became Mrs. Max Lander, the commander of *The Flying Scud* had no cause to be discontented with this arrangement.

No. 84, Camford Street is still without an owner. It appears, from the story told by the girl, Susan, that on reaching England, her father hurried her from place to place, seldom stopping for more than two or three days under one roof. They seem to have made their most lengthy stay in a barge in one of the lower reaches of the river. No doubt the notion of concealment was present to his mind from the first. Though how he lighted on the house in Camford Street is still a mystery. Nor has anything transpired to show by whose orders it was fortified in such ingenious and elaborate fashion; nor by whom the work was executed. Nothing has been found which goes to show that he had any right to call the house his property. Its actual ownership still goes begging.

The document purporting to be a will was possibly drawn up by his own hand. The letter signed "Arthur Lennard, Missionary," pretending to announce his death on that far-off Australasian island, was probably concocted, at his instigation, by one of the miscellaneous acquaintances whom he picked up during his wanderings among the riverside vagabonds. From such an one he might have acquired Mr. Paine's name, together with some side-lights on that gentleman's character. Miss Batters made it abundantly clear that her father was the "freak" to whom Mr. Paine was of service by rescuing him from the too curious crowd in the Commercial Road.

His exact object in making his will has never been shown. No doubt the man's brain was in disorder. He was actuated, perhaps, by three considerations. The desire for concealment; the consciousness that he and his daughter would fare very badly if shut up in a house alone together; the wish to avail himself of his niece's services. To have gone to her with a straightforward tale would have been in accord neither with his character or policy. He had lived too long in what, for civility's sake, may be called a diplomatic atmosphere, to be able to breathe in any other. Also, he knew nothing of his niece. Suspected that she knew nothing good of him. Was moved, possibly, by a very natural unwillingness to make himself, or his story, known to her until he had learned what kind of person she was.

So he invented his own death, making her his heiress, for the sole purpose of getting her inside the house. It is impossible to say what might have happened had she proved amenable to his wishes; and events moved along the road which he had laid down for them. The presumption is that, sooner or later—probably sooner—he would have made himself known to her, and endeavoured to purchase her fidelity, and services, on terms of his own.

As it is, the uncle is the constant theme of the niece's conversation. Miss Blyth is now Mrs. Cooper. The Coopers are residents of one of the smaller south coast watering places, where they are regarded as leading lights among local social circles. Mr. Cooper is a vice-president of the boat-club, yacht-club, swimming-club, cricket-club, football club, and so on; his wife is the mother of an increasing family, and a lady with a tale. Its subject is Uncle Benjamin. That gentleman lived a life of strange and varied adventure. His history loses none of its marvels at his niece's lips. Either because they are a trifle tired of the theme, or are merely jealous, some of the more frequent hearers have been heard to doubt if there ever was an Uncle Benjamin. If these doubts are serious they do the lady less than justice.

Mr. and Mrs. Lander are also happy. One would be reluctant to doubt it. Yet, at the same time, one cannot refuse to admit that there are occasions when the outward and visible signs of their happiness take a somewhat boisterous shape. He has a temper; she has a temper. There are moments when it would appear as if there was hardly room for the two tempers in a single house. Since they seldom remain in one place for more than three months, they can scarcely be said to live anywhere. In selecting their next abiding-place, they seem to act on the principle of letting it be as far from the present as possible. Mr. Lander has not pursued his profession since the last eventful voyage which he has herein set forth. Possibly by way of killing time he is apt to be a trifle too convivial. Nothing makes Mrs. Lander more indignant than an even hinted doubt of her positive assertion, made in and out of season, that every drop of blood in her veins is English. As her complexion is a little dusky, her aggressive attitude upon this point makes her rather a difficult person to get on with.

Mr. Frank Paine, oddly enough, has married Miss Purvis. And, what is perhaps still more odd, theirs is the happiest match of the three. About their complete and absolute content with their condition there can be no possible doubt whatever. He worships her; she worships him. If there is any finer recipe for matrimonial happiness than that, it has not come in the present writer's way. His practice as a solicitor has grown large. Mrs. Paine is of opinion that he is rightly regarded with even fulsome reverence by the entire bench and bar. Since he would not dream of contesting any opinion which happened to be his wife's, the position of affairs could not possibly be improved.

Mr. Benjamin Batters lies in Kensal Green Cemetery. In a deep grave, and in a full-sized coffin. Surrounded by dignitaries and respectabilities. In his coffin were placed the broken pieces of the curiosity which he called the God of Fortune. So they are still together. A handsome monument has been raised above him. There is no hint, in the inscription, that below are but the mangled fragments of what was once a human body; or any reference to the fact that he ever posed as a joss; or a god; or was ever believed, even by savages, to have put on immortality before his time. It simply says:

> "BENEATH THIS STONE
> REPOSES
> BENJAMIN BATTERS,
> WHO,
> AFTER A LIFE OF VARIED ADVENTURE
> IN DIFFERENT PARTS OF THE WORLD,
> SLEEPS WELL."

We will hope that it is so.